IT ENDS NOW

TY HUTCHINSON

ONE

COMING HOME FELT like a death sentence.

Not that I knew what a death sentence felt like, but I imagined it to be kind of close to how I felt. I knew I was being over-dramatic and childish. But I had spent the last twelve years living a life that made me happy. I had a reason to wake up every day. I smiled and said, "Hello" to people in stores and on the street. I went to bed each night content, knowing I would wake up to the start of another fantastic day. But now...well, I was back home. And the reasons why I left were quickly surfacing like bubbles in a pot of boiling water.

My mother had passed away two weeks ago from a sudden heart attack. I was halfway around the world when I got the call, and I did my best to get home as soon as possible. I arrived back in town on the morning of the funeral.

Since landing at San Francisco International Airport, there had been a constant drizzle. I couldn't recall the weather in Danville ever being this wet while growing up, especially not in the summer. I was used to the occasional fog, and downpours were common, but gray skies and drizzle were a rarity. I added that to my list of things I noticed had changed in my hometown.

I adjusted my grip on the umbrella handle as I stood there staring at my mother's casket, a beautiful hardwood cherry. My mother was one of those people who paid for her own funeral in advance, even picking out the casket and plot where she wanted to be buried. It was an older cemetery, and the only people who could be buried there were families who had purchased plots long ago, like my mother had. There was simply no room left. My father was already buried there. The other plot was for me, though I wasn't sure I wanted to lie in Danville when the time came.

Gary Holmes, my mother's lawyer and longtime friend of the family, had picked me up at the airport and driven me straight to the cemetery. Aside from stating how good it was to see me again and that I had grown into a beautiful young lady, he didn't talk much during the drive. I didn't feel like conversing anyway. He stood to the left of me at the graveside.

Netty was to my right. I called her Aunty Netty while I was growing up. She was my mother's best friend and had handled the funeral arrangements.

"You look so grown up," she'd told me when she first laid eyes on me again. "I almost didn't recognize you."

She gave me a long hug, and for the first time since making the trip home, I experienced a positive feeling. But after the hug, reality set in. I was back in the place I had escaped from.

The only other person in attendance was the priest, whom I'd never met. I didn't expect there to be a large crowd. My mother was an introvert and content to have only Netty and me in her life. It was normal, and all I had known since I came home with Mr. and Mrs. Baxley, my new parents.

They adopted me at age four. Six months later, the man I was told to call "father" passed away. From then on, people around town referred to us as Wendy Baxley and her daughter, Addie.

Of the three of us standing there, Netty was the only one wearing all black. I knew I would be heading straight to the cemetery from the airport, but I didn't want to wear an all-black outfit during my travel. Instead, I wore my favorite pair of jeans, a cashmere sweater, and leather boots. Not exactly rainy weather fashion, but I had expected clear skies with a warming sun. Gary always wore various shades of brown suits. That day it was copper.

I was only half listening to the priest. I knew my mother would not have wanted any fuss to be made over her death. Even a funeral with three people in attendance would have been too much for her. It could have been two, as I almost hadn't come home. But a phone call from Gary changed my mind. He insisted that I return to settle my mother's estate.

It may sound like my mother and I weren't close, but we were. We simply had our own way of showing our love to each other. People might think otherwise, because I hadn't returned for a visit in the last twelve years. But my mother knew it would be this way when I left. She knew why I ran. I had to get far away if I was going to have my life back.

After Gary convinced me that my physical presence was necessary, I devised a simple plan. And I promised myself I would stick to it and let nothing derail me.

Get in. Get out.

I had said those words over and over during the multiple plane rides. I told myself to remain focused and treat this like a business trip—which, in a way, it was. I wanted to keep my time at home to a minimum. I had planned a week's stay. There was no rhyme or reason to it, except that it seemed like enough time to finalize my mother's estate.

I allowed my gaze to drift away from the casket and across the cemetery. Most of the tombstones in that particular area of the grounds were flat granite blocks; very few were upright. All the better for a view of any looky-loos who might dare show up. I wasn't sure what to expect with my return. Would things pick up where they'd left off?

Get in and get out, Addie. There shouldn't be any problems if you do that.

Danville, California lay east of San Francisco, across the bay and on the other side of a low mountain range. It was one of those towns where everyone knew everyone. I was sure my mother's death had already made its way through the gossip mill. And I imagined there were discussions about whether I would return, among those who thought I was alive. Many thought I'd met my maker, and there were a lot of theories floating around on how. A good contingent of people believed I had gone mad and was institutionalized. Even a select few had somehow come to believe I'd settled in with the Romani and roamed around Europe with them. This is what happens to wandering minds when you deny them information.

I had given my mother specific instructions before I left home: Never discuss me with anyone in that town. During our phone calls, she'd kept me abreast of any new rumors about me that had surfaced. I did get a kick out of them.

After the service concluded, Netty hugged me once more. I knew she missed my mother as much as I did. Since I'd arrived, she'd been sniffling and dabbing at her eyes with a crumpled-up tissue. But my childhood had taught me how to hide my emotions. I'd learned to cry on the inside.

I wouldn't say I regretted not seeing my mother during those twelve years, but I was saddened that it had to be that way. My mother wholly understood. When I told her I was leaving, she'd smiled and cried simultaneously. She knew what leaving meant, and at the same time, she knew what it could do for me. She believed it was the only way to get out of the situation I had been placed in.

"Addie, there's some paperwork I have to handle with the mortuary," Netty said. "You don't need to stick around for it. I know you're probably tired and want some time alone to process. We can meet again in a few days."

She had read my mind.

"Thank you, Netty. Are you sure there are no expenses I can help cover?"

"Your mother had everything paid for in advance. She didn't want you to have to deal with it when the time came."

I gave her another hug. "Thank you so much for handling all of this. I don't know what I would have done without you here."

Gary was waiting to drive me to my mother's home. He had put a lock on the front door so no one could enter until I returned. As far as I knew, no one had. We parted with Netty and made the walk back to his car. I still kept a lookout for other people. Were they lurking behind trees? Perhaps they were crouching behind a tombstone. I had told Gary not to print an obituary for my mother. My mother's surviving relatives were no one's business but hers. And anyway, the people who truly cared about her were at the burial that day. That was all that mattered.

"I know I asked already, but how are you doing, Addie?" Gary glanced over at me as he drove.

"I'm fine, really. Thank you so much for everything you're doing."

"Your mother had given me explicit instructions on what to do in the event of her untimely death. I'm just fulfilling her wishes."

"My mother didn't trust many people, but you were always someone she could count on. She was very fond of you."

"I'll miss her. She had a kind heart."

"What happens now?" I asked.

"There's a lot to go over, and it's probably best we do it at my office. When you're ready to come in, call me, and we'll set up a time. Sound okay?"

"That's fine."

Gary made a left onto my old street. The road leading to my childhood home was a gradual slope. You'd notice it if you walked, but not so much while driving. Seeing my home again after all this time gave me chills. It sat at the very end of a cul de sac. Because of the size of the property and the shape of the hill, my mother's home was the only house that actually sat *in* the cul de sac. The other homes were located where the road started to form a circle at the end. She had loved it because of the privacy it afforded. If someone wanted to eavesdrop or peek through our windows, they'd have to walk right up to our house.

The house was a blue and white Victorian. It was two stories with a basement and an attic, four bedrooms, and three bathrooms. For a single woman and a small child, it was a large house to live in.

The house sat on the side of the hill and overlooked the neighborhood. It gave the impression that we were royalty over-looking our subjects—only living there was nothing like that. Gary brought his car to a stop and set the parking brake.

We climbed out of the car, and Gary helped me carry my luggage to the house. I looked over the front yard; the grass was overgrown, and the hedges along the property's edge were scrag-gly. The yard hadn't been maintained properly in a while. The paint on the house had dulled since I left and could use a fresh coat. The steps leading up to the porch were worn, and one bowed under my weight. On the left side of the porch, I spied the same bench swing where my mother sat in the evenings and as she looked out across the neighborhood.

Gary fished a set of keys out of his pocket and unlocked the metal case covering the doorknob.

"I didn't change the locks on the door, in case you're wondering," he said as he pushed. It stuck, and he had to give it an extra shove. "There we go. Looks like all this rain has made the door swell a little. Will you be fine here?"

I took the keys from his outstretched hand. "I will. Thank you again, and I'll be in touch."

I hugged Gary quickly and waited outside as he walked back to his car. I waved at him as he reversed down the driveway and kept watch until his car disappeared from view. It had been years since the last time I stood on this porch, but at that moment, it felt like only a day had passed. I drew a deep breath as I eyed the neighborhood, wondering when it would start again. Because I knew it would. While my mother believed it ended the day I left home, I wasn't foolish enough to buy into that. Nightmares don't disappear. They simply wait for you to crawl back into bed again.

TWO

I stood in the doorway for a few moments before stepping inside. I drew a deep breath, half expecting to smell my mother's perfume, but instead smelled only old wood with a bit of mildew. The place was stuffy, so I threw open the front windows. The living room hadn't changed. My mother still had the same furniture, and the photos on the mantle were the same. A sizable built-in wall cabinet ran the entire length of a wall. And it was filled with more knickknacks than I cared to count. I wouldn't call my mother an outright pack rat, but people might suggest she was on her way. The area rug on the floor was tattered around the edges, and a worn trail was visible where she had habitually walked. While the yard was a hot mess, the inside of the house was spotless, aside from needing to be dusted. I switched on a lamp.

The electricity is working; that's a good sign. Let's hope there's hot water.

Netty had mentioned to me that Gary had locked the house as soon as my mother's body was removed. And it stayed that way until I returned—per my mother's wishes.

I flipped on every light switch as I passed through the dining room and went into the kitchen to check my food supply. Condiments and containers of unidentifiable leftovers filled most of the fridge. There was also a half gallon of spoiled milk, an unopened container of orange juice, a couple of eggs, and a half dozen bottles of salad dressing. The cupboard, where my mother kept her dry goods, was still stocked with a decent amount of food. I'd only have to replenish the perishables in the fridge. I had every intention of cooking all my meals at home. The last thing I wanted was to be seen sitting in a restaurant by myself. It would invite curiosity.

At the rear of the house was a bathroom. Next to it was a small room my mother used as an office. She rarely went in there but liked the idea of having an office. I unlocked the door that led to the backyard and stepped outside. The paint on the porch was much flakier than I had remembered it, and the lawn here was just as overgrown as the front yard. There was a tall hedge to the rear of the yard, where the slope of the hill rose.

I turned back inside, shut the door, and locked it. I also checked all the windows at the back of the house to ensure they were securely closed.

My bedroom was on the second floor at the front of the house. It had a clear view of the front yard and the neighborhood below. I grabbed my suitcase and headed up the stairs. I stood at the top of the landing, looking left toward the rear of the house, where my mother's bedroom was.

I'll look at it later.

Straight ahead was another bathroom. To the left of it was a guest room.

I pushed the door to my bedroom open, turned on the lights, and rolled my luggage in. What I saw didn't surprise me. My mother had kept my room exactly as I had left it—a snapshot in time. Part of me wished she had turned it into an exercise room or another sitting room. Seeing it preserved that way only brought back painful memories of my previous life. I crossed the room, opened the window that overlooked the front yard, and poked my head out. The overcast skies had darkened. A quick glance at my watch told me it was near sunset.

Just as I pulled my head back inside, my eye caught sight of movement along the hedges to the left of the property. I stuck my head back out for a better look, but I didn't see anything. I focused on the hedge, squinting for clarity. Suddenly, a cat darted out from it and crossed the lawn, causing me to jump. Goose pimples erupted on my arms.

Sheesh, relax, Addie. You just got here.

But as far as I knew, *they* were still in town. I shut the door and drew the sheer curtains closed.

I really wanted to believe that coming home would be different. I wanted to think that the passage of time had changed things, and this visit would be boring and uneventful. That would have been ideal. But history proved it could go the other way.

Remember, Addie, the plan is to get in and get out. Stick to that, and you'll be fine.

I headed into the bathroom and drew back the shower curtain, revealing a large claw-foot tub. I turned the faucet knob marked "H," and waited. After a few seconds, the water grew warm, and a smile formed on my face. The water heater worked.

You see, there's nothing to worry about. Your imagination is what's making it weird. Twelve years have passed, and you've grown during that time. Don't you dare revert back to teen behavior, Addie.

And that was the truth. My time away from home had changed me into the person I knew I could always be: independent, decisive, and strong-willed, with a hunger for discovery.

Nothing about the current me resembled the quiet, shy girl who grew up in this house.

I'd traveled nearly twenty-six hours to make it home in time for the funeral, and I was exhausted. I decided while soaking in the tub that I would look over the rest of the house later. After I finished my bath, I switched off my bedroom light and crawled into bed. I told myself everything would be fine. But I knew that was a lie.

THREE

THE SUMMER WHEN I WAS 10

I'D ALWAYS BEEN a bit of a loner. I guessed I picked it up from my mother. It didn't bother me at all; I never felt lonely. When my mother needed her space, I happily entertained myself, even without a television in the house. She thought TV was a terrible way to pass the time. She preferred that I play outside, and if I was indoors, she wanted me to read.

She was a big reader, and when she first brought me home, she insisted I read with her. So, every Saturday, she and I would make a trip to the local library, where we'd spend hours browsing the shelves before checking out an armful of books for the week.

One day during the summer, I was in the living room, lying on the sofa and humming a tune, when she appeared.

"Addie, what are you doing?"

I shrugged. "Nothing."

"Well, why don't you go outside and do nothing."

I lifted my head and looked at her. "How can I go outside and do nothing?"

"Figure it out. Now scoot."

I picked myself up off the couch and headed outside. I

walked straight over to the hedge in the front yard. Sometimes I'd see a caterpillar on one of the branches and catch it. But that day, I didn't see any. I walked around the yard, kicking the tops off of mushrooms that had sprouted up overnight, but eventually I got bored with that and decided to go to the park near my house. There were swings there that I enjoyed, and I guessed my mother had something like that in mind when she told me to "figure it out."

I recognized a couple of kids from my school playing on a jungle gym. There were also a few joggers and people walking their dogs. Most kids my age were signed up for some sort of activity to keep them busy. Summer camp was a popular one; summer school wasn't. Nothing like that interested me. I loved my time alone. And plus, we always took one big trip during the summer. When I say "we," I mean my mother, Aunty Netty, and me. That year, she planned on driving down the coast to Los Angeles. Aunt Netty had put the idea into my mother's head. She insisted it would be a good experience for me. I just knew Disneyland was somewhere around there, and that's where I wanted to go. Aunty Netty wasn't my real aunt; I just called her that. She was my mother's best friend and was always around. I liked her because she was different from my mother. Netty was louder, less shy, and always spoke her mind. I secretly admired her.

I hopped on an empty swing and started back and forth. It didn't take long before I began to daydream—nothing in particular, just whatever popped into my head. I can't remember what thought I was lost in that day, but it took a moment or so for me to realize someone was talking to me.

Standing off to the side of the swing were two girls I'd never seen before. They must have attended a different school than I did.

"I asked you your name," the one with blond hair said.

She had a hand resting on her hip and a scowl on her face. She was dressed in a short skirt and blouse, and she had a purse slung over her shoulder. I didn't even own a wallet. The girl next to her had black hair and the same look on her face. She also had a purse, but she wore it across her chest.

"My name is Addie," I said as I continued to swing. "What's your name?"

"I'm Virgie, and this is my best friend, Felisa. We've never seen you before."

I shrugged.

"Don't you know it's rude to swing when someone's talking to you?" Virgie said.

"Yeah, don't you know that?" Felisa chimed in.

I brought the swing to a stop, and they moved in closer.

"You must go to the other elementary school in town," Virgie said as she smirked. "That's where the uncool people go."

I had no idea what she was talking about. The kids at my school were perfectly okay. There were two elementary schools in the area, and they were located on opposite ends of the town. It was in middle school when all the kids in town were funneled into one school together, and it would stay that way throughout high school.

"We don't go to the same school now, but we will when we get older," Virgie said. "I hope you don't think we'll be friends then, because we won't."

"Yeah, we already have plenty of friends. And they're all cool," Felisa said with a smile.

Fine. I didn't want to be friends anyway.

A boy I had never seen before walked up to us.

"Ugh," Virgie said as she looked at him.

Clearly, they knew each other.

"Leave her alone, Virgie," the boy said.

"Why? Is she your girlfriend?"

Virgie and Felisa both laughed.

"Oh, my God. He totally likes her," Felisa said.

"Come on, Felisa. Let's leave Romeo and Juliet alone." She hooked an arm around Felisa's and then shouted at me as they walked away. "You dress like a boy!"

"Don't mind them," the boy said. "I'm Spencer. What's your name?"

"Addie."

"Virgie and Felisa always think they're so much cooler than everyone else." He took a seat on the swing next to mine. "Can I swing with you?"

I nodded. "Do you go to school with them?"

"Yeah, unfortunately. They're always teasing me, too. I just ignore them."

Spencer quickly picked up speed until he swung all the way to the back and front. I timed my swings so that we were in sync and could talk more easily.

"Why do they tease you?" I asked.

"Because they're mean. They always call me Spence the Dense."

"Really? You don't sound dense to me."

"I'm not. They just say it because it rhymes. It's so stupid. But you won't have to worry about them until middle school."

Spencer would be wrong about that. There was still a month left of summer, and I'd have many more encounters with Virgie and Felisa. Later, I would refer to that time as the summer I met my bullies.

FOUR

I woke the following morning feeling like I'd slept for an eternity, for which my body was grateful. I swung my legs over to the side of the bed and stood. My room didn't seem as bright as I remembered it usually being from the morning sun. Of course, a quick look outside my window and I saw overcast skies with rain falling.

I slipped on a robe and went downstairs, still ignoring the bedrooms at the other end of the hall. My body needed coffee, and I prayed my mother had some in the cupboard. She did, but it was instant. It would suffice until I could get better grounds. Surprisingly, my mother still had the coffee maker. I was the only one who used it, so I half expected her to have gotten rid of it. I started drinking coffee during my junior year in high school. It never bothered my mother, as she loved the smell of it brewing. She just couldn't stomach the taste. Black tea with milk and sugar was her daily vice.

I went through the dining room and into the living room with a hot cup of coffee. That's when I realized why it was cold in the house. I had forgotten to close the front windows before heading to bed.

Smart move, Addie.

The floor below each window had a coating of dew. I shut the windows and wiped away the moisture before plopping down on the sofa and making a checklist of things I needed to do. Because I had no intention of moving back in, I immediately thought of selling the house. I wasn't interested in maintaining it as a rental, so I was left with clearing it out. No easy feat, as my mother had lived here a long time and acquired a vast collection of belongings.

I highly doubted there was much I would want to keep, including the items in my bedroom. I'd taken anything important to me when I left. So it would be a matter of separating items into two categories: donations and trash. I wasn't interested in a garage sale—that meant visitors.

The job was easy enough and something I could do within a week. If I achieved that, I'd be on track with my plan of getting in and out.

While I drank my coffee, I mentally envisioned how fast I would breeze through each room in the house, separating donations from trash. Of course, I would have to leave the house at some point during the day, as I needed to stock up on food. And I figured since I was heading out, I would call Gary and see if he had time to see me.

I waited until nine to call and was able to schedule an appointment for 1:00 p.m. Maybe the rain would stop by then.

With caffeine in my system, it was time to get started. And what better way to start than by tackling my mother's bedroom? I climbed up the stairs and walked past the guest bedroom, which had the door closed. I pushed open the door to my mother's room, and her scent hit me. Immediately, tears welled in my eyes and I started bawling, dropping to the ground. It finally hit me that my mother was gone.

I'm not sure how long I cried, but I needed it. It brought

some sense of closure to my mother's death, acknowledging its finality with a good cry. I don't know why I thought I had to be strong and show no emotions. I'd put on a stoic front ever since I arrived. And for what? Who would I impress? Not Netty or Gary. When I thought about it, I realized I'd done it for my bullies. I didn't want them to see a weak Addie. I had told myself I would remain the new and improved Addie when I came home, but I could already feel myself slipping back into the past.

Pull yourself together, Addie. Be the person you know yourself to be.

My mother's room looked just how I remembered it. She even kept the same bedspread all these years. Her dresser top was covered with the same perfume bottles and makeup containers she always used. The dresser drawers were filled with neatly folded clothing. My mother was a stickler for folded clothes. I walked over to the window and pulled the drapes open.

That's when I saw him: a man standing near the edge of the property. A few blinks later, he'd disappeared. I couldn't get a good look at his face, as the window was dirty and covered with rain spots. I opened the window and stuck my head out, looking in both directions, but he was gone.

Probably one of my nosy neighbors.

It dawned on me right then that I wasn't even sure if my neighbors were the same people they had been when I was growing up. If the man was one of them, I was sure I would have recognized him. But this man wore a ball cap with his hoodie pulled over his head, which helped shield his face.

I shut the window. I certainly hadn't moved away from Danville to grow into the woman I was proud to be, only to return and revert to being a timid little girl.

I hustled down the stairs, grabbed a large knife from the kitchen, and marched out the front door, waving the knife around in full view. This was my property, and I had every right to stick someone. I walked over to where I saw the man standing. The area was grassy, so there were no shoe prints (not that it would help me identify him).

I circled the house, looking for signs of someone having walked around the property, but found none. A shiver ran through my body when I remembered I had slept through the night with open windows.

Did this person visit me last night? Did he set foot inside my house?

I hurried back inside and checked around the windows for signs of shoe prints or anything that might tell me if someone had come inside. I didn't remember seeing footprints in the moisture on the floor. Once again, I checked all the windows and the back door to ensure everything was tightly secured.

From now on, you only go out the front door and don't open the windows. Got that, Addie?

I headed back up to my mother's bedroom with renewed determination. I was going to power through as much as possible before meeting with Gary. Armed with a box of trash bags, I started with her closet. Most of it I thought I would be able to donate. Whatever wasn't current would be a nice haul for someone thrifting vintage. When I finished with her closet, I moved to her dresser drawers and had them empty in no time. It was an easy decision on what to do with all the grooming and makeup accessories on the dresser top. They all went into a bag marked for trash. Even the perfume bottles went. Next, I stripped the bed.

Should I trash or donate? Do people even donate used linens?

I threw them out, considering my mother had died while taking a nap, even though she always napped on the covers.

On a lark, I got down on my knees, peeked underneath my mother's bed, and spotted a shoebox. I pulled it out, flipped off the cover, and found something I would never have expected to find in a million years.

Inside the box were old newspaper clippings about Kam McDermitt's murder. She and I had gone to high school together. Five days before we graduated, Kam was found strangled on campus. I looked through the clippings, confused as to why my mother would keep them.

Kam's death had been a big deal in Danville, and there were always two or three articles a day devoted to it. Some focused on Kam and her family, while others were strictly about the investigation. Of course, there were numerous editorials and op-ed pieces on her murder. It seemed as though everyone had an opinion and wanted to voice it. Social media didn't exist back then, and I was glad for it, because I had been considered a prime suspect during the investigation. The speculation and bullying could have been much worse.

It wasn't just newspaper clippings—my mother even had the transcript of my interviews with the police. I simply could not understand what compelled her to keep it, especially after all these years. Throughout the ordeal, she had told me not to worry and to put everything behind me. If that was what she thought, why keep all of this? I threw the entire shoebox into a trash bag.

I glanced over at the clock and saw it was 12:30. My appointment was in thirty minutes. I took a few moments to freshen up before heading downstairs. My mother owned a car, a silver Honda Accord. I had just assumed she kept it and it was parked in the garage. I hadn't bothered to look. I retrieved the keys from the drawer of the table next to the front door, where she'd always kept them.

I opened the garage door, and there was the car. It looked fine, dusty windows aside. I climbed inside, inserted the key into the ignition, and turned. The engine turned over on the first try.

Yes!

Who would have thought a car starting would be a win?

FIVE

GARY HAD a practice that he shared with two other men. I had never met them, nor had I ever visited his office before. The size of the building surprised me. For some reason, I imagined three men sitting in one large space behind three desks. I waited in reception for a few minutes before a young woman led me to Gary's office.

"Addie, how are you doing?" He greeted me as I entered his office. "Please, have a seat. Can I get you anything to drink? Coffee, mineral water?"

"I'm fine, Gary."

He took a seat behind his desk. "Let me give you a quick overview of what you're facing. Being an only child, you stand to inherit everything your mother owned. What you do with those items is completely up to you. Let's talk about the house. You'll need to sign some paperwork to transfer the deed into your own name. You won't trigger any taxes on the house, but if you do decide to sell it, you'll need to pay capital gains on the gains the home has made since coming into possession of it."

"I plan to sell it as soon as possible. Do you have any idea how long that will take?"

"Well, a realtor would be better equipped to answer that question. I know a perfect one that I could put you in touch with."

"Great, can you set that up? The sooner we can list the house, the better. I plan on cleaning it out and leaving just the appliances—so, unfurnished."

"Okay."

"I want to leave Danville within a week. Can we finish all the paperwork by then?" I asked.

"A week? That's quick. I might need more time than that. Selling the house could take some time as well."

"Why is that?"

"Well, if I may be frank, the house comes with history. It'll be difficult selling to someone from Danville. But again, the realtor would have a better assessment of the best way to sell the home."

"So, how long do you think it will take to finalize my mother's estate?"

"Six months, if there are no problems."

My stomach sank. I wasn't sure I could stay in that house for that long, let alone in this town. "You're kidding, right?"

"I am not. I had advised your mother to set up a trust for you, which would have made it easier and faster to settle her estate, but she kept putting it off. As it stands, we must go through the probate process. This takes time, but I promise to expedite the process as much as possible. Any other questions about the house and property?"

"No."

"Okay. Outside of the house, your mother did not own any other property, but she did have a significant amount of money in the bank."

"Really?"

While I was growing up, my mother had always pinched

pennies. I was rarely given the latest and greatest must-have toys and clothes. We didn't even have a television in the house, and home computers weren't a thing when I was growing up.

"Her assets are spread out over stocks, bonds, and cash in various accounts."

"How much did she have?"

"All together, it's roughly five million dollars."

"Five million dollars!" I choked on a breath of air.

"I'm guessing from that reaction you had no idea."

"I grew up thinking we were poor."

"Well, your mother was a thrifty one. I imagine the value of the house and the land will probably add another two and a half to three million. I believe the location at that end of your street is prime property—lots of privacy. Now that I think of it, your house could sell quickly because of the land."

"You mean they'll buy it just to tear down our home and build something else?"

"That's right. You could fit two houses on that lot, or one huge mansion."

I sat in shock. I had half expected Gary to tell me I owed taxes.

"The stocks and bonds will need to be transferred into your name. You can choose to keep them as is or sell them. It's your decision. About half of that five million are in stocks and bonds. The remaining is in cash."

"What about your fee?"

"It's all taken care of by your mother. I've essentially been paid to do this work already. Money has also been set aside to pay the probate fees. You have nothing to worry about."

I left Gary's office learning two new things: One, I had a lot of money coming my way. Two, I wouldn't be leaving Danville in a week.

As I drove to the nearest grocery store to stock up, I grew

anxious about running into someone I knew. I thought avoiding people I knew for a week was doable, but now that it looked like I'd be in town much longer, an encounter was bound to happen. It was only then that I wished I had a pair of dark sunglasses and an oversized hat with me.

I lowered my umbrella close to my head and remained hopeful.

My hair was lighter, and I was no longer boney; I had curves. My makeup and outfits had improved. I wore color and no longer resembled a goth wannabe. If someone didn't *really* know me back then, there was a good chance they wouldn't recognize me now. At least that was the bull I wanted to spoon-feed myself.

I did well in the grocery store. I knew exactly what I wanted, kept my head down, and, most importantly, didn't dilly-dally. I shopped like a man. I went in, got what I needed, and headed for the checkout. I was pleased as I rolled my shopping cart back to my car. Even the front wheel pulling the cart to the left didn't bother me.

I loaded my groceries into the trunk and returned the cart to the collection area. As soon as I turned back to my car, a woman appeared in front of me.

"Addie? Addie Baxley?" she asked.

Oh, my God. Who is this woman smiling at me with her super-white teeth and a perfect blond blowout?

"It *is* you, isn't it?" she asked as she lifted her umbrella a little higher and leaned forward for a better look.

"I, uh…"

"It's me, Virgie. Virgie Gillis."

What were the odds that the first person to recognize me would be my bully? Virgie was the OGB, the original gangster bully who started it all. She was the catalyst that forced me to leave Danville the summer after graduating high school. Before

I could manage another round of gibberish, Virgie threw her free arm around me. She pulled me in for a hug, causing our umbrellas to bang against each other.

"I can't believe it's really you!" she shouted. "I thought you were…"

What? Dead? Institutionalized? Traveling with the Romani? Which rumor did you start?

"Oh, never mind." She pulled away and stared at me with bright blue eyes. "How have you been?"

Really? You're going to pretend those eight years of terrorizing me didn't happen?

"My, my, my, what a treat. I mean, I sort of knew there was a chance you might return. I'm sorry to hear about your mother's passing. My condolences to you."

"Thank you."

The smile on her face dimmed as she crinkled her brow. "I'm just going to get this out of the way, because I know we're both thinking it right now. I'm serious when I say this… I am truly sorry for how I treated you when we were younger. It wasn't right, and I was a hundred percent responsible for it. You did nothing to deserve that appalling treatment from me."

Wait, what? Was Virgie actually apologizing to me?

"I feel bad about the teasing," she said as she looked away briefly. "I wish I could take it back. Look, I'm not expecting you to come right out and say 'I forgive you' or anything. But I just want you to know I realize what a bitch I was to you. And I was wrong. Part of me is so glad I could tell you this to your face."

Why? Because it dampens your guilt?

"I know this is asking a lot, but if you could one day find it in your heart to forgive me, it would mean a lot."

"I don't know what to say," I said.

"Don't say anything. It's me who has the explaining to do."

"Okay."

I wasn't sure what was supposed to happen next. Were we supposed to get coffee together and catch up? Were we supposed to exchange phone numbers? I didn't want to do either if those things.

"How long are you in town for?" Virgie asked.

"I'm not sure."

"Sure, of course. You're probably busy dealing with your mother's estate, and I'm holding you up."

"Yes."

Virgie opened her mouth to say something but stopped short. She looked around briefly. "I am really sorry. And if you give me a chance to prove myself to you, I would love to start over and get to know the real Addie."

Is that so?

"I would love to hear all about what you've been up to the last twelve years. But I understand if you're not ready for that." Virgie dug into the Louis Vuitton handbag that hung off her shoulder and retrieved a business card.

"This is my business, the Cubbyhole. It's a co-working space. You're welcome to come in if you need a place to get work done. You won't have to pay. You'll be my guest as long as you're in town. Just let me know."

I took the card from her, thinking that perhaps my biggest bully had changed. But did that mean I had to forget everything she'd done to me? Could I forget about the childhood she had stolen from me? I wasn't sure. I briefly wondered what I would do if the situation were reversed. Well, it didn't matter what I would do, because I would never bully someone like that.

"Thank you, Virgie. It's a nice gesture."

"Call me, email me, message me. Whatever way works for you is fine with me. I'd love to host you."

We looked at each other for a few more awkward seconds

before Virgie gave me a friendly squeeze on my arm. "Bye, Addie."

I was still at a loss for words as I watched her walk away. The Virgie I remembered was mean, conniving, bitchy, and more. She'd made my life unbearable. She'd stolen a good portion of my teen years away from me. What would my life have been like if I hadn't spend a large part of it enduring her terror or avoiding her? What experiences would I have had if I didn't have to factor Virgie into every decision I made? I climbed back into my car and drove away.

Focus, Addie. You didn't come back for a therapy session. The plan is still to get in and get out.

SIX

I DROVE straight home and hurried into the house with my groceries. I just had a feeling that the second Virgie was out of my sight, she'd gotten on her phone and called the other bullies to let them know I'd come back. Why wouldn't she? She was always the one making sure I was the outcast.

Maybe she's changed, Addie.

Maybe, but why do I have to accept it?

Nothing about that interaction in the parking lot made me feel better. In fact, it made me feel worse. Virgie wanted my forgiveness for her benefit. The apology only served to make her feel better.

But isn't it nice to hear her admit she was wrong?

I already knew Virgie was wrong. I didn't need to hear it from her. I decided to forget about it. It wasn't worth wasting energy on.

Before heading to the dining room, I made a tuna sandwich and grabbed a bag of chips. While I ate, I tried my best to focus on the task at hand: the house. But I couldn't get Virgie out of my mind. She had also changed with age. She had the same eyes and facial expressions, but much like me, she had grown into a woman. But I doubted that enormous chest was real.

I wonder if she's married with kids...

Wait, why are you wondering? You're supposed to not care.

But I did. Isn't it normal to be curious about what happened to one's bullies? Would karma take care of them like everyone said it would? While I was away, I had never thought about Virgie. Ever. I had focused entirely on myself. Self-love had been my priority.

Dammit, why did I have to see Virgie? And why did she have to be friendly and apologetic and appear genuine about it all? She even invited me to work at her co-working space for free.

I did work, but not at a desk job. For the first three to four years after high school, I did whatever work I could find: waitressing, retail sales, or just odd jobs to sustain myself. But one day, I met this woman who turned me on to e-commerce. The internet had exploded, and so had e-commerce. In the beginning, I started with the idea of monetizing a blog. I wrote about my adventures but kept my identity a secret. I was a mysterious woman solo traveling the world. People could easily imagine themselves in my shoes. That blog soon became a solid money-maker for me.

After that, I started other online businesses related to travel, specifically for women. I even created a bikini line specifically designed for small-chested women like myself. My companies fed off each other, and I did very well. I never once called my mother for money during those twelve years. She offered every single time we talked, but I always turned her down. It was vital for me to take care of myself. It was empowering. I now maintain three businesses, all from my laptop. I could work and live anywhere in the world. There was zero need for me to be in Danville.

The landline rang, startling me. I hadn't realized it was still connected. My mother kept one phone in the house, and it was in the living room next to the sofa.

"Hello?"

"Hi, Addie. It's Netty. How is everything?"

"Everything is fine. I just got back from grocery shopping."

Netty knew all about Virgie. It was no secret, but I decided there was no need to bring up our encounter.

"So the car is working. That's good. What about the house? Do you need any help clearing it out? You know you can count on me for help."

"I know that, and I'm grateful, but I think I'm good for the moment. I made a lot of headway this morning. Oh, I met with Gary today. He said I should expect the probate to take a while."

"It always does. It's such a complicated process. Have you decided what you're doing with the house?"

"My initial thought was to sell it, but Gary thought it would take a while because of its history. Meaning me."

"Oh, what does Gary know? A good realtor should be able to move that house no matter the history."

"We'll see. He knows a good realtor and said he would give me their information. Tell you what, why don't you come over for dinner tonight? I'll fix us something delicious."

"Oh, that sounds wonderful."

"Great, come by at seven."

After getting off the phone with Netty, I finished my sandwich and thought I would do some work. The house didn't have Wi-Fi, and as luck would have it, there was nowhere in the house where my phone had a signal stronger than two bars. Using my phone as a hot spot wasn't helpful. Tasks that would usually take ten minutes to do now took twenty minutes. I needed a stronger signal to be more efficient.

No, you're not taking Virgie up on her offer. You've worked in plenty of coffee shops around the world. No reason why you can't work at one here. Taking her up on her offer would only signal that things are okay between you two.

That much was true. But I also didn't have a beef with Virgie. It wasn't like I came back with a plan for revenge. I'd probably never, ever see her again when I was finished here. And if that was the case, why not take advantage? Really, it would be me using her for my needs. I'd never thought I would be in a position to do that.

That settled it. I fired off an email to the address on the card, being sure to use the email address I had for subscriptions or anything that could end up spamming me, like Virgie. A few minutes later, she responded, "See you soon."

SEVEN

WAS IT A POWER STRUGGLE?

Virgie held power over me while we were younger. Did allowing me to work at her co-working space also demonstrate she still had the power, but in an adult way?

Stop it, Addie. Stop wasting time and energy thinking about this. You have much better things to occupy your mind, like how to shrink that six-month timeline Gary gave you.

I did have better things to think about. And if using Virgie's co-working space could help, why not? I had work to get done, and it didn't matter much where I did it.

From the minute I arrived in town, I had noticed the change. The downtown area looked three times bigger. There were many new shops, restaurants, and even a new building that housed five floors of shopping and eating. There was even a large cinema complex. The town had definitely changed. Maybe Virgie had, too. Maybe I had her all wrong, and she was genuinely sorry.

I parked my car in a parking structure and walked to the Cubbyhole. According to Google Maps, it was situated smack dab in the middle of town in a new building.

I bet her dad built it.

It was no secret Virgie's family was wealthy. Her dad was a prominent developer, and Virgie was a big-time bragger. All she did when we were younger was make sure everyone knew how rich her family was. At school, she would hand me her old clothes, shoes, notebooks, pencils—anything she no longer wanted—and then ask for a charity donation receipt. People would always laugh.

On the walk there, I bought a cup of coffee. Exiting the café, I realized I was across the street from a children's clothing store called Playground. The owner of the shop was Mrs. McDermitt, Kam's mother. She was inside but busy with a customer, so she didn't see me. I doubted she would have recognized me from that distance.

Mrs. McDermitt was my most vocal critic during the investigation. She wholeheartedly believed I was responsible for murdering her daughter. She went around town telling anyone who would listen that I was envious of Kam and killed her out of a jealous rage. Even with the police clearing me, she continued to blame me. Whenever she'd see me out in public, she'd shout, "Murderer!" I hurried along.

The Cubbyhole was a modernized two-story warehouse. Very hipster. I could already see it. Everyone inside would be working on a start-up that was their entire identity. Virgie was talking to the receptionist when I walked inside.

"Addie! Welcome to the Cubbyhole. I'm so glad you decided to give us a try. I'm sure you'll get a lot of work done here. By the way, you never told me what type of work you do."

I know. That was on purpose. "I'm writing a book."

I really didn't want to get into it with what I did. One answer would only lead to more questions about my personal life, and I wasn't ready to share.

Virgie pointed at me. "Look at you, an author. What kind of book are you writing?"

"It's about travel."

I wasn't lying entirely. Writing a book was on the list of things to do.

"Is that what you've been up to all these years? Traveling?"

"More or less. Um, where can I sit?"

"I'm sorry. I'm blabbing and keeping you from your work. I've already set aside an office for you on the second floor. Follow me."

I followed Virgie through an open floor plan where I saw people sitting at a large communal table or at individual desks.

"Anyone can work in this area, so long as there's a free space. Nothing is reserved. Over there is a coffee bar. Getting your caffeine fix is free. We also have organic smoothies and fresh-pressed juices, and we make our own kombucha. Those drinks aren't free, but the price is minimal."

"Is that you, Addie?" I heard a voice say behind me. I turned around and saw Felisa Chu, Virgie's best friend and my second bully.

"I'm not sure if I told you, but Felisa co-owns the Cubbyhole with me," Virgie said.

Felisa looked the same as she did in high school. Not a wrinkle in sight. But instead of wearing her black hair straight and down to her shoulders, she had it pulled back into a French braid.

"When Virgie told me you were back in town, I couldn't believe it," Felisa said. "I mean, one minute you were here, and the next you were gone." She reached out and gently grabbed my arm. "I am so sorry about your mother."

"Thank you."

"Oh, and..." Felisa lowered her voice. "I also want to take

this opportunity to say I'm sorry for how I treated you in high school."

What about middle school and the summers in between?

"I feel horrible that I was one of those people. I can only imagine the hurt you must have felt throughout all those years. I truly am sorry."

That was two of them owning up to what they did. I knew I couldn't change the past. It was what it was. But seeing this new side of Virgie and Felisa... Maybe they did deserve a second chance. Their words certainly seemed sincere.

"I appreciate that," I said. "Thank you. Thank you both for telling me this."

Virgie and Felisa escorted me up to the second floor, which was filled with offices of various sizes divided by glass partitions and a few solid walls.

"Here we are." Virgie pointed to a small office. "I hope it suits your needs."

The office was large enough for one person, with a window giving me a partial view of Main Street. There was a desk, an executive chair, and one guest chair. The front was all glass, but luckily, the other three sides were solid, giving me some privacy.

"This is perfect. It'll totally work."

"Great. That's your welcome packet on the desk. It has the Wi-Fi password and the code to get inside the building. It's open twenty-four hours. Information about receiving and sending mail is included, as well as how to print on the copier machines and book a meeting room. Feel free to leave personal belongings here. You can lock the door to the office. The keys should be in the top desk drawer. Any questions?"

"Not at the moment."

"I hope I'm not too forward by asking, but Felisa and I would love to take you to dinner. What do you say, Addie?"

"Sure."

"How does tomorrow night sound?"

"I can do that."

"Great. Happy co-working."

After they left, I took a seat behind the desk. I may have had this visit all wrong, I thought. Maybe I was making it out to be worse than it was. Because it didn't feel like I was having a terrible time. In fact, I felt okay. Getting in and getting out might not be that rough after all.

EIGHT

THE SUMMER WHEN I WAS 11

I HAD FORGOTTEN ALL about Virgie and Felisa until summer came back around. I had made plans to meet Spencer at the park, but he was late, so I ended up swinging by myself. I was eating an overripe banana and singing to myself when a voice called out.

"Oh, it's you again."

I slowed my swinging so I could see who it was. I wished I hadn't. Virgie and Felisa were standing there looking at me as if I had leprosy.

"Still dressing like a boy, I see," Felisa said.

They walked around to the front of the swings.

"Did you pass your grade this year?" Virgie asked.

"Yes, why?"

"Oh God, we'll go to the same school next year." Virgie stuck her finger into her mouth and pretended to vomit.

"What are you eating?" Felisa asked. "It's so gross looking."

"It's a banana."

"A rotten banana. Don't you know you're not supposed to eat it when there are black spots on it?"

"It's perfectly fine. It's just sweeter, that's all."

"Oh, my God, you're so dumb."

She and Felisa then said "Ewww" for a solid fifteen minutes. The next day, they would throw a rotten banana at me. In fact, from that point on, whenever they had an opportunity to throw a rotten banana at me, they didn't hesitate.

Just then, two boys I'd never seen before showed up.

"Hi, Virgie. Hi, Felisa. Sorry we're late."

I would later learn that boy's name was Jude Akers, and he had a crush on Virgie. I remember him having his hair neatly gelled back. Not many boys his age did that. His friend was Reed Holland. He had orange hair and freckles covering his face. All four of them went to the other elementary school in town.

"Hi, Jude."

Virgie smiled and batted her eyelashes. She was so fake.

"I'm so glad you guys are here," she said. "We were getting bored talking to Addie. She's so weird."

"Yeah, and she's poor, so she has to eat rotten bananas," Felisa said.

"Ugh," Reed said. "That's disgusting. Even monkeys don't eat rotten bananas. I think I'm going to be sick." He grabbed hold of his stomach and pretended to vomit.

"That's what we were saying," Virgie said. "Let's go. We have better things to do than be grossed out by her."

I continued eating as they walked away, confused about why I shouldn't eat a ripe banana. My mother ate them, and so did my Aunty Netty. What was the big deal?

"Hey, Addie."

I looked up and spotted Spencer walking toward me.

"You're late."

"I know. I'm sorry."

"I was here alone with Virgie and Felisa. They said I'm gross and weird for eating this banana."

"Don't listen to them, Addie. They're jealous that they don't have one to eat."

"They got two other boys to tease me."

"Really?"

"Yes. Spence, if we meet here again, you can't be late, okay? I don't want to be here by myself with them."

"I promise I won't ever be late again. Hey, I have an idea. Follow me."

Spencer and I left the park, cutting through the backyards of several homes. After about twenty minutes, he led me down a wooded trail that he eventually veered off of.

"Spence, where are you taking me?" I asked as I walked beside him, holding onto his shirt. "I don't want to get lost."

"You'll see. It's just up ahead."

Spencer pushed through a few bushes, and we popped out onto the banks of a creek.

"What do you think?" he said with a proud smile.

I stared at the isolated spot along the creek, with its large, smooth rocks along the banks, perfect for sitting or lying on. I jumped over to one.

"I love it. What is this place?" I asked as I twirled around.

"It's my secret spot, and now it's our secret spot. We're the only ones who know about it, so you need to keep it a secret. If you or I get into trouble, this is where we can come. If you're here, I'll come and meet you. It's the same if I'm in trouble and come here."

"I like it. But how will we know if one of us is here? We don't have phones."

"Hmmm... I think we'll just know. We'll feel it inside, because we're friends, and that's what friends do. They're always there for each other."

From that day forward, the creek became our hangout spot. Spencer and I would pack lunches and spend entire days there, exploring, talking, and doing whatever else came to mind. Having Spencer and the creek in my life made me feel much better. What made it even better was that we rarely saw Virgie and Felisa. I was having the best summer ever.

Of course, my life would take a drastic turn when school started later that year. I'd have to face Virgie and Felisa daily, and it wouldn't just be them I'd have to deal with. The awesome summer when I was eleven would also be known as the summer Jude and Reed joined the bully group.

NINE

I SPENT two productive hours at the Cubbyhole before leaving.
I could have worked a few more hours, but I needed to get home
and prepare dinner for Netty and myself. I had already decided
to make a pasta dish with a nice salad and garlic bread. I parked
my mother's car in the driveway; I had to pee and didn't have
time to squeeze it into the small garage.

I was hurrying up the porch steps, fumbling with my keys,
when I came to a quick stop. I couldn't believe what I was
looking at. Someone had left a bunch of rotten bananas on the
porch. Next to them was a note in red paint that read: *We
haven't forgotten about you.*

*I knew their smiles and words were fake. They were just
setting me up so they could tear me down again.*

But there was something different about these rotten
bananas. I leaned in to take a closer look. Razor blades had been
buried deep inside each one, so only the sharp tips were sticking
out. I could have easily picked up the bunch and sliced my hand
open. These bananas weren't only meant to tease me; they were
there to cause harm. I looked over my shoulder to the front of
the property. *Is someone watching now to see if the plan worked?*

I picked up the note for a closer look. It was written with a paintbrush, and tiny bits of the paint were still wet, meaning it wasn't written very long ago. I brought it up to my nose and took a sniff. It had a metallic scent to it. I dropped the note immediately.

Is that blood?

I couldn't be entirely sure, but it looked like blood and smelled like it.

If this is how they want to play it, fine. But I'm not letting them get to me.

In fact, I'd continue working at the Cubbyhole just to spite them. The way I saw it, every day I occupied that office for free was another day of lost revenue for them. I carefully picked up the bananas and threw them in the trash container on the side of the house before heading inside.

Nothing in this town ever changes.

———

Netty showed up a little before seven in an upbeat mood.

"I brought wine," Netty said as I opened the front door. "I hope you like red."

"I love red. It'll be perfect with the pasta I'm making."

Netty came inside and took a deep breath. "Smells delicious. Did you make your own sauce?"

"I did," I said proudly. "I learned to cook during my travels, especially while in Italy. I took cooking classes there. I've prepared pasta alla norma, a Sicilian dish, Italian sausage and peppers, and an Italian salad for dinner."

"That sounds yummy."

Netty knew from my mother that I'd been traveling worldwide, but she wasn't aware of the nitty-gritty.

"Everything is ready and out on the dining room table. Have a seat while I fetch us glasses for the wine."

"This looks wonderful," Netty called out from the dining room. "I'm glad you made it to Italy."

I returned with glasses and a corkscrew.

"Do you think you'll go back to roaming, or will you settle someplace?" she asked as she took a seat. "I would think by now you've discovered a few favorite spots."

"I have, but settling down... I'm not so sure I would want to do that permanently."

I popped the cork on the bottle and poured us each a glass.

"Here's to us," I said as I raised my glass. "Family."

"I'll cheers to that."

She clinked her glass against mine and took a sip.

"You said you weren't sure about settling down, but what if you meet someone?" Netty gave me a playful wink as she lowered her glass.

"I'll cross that bridge when I get there."

I served Netty the Italian salad.

"This is delicious," she said.

"It's so easy to make. Romaine lettuce, cherry tomatoes, red onions, pepperoncini, and olives all tossed in Italian dressing. Then top off with grated Parmesan cheese."

Netty was too busy eating to respond and simply nodded. I realized right then how much I'd missed her.

"What have you been up to since you've been back?" Netty asked. "It doesn't look like you've gotten much done with the house."

"I know. I got caught up reminiscing while I was cleaning."

"That'll do it."

"Guess what?" I asked.

"What?"

"I ran into Virgie Gillis today."

Netty stopped mid-bite. "Is that so?"

"Yup, outside the grocery store."

"Such rotten luck. So what happened?"

"Believe it or not, she apologized to me for the bullying."

Netty paused the bite she was about to put into her mouth. "Was it genuine?"

"At first, I thought she was just saying it out of guilt, you know, to make herself feel better."

"But?"

"She then offered to host me at her co-working space for free. Did you know she owned her own business?"

"I'd heard about it but never been there," Netty said. "Well, that's nice of her."

"I know. I took her up on that offer. Turned out the other owner was Felisa Chu. You remember her?"

"How could I not? Both of those girls were so mean to you. They deserved a good spanking."

Netty served us each some pasta. "I don't see either of them that much since I only go into town when I need to. But I guess people change over time. So how did it go at the co-working space?"

"Fine. Felisa also apologized for her past behavior," I said as I forked some ribbon pasta into my mouth. "She seemed just as genuine as Virgie. I honestly believed their intentions were sincere until I returned home. I found a bunch of rotten bananas on the porch."

"Unbelievable. You think it was them?"

"When I was a kid, they tormented me with rotten bananas."

I decided to leave out the part about the razor blades and the message written in blood. It would just upset Netty and spoil our dinner.

"I could be wrong, but those two are the most likely

culprits," I continued. "But you know what? I'm not going to let it get to me. I'm going to keep going to that co-working space. Things are different now. I'm not little Addie anymore."

"I'm proud of you." Netty poked her fork at me. "You'll be the winner when they see that their bullying has no effect on you."

"And you know what else? They also invited me to dinner."

A devious look popped onto Netty's face. "Please, please, please tell me you accepted," Netty said.

"Of course I did. I was initially on the fence, but after this banana bull, I'm definitely having dinner with them."

"Good for you, Addie. I wish your mother could see you now. She'd be smiling from ear to ear." Netty eyed the sausages and peppers before serving herself. "Oh, to be a fly on the wall and see the look on their faces when you show up and they realize the bananas had no effect on you."

Netty and I spent the rest of the evening chitchatting, mainly reminiscing about our good times with my mother. She talked about how she and my mother had started to take trips together, which surprised me, because my mother had never mentioned it during our phone calls.

"They weren't anything big," Netty said. "Sometimes it was a day trip to Napa Valley, and sometimes we'd spend the weekend in San Francisco, playing tourist. Your mother was able to come out of her shell during those trips. I wish you could have been there with us."

"Me, too."

I felt a pang of guilt.

"I can see it on your face. Don't beat yourself up for not visiting. Your mother wouldn't have it any other way. She knew what this town had done to you, and the only way for you to heal and get your life right was to leave and stay away. Addie, I want you to know if you have any trouble while you're back in

town, you can come to me. I promised your mother that I would
always look out for you. I love you like you're my own daughter.
I may be getting up in my years, but I still have some fight in
me." She shook her fist.

I chuckled. "Thank you, Netty. I love you, too."

Netty left a little after ten. I walked her out to the car and
said goodbye, promising to give her all the details of my dinner
with Virgie and Felisa. I quickly headed back inside and
ensured all the windows and doors on the first floor, including
the back door, were locked. I then grabbed a large knife from the
kitchen and ran upstairs straight into my bedroom, leaving the
lights off.

I peeked out the window—he was still there. A blink later
and he had disappeared.

I'd spotted the mystery man in the shadows near the edge of
the property while seeing Netty off. I assumed this was the
same person I had seen the day before.

No, nothing ever changed in this town. But I was ready for
it this time.

TEN

THE FOLLOWING DAY, I kept sorting items, moving on to tackle
my mother's office. I still needed to figure out how to drag the
furniture to secondhand stores. I wasn't even sure they would
take it. Holding a garage sale would be the easiest way to get rid
of it, but having everyone in the neighborhood show up was the
last thing I wanted. Or worse, no one might show up.

Virgie sent me an email confirming dinner that night, to
which I said yes. She said she knew of a great restaurant in town
and couldn't wait to meet.

Fake.

Dinner reservations were set for 7:30. I almost pushed for
6:30 in hopes we could end the night early, but I decided to let
the timing stand. It took a while for me to figure out what to
wear. I definitely didn't want to wear anything that would trigger
a discussion of my fashion sense of yesteryear, so even though I
had packed a cute black dress, I ruled it out. I ended up wearing
jeans, a floral blouse, and leather boots. I had to do me. I knew
Virgie and Felisa would show up dressed in designer casual.

At 7:00, I made the drive into town. The name of the

restaurant was Cut, as in cuts of meat. Virgie had mentioned in the email that it was a steakhouse and stated, "Hope you're not a vegetarian, ha ha ha."

The restaurant was in a standalone building with its own parking lot. I walked in a few minutes after seven. The hostesses told me my party had already been seated, which surprised me. I had half expected Virgie and Felisa to arrive late, make me wait, and then laugh it off.

Sitting at the table were three people. I recognized Virgie and Felisa right away.

"Addie, welcome to Cut." Virgie popped out of her chair and gave me an awkward hug. "You remember Felisa, of course, but can you guess who this is?" She gestured to the man with a serious look on his face.

I had to take a second, but then it hit me. *Reed!*

His red hair had turned a reddish brown, and his freckles didn't pop as much. He also looked like he had bulked up from weight training.

"Reed..." I said.

"That's right. It's hard to forget a beautiful face like mine," he said.

Or an asshole personality.

Reed didn't extend a hand or bother to stand. Instead, he picked up his drink and finished it before calling a server over to the table.

"Felisa and I are enjoying this wonderful red. Can I pour you a glass?"

"Sure." I slipped my purse off my shoulder and placed it on the back of the chair before sitting.

"How exciting is this?" Virgie said. "The four of us having dinner."

"Yeah, who would have thought, right?" Reed quipped.

Even if Virgie and Felisa were faking it, at least they were faking it. Reed remained the same rude idiot I'd grown up with.

Virgie placed a hand on my shoulder. "I have another surprise for you."

What? Do you plan on making me pick up the bill?

"Hello, Addie."

A handsome man dressed in a fitted suit walked up to the table.

"You remember Jude, right?" Virgie said. "He's the owner of this fabulous restaurant."

Jude bent down and gave me a hug with a pat on the back. He smelled wonderful.

"I almost didn't recognize you," I said.

It was mainly because he looked nothing like the pimple-faced boy who had made high school hell for me. I hated to admit it, but aging was a positive thing for him. He had clear skin, a chiseled jawline, and a strong brow that enhanced his icy-blue eyes.

Wait a minute, Addie. Don't let his looks fool you. He was part of the bully group.

"I can say the same for you too, Addie. You look beautiful."

"Jude, dear. Could you please get us another bottle of the red I absolutely love?"

"Sure, I'll be right back."

Virgie cleared her throat. "Jude and I are together and have been for a while. I think it's been five years now."

Two minutes in, and she's already threatened by me. This might turn out to be a great dinner, after all.

"Will Jude be joining us for dinner?" I asked.

"Don't be silly," Virgie said. "He just said 'Hi' because I asked him to."

Hate to break it to you, but your man didn't need any convincing.

"He's got a restaurant to run. It takes a focused person to run a profitable business."

Things calmed down after that and went about as well as I expected. Reed wanted nothing to do with me and concentrated on drinking and his phone. Virgie and Felisa, on the other hand, were doing their best to pull information out of me. It was as if they needed to account for every minute I'd been gone. But mostly, they wanted to know what I did for a living, primarily my financial status. Clearly, they weren't buying the author thing.

"So, Virgie tells me you want to be an author," Felicia said. "That's so cute. Writing a book seems like an impossible feat. So many words to string together."

I remember back when we were fifteen. You had the same problem with sentences.

"It's a travel memoir, so it's mostly just writing down my experiences," I said.

"Traveling—wow, that sounds so expensive," Virgie said. "Not to mention the time off needed."

"My work is flexible."

Virgie sat up straight. "So you do have another job besides writing?"

Deflecting and avoiding their questions became a chore. I eventually gave them a tidbit.

"I manage websites."

"I knew it. You had to have some type of work that required only a laptop. What company is it?"

"It's a small, foreign firm. You've never heard of them."

For the remainder of the evening, I asked questions that allowed Virgie and Felisa to brag about their lives, which was fine. That way, I didn't have to divulge anything more about myself.

Reed was not nearly as talkative. Every once in a while, I'd catch him looking at me. And not in an inquisitive, you-have-something-interesting-to-say kind of way, but more like a wolf eyeing his next meal. There was no mistaking Reed's feelings for me; they hadn't changed since high school. So far, the only thing he talked about was successfully managing his father's two car dealerships and that he had recently bought a Porsche.

Whoop dee do!

"So, Addie, have you had a chance to stop by Kam's grave since you came home?" he asked as he tossed back his drink.

I couldn't believe he had just asked that question. What a dick. He knew how touchy a subject Kam's death would be, especially since I'd been considered a suspect. Virgie and Felisa clammed up, but I wasn't about to let Reed have his way.

"I haven't," I said. "Have you?"

"I'm not the one visiting."

"So, no, I take it?"

Reed held up his empty glass and motioned to a nearby server for another drink. "I just thought you might want to see it."

"Why is that?"

A look of surprise fell over his face. "Because of what happened. Sheesh."

"I still have no idea what you're talking about."

Of course, I did. Everyone at the table knew I had been suspected and been cleared of any wrongdoing. This was Reed continuing his bullying ways.

"How about dessert?" Virgie said. "The chocolate mousse is to die for."

That interjection was enough to stop Reed and had Virgie scoring more brownie points with me.

Jude stopped by the table again after we finished dessert to see if we'd enjoyed our meals. Of the four of them, Jude came across as the most sincere. He wasn't over the top like Virgie or Felisa; his demeanor was chill and down-to-earth.

When I stepped away from the table to use the restroom, Jude caught up with me and apologized for his behavior when we were younger. I believed him right away—and not because he was handsome. The way he looked at me, and leaned in just a bit with his head turned slightly. His eyes pleaded with me to accept his apology.

When the bill finally came, Virgie snatched it up. Felisa didn't blink an eye, and Reed never even looked up from his phone. I offered to chip in, but Virgie insisted it was her treat.

She definitely deserved an "A" for effort. By the night's end, she had me thinking she was the real deal. Maybe she had nothing to do with the bananas. Perhaps it was someone else. *Like Reed.*

"Are you okay to drive?" Virgie asked me with concern in her voice.

"I'm fine, but you might want to check on Reed," I said.

"Hey, I can drive," he shot back. "Don't worry about me."

Virgie and Felisa told me they wanted to hang out until Jude closed up. As luck would have it, Reed and I had nothing else to do but leave simultaneously. I did my best to stay a couple of feet ahead of him. I turned right outside of the restaurant, and he turned left. Thankfully, we weren't parked near each other.

I let the engine run a bit before backing out of the parking space and driving off. During my drive home, I got lost in my thoughts about the night and how I might have been wrong about Virgie and Felisa. They were definitely trying to get past the walls I had thrown up. Initially, their interest in me had been over the top, probably due to nervousness and wanting to make amends. I couldn't say the same for Reed. On the other hand, Jude was friendly and professional, though I was also a guest in his restaurant. I had noticed that he made sure to stop at everyone's table and see how they were doing.

On my drive home, I had to keep squinting. The car behind me either had its high beams on, or they were at the right angle to hit my rearview mirror perfectly. I flipped the tab on the mirror, dimming the glare from the headlights. I made a left, and so did the car. Then it moved abnormally close to me. With the rearview mirror set for night driving, I couldn't make out what kind of car it was.

Is this car following me?

I made a right where I should have, and the car behind me did the same. I then made a left, and it followed. I sped up, and it increased its speed.

If this is Reed, I swear I'll let him have it. What a jackass.

I slowed down and brake-checked the car. The other car backed off but quickly caught back up with me. Reed knew where I lived and would realize I was driving in circles. But I didn't want this person following me home if it wasn't him.

The police station was coming up. I turned into the parking lot near the front of the building and parked. The car that had been following came to a stop on the road. It sat there with its engine idling. I still couldn't tell the make or model; it didn't look like a Porsche, but I wasn't a car expert. A few seconds later, the car did a U-turn and sped off.

ELEVEN

I WOKE EARLY the following day with a slight headache, but nothing a couple of aspirins and a cup of hot coffee couldn't take care of. My challenge for the day was to tackle the basement. The last time I had set foot in there was shortly after I came to live with my new mother and father.

I'd never lived in a house like the one they owned. At the time, I remember thinking it was a castle. It was so big, and there seemed to be so many places I could hide. My new parents never told me a room was off-limits, so I explored everywhere.

However, one door remained locked. I recalled asking my mother what was behind it, and she said it was stairs leading to the basement. I'd accepted her answer at the time and gave it no more thought until, one day, she left a note in my bedroom telling me where the key to the basement was kept. I quickly fetched it, unlocked the door, and went down the creaky steps.

It was much colder in the basement than in the rest of the house, and I remembered the air smelled funny. There wasn't much to see, just a bunch of stacked boxes, shelves filled with tools and other metal objects I'd never seen before. I didn't understand why they kept it locked. And then I heard a low rumbling noise coming from the corner, where a tall, cylindrical thing stood. I walked up to it, and it rumbled again. I reached out and was about to touch it when I heard my mother.

"Don't."

I spun around, and my mother was standing on the stairs.

"That's the water heater. It's feisty, and your father is the only one allowed to touch it. Is that clear?"

I nodded and followed her back up the stairs. I never went into the basement again.

Cut to me at age thirty, standing in front of the basement door. It was locked, but now I knew where the key was kept. I unlocked the door and made my way down. It was still colder than the rest of the house, and the air smelled dank. Nothing much about it appeared to have changed. It stood frozen in time —except for one thing. A new water heater stood in the corner, and it didn't rumble.

I knew my father's tools might be helpful to someone, so I mentally earmarked them for donation. As for the stacks of boxes, I had yet to learn what they held, but it was apparent they'd been sealed for years. I pulled a box off the pile and placed it on the floor. The tape sealing it was cracked and yellowed. The tip of the basement key easily sliced it open. Inside, I found something I never, ever would have expected: baby clothes.

They couldn't have been for me. I was four when my parents brought me home, and these clothes were clearly for a newborn. I quickly opened up another box and found more baby clothes. Some other boxes held toys, stuffed animals, baby blankets and towels, and linens for what I imagined had to be a crib. I spied a larger box, and inside I found a disassembled crib.

Do I have a sibling?

I quickly shook off that thought, realizing what had really happened. My parents had been expecting, and something terrible had happened. A miscarriage, most likely. I couldn't believe my mother had kept this from me all these years. Was it too painful for her to talk about? Was that why she never wanted to leave the house and often kept to herself? Were those mood swings really depression?

Tears began to well in my eyes as I thought about my mother and how she kept that bottled up. It made me sad that she couldn't talk to me about it. It made me feel guilty because I had problems growing up—my bullies—which, of course, became her problem. She'd always felt helpless against them.

Was this why I was adopted? Because my mother couldn't have children, or worse, didn't want to risk another miscarriage? I wished I'd had an opportunity to talk with her about this.

I held up a blue onesie. They were expecting a boy. When I turned six, I remember picking at the paint on the wall near the side of my bed and discovering the color underneath was a light blue. I had taken his room.

I spent twenty minutes sitting on the floor and looking through the clothing. Every single item was brand new; some still had price tags. I wondered if she'd bought any from Mrs. McDermitt's shop. All the baby items were in excellent condition, and I couldn't bring myself to throw any of them out. Some other family would appreciate them. I folded a yellow T-shirt with a sailboat. I'd never known my mother to like sailing, but perhaps my father did.

As I stood, a shadow passed across the basement. My gaze shot up to the narrow windows at the top of the basement wall, and I saw someone walking by the last window.

I quickly ran upstairs, trying to recall whether or not I had gone out on the porch that morning—and if I had, did I lock the door behind me when I came back in? I ran straight into the kitchen, grabbed my large knife, and quietly went to the front door. A quick check of the knob, and relief washed over me. It was locked. I looked out through the sheer curtains but saw no one. I looked out the windows at the rear of the house. Nobody was in the backyard.

I swear, if this is Reed planting more rotten bananas on my porch...

I hurried back through the house and out the front door. No bananas, and no one in sight.

I know I saw someone. Not a chance I imagined it.

I walked the property looking for signs of vandalism or a break-in. I saw none, but I could clearly see inside the basement through the windows. Had this person watched me? And if so, why?

TWELVE

I MOVED ALL the boxes containing the baby items up to the living room and taped them shut. But by that point, I'd become irritated and decided to take a break from the basement. While snacking on a yogurt cup, I thought about calling Netty and asking her if she knew about the baby. She was my mother's best friend, after all. But then I thought, why dredge up the past unnecessarily? Clearly, it wasn't something my mother had wanted to discuss. I tabled the subject for the time being.

Speaking of dredging up the past, ever since Reed had mentioned Kam's grave, the subject had continually popped into my head. Before I left town, I'd had no desire to visit Kam's grave, and no real reason to. I didn't attend the funeral, even though everyone else in town did. Kam had bullied me, and I didn't like her. And while I was sorry that she was dead, that didn't mean I needed to feign sadness. Because, well, there wasn't any.

My mother had also declined the open invitation from Kam's family, but Netty hadn't. But I knew her only reason to go was so that she could come back and dish the dirt to my mother.

But after twelve years, there was a little curiosity on my end. In fact, she was buried at the same cemetery where my mother had just been laid to rest.

I should refresh the flowers on my mother's grave. If I notice Kam's grave, I might have a quick look. But only if I happen to see it.

I changed from my shorts and T-shirt to something more fitting for a grave visit. I took two steps out the door, felt the drizzle, and went back inside for an umbrella and a coat.

Some cemeteries allow cars to drive throughout the property. This wasn't one of them. I had to leave my car in the parking lot and make the trek on foot to my mother's grave.

The flowers were still in decent condition, probably because of all the rain. I changed them out for the fresh bouquet I'd purchased on the way over. I stood quietly under my umbrella, staring at the plaque. I wasn't big on talking to graves, but I did a little thinking, mostly about why my mother didn't mention the baby.

Inside the office of the cemetery's caretaker, I knew there was a directory of every burial plot. I could quickly look it up if I really wanted to find Kam's grave. So I did. Why? Curiosity.

A few minutes later, I had tracked down her grave. She didn't have a flat plaque like my mother's; it was part tombstone and part bench. I didn't sit, as that would have been too weird for me. What I really wanted was to see how I felt. Would there be animosity, or would I feel nothing?

If Kam were alive today, would she have apologized, too? She wasn't the worst one in the bully group. In fact, she had been nice to me the first time we met. Virgie ruined that by recruiting Kam into the bully group. Virgie was no doubt the queen of mean and wore that crown proudly. I wanted to believe that Kam would have apologized. She was different from the others.

With Kam, sometimes the bullying was intense, and some-times it was barely an effort. I had noticed the intensity was largely dependent on who was with her. If Virgie was there, it was a twenty on a scale of one to ten. If it was Jude, it could be a five. But if Kam was just passing me in the hall and no one was around, it was a zero.

I wondered if Kam had been projecting. Did she have a hell of her own she was dealing with? I had no idea what her home life was like, but if the nastiness Mrs. McDermitt had displayed toward me when I was young was any indication, she might have had problems at home. And if that had been the case, I might give Kam a pass for how she treated me.

Did you know your murderer, Kam? You were strangled, so there's a good chance you could have identified the person. I know you know it wasn't me. And if you could, you'd tell everyone in town the truth.

I'd always thought the police didn't do enough to catch Kam's killer. In fact, I didn't think they had any suspects besides me. I ended up leaving town before the investigation officially went cold. I never once asked my mother about what had happened after I left. I was too busy healing and starting a new life. I just wanted to move on.

But now that I was back, I did wonder what exactly had happened. Murder wasn't an everyday occurrence in Danville. Kam's death was the first I'd heard of since living here.

A breeze blew, and I suddenly felt like someone was watching me. I looked around but didn't see anyone. It could have just been the wind that triggered the feeling. With the lower half of my jeans feeling slightly damp, I decided my time at the cemetery was up, and I walked faster than usual back to my car.

Before returning to the house, I picked up an iced coffee in town. I found street parking near a coffee shop, and the door opened as I reached the entrance.

"Thank you," I said, nodding at the man who had held it open for me.

"Addie Baxley? I'd heard rumors you were back in town."

I focused on the person holding the door open and recognized him immediately.

"Officer Abbott."

"It's Chief Abbott now." He smiled at me.

"Congratulations on the promotion."

Abbott was the police officer who had interrogated me during Kam's murder investigation. Just fifteen minutes ago, I'd been wondering what had happened with the investigation, and now the guy responsible for it was standing in front of me. It's funny how the universe works.

"I can tell by the surprised look on your face you weren't expecting to hear that," he said.

"I've been gone for a while."

"Well, allow me to welcome you back to Danville. A lot has changed here, but you can see that. I heard of your mother's passing. My condolences. She was a kind woman."

"Thank you."

"Are you back for good?"

"I'm just here to handle my mother's affairs."

"Of course."

"The downtown looks like it tripled in size," I said.

"Just about."

"Has crime gone up?"

"Petty crime has."

Did you figure out who killed Kam?

"I guess it's expected," I said.

"I still consider Danville a safe place to live. You can still walk around at night without worry."

"I've been spending time at the Cubbyhole, so that's good to know if I work late."

"Isn't that Virgie Gillis's place?"

Chief Abbott had known all about my bullies, but there wasn't much he could do about it. There was nothing overtly violent about their bullying. It was mainly them messing with my head. I think I would have preferred a fistfight to end it all.

"She and Felisa Chu both own it. I bumped into Virgie the second day I was back, and she offered to host me for free."

"That's nice of her. Let bygones be bygones."

If that's true, why are your beady eyes looking at me like you still believe I killed Kam?

"I don't want to hold you up," Chief Abbott said. "It was nice seeing you, Addie. If there's anything I can do for you while you're back in town, just holler."

THIRTEEN

THE SUMMER WHEN I WAS 12

EVER SINCE I had met Spencer, I looked forward to summer. Now that we were all in the same school, it was also my escape from my bullies. Because they had no idea about the secret spot by the creek, they were easily avoided.

I'd wake up every morning, stuff a bunch of food and a couple of books in my backpack, and leave shortly after breakfast. Spencer would always bring a pack of cards and board games, so we had something to do if we ran out of things to talk about or got tired of reading.

Spencer and I pretty much lived at the creek. We both considered it our home away from home. My mother knew nothing about it, not that she would mind. I just had to be home before the streetlights came on.

I don't think Spencer's parents knew, either. He always told them he was hanging out at my house, which was funny because I still hadn't invited Spence inside. I never would. I didn't want to mess things up between us.

Before I met Spencer, my mother would invite the neighborhood kids over. But each time she did that, they stopped being my friend after. I was convinced the house was cursed.

And since Spencer was my only real friend, I didn't want to lose him.

I'd been to Spencer's house several times, but I preferred our spot at the creek. We could be ourselves there and didn't have to mind our manners or our mouths.

One day before I left the house, my mom asked about Spencer.

"Why don't you invite him over for dinner? I'd like to meet this boy you spend your summer days with."

"Aww, Mom, we don't do anything special. We just hang out and talk about random stuff."

"I'm just letting you know he's welcome."

"Okay, I'll ask."

I didn't, not that day. But the next day, I did. I knew Spencer didn't care about being invited to my house; he just cared about hanging out with me.

"Hey, Spence, do you want to eat dinner at my house tonight?"

"Depends. What's your mom cooking?"

"I don't know. Food."

"Do you want me to come?"

"It's up to you."

Spencer took a moment to think before answering. "Nah, I like it the way it is. I don't want to screw things up."

I couldn't believe he had said that. It was like he read my mind.

"Yeah, you're probably right. We got a good thing going here."

That summer, I also started to read more. Really, it began during the last half of the previous school year. Spencer had turned me on to fantasy books, and I fell in love with them. Anything about fairies, unicorns, elves, or any magical forest creature caught my attention. I couldn't get enough of it.

Spencer liked the books with fire-breathing dragons and witches that practiced dark magic. He especially liked the book if it had ogres and trolls warring with people.

The downside was that people at school saw me carrying these books around—people meaning Virgie and Felisa. I don't know how it started, but Virgie started calling me "Addie the Maddy." At first, I thought she was calling me a maiden, which made sense because there were maidens in the books I read. It wasn't until later that Spencer explained that she was saying "maddy," not "maiden," and that "maddy" meant I was mad, which I still didn't understand.

"It's so stupid," I told him. "I'm not even mad."

"No, not that type of mad," Spencer said. "Mad can also mean crazy. You get it?"

"Ohhh. I get it now. Well, it's still stupid, because I'm not crazy."

"They just want you to have a stupid nickname like the one they gave me."

"Whatever." I held up a hand for a high-five. "Here's to Addy the Maddy and Spence the Dense."

Little did I know, the name would catch on permanently when Virgie discovered my mother had adopted me. She made up a story that I had been in an institution for insane people since birth. Carrying around books about black magic and having a best friend who believed in dragons didn't help.

FOURTEEN

I HAD TAKEN time off from the Cubbyhole and hadn't seen Virgie or Felisa since the dinner at Cut. But I knew I needed to buckle down and make sure my businesses were still running smoothly. I walked into the co-working space and smiled at the receptionist before turning left and heading up the stairs. As I settled into my office, Virgie and Felisa appeared in the doorway.

"Hi," I said, noticing the sour looks on their faces. "What's wrong?"

"Someone slashed the tires on our cars," Virgie said.

"Really? I guess petty crime is up. I ran into Chief Abbott a few days ago, and he mentioned—"

"It's not a petty crime, Addie. Someone deliberately slashed *our* tires. No other cars in the lot had their tires slashed."

"Oh, well, that's terrible. Um, is there anything I can do?"

"No. Reed's coming by to change our tires."

"That's good."

I opened my laptop, hoping they would take the hint that I had work to do. And honestly, I didn't really care about their tires. Plus, I hadn't forgotten about the razor-bladed bananas on my porch.

I looked up from my laptop after I realized they were still standing there. "I'm sure Reed will handle everything just fine."

"Of course he will," Virgie said.

It wasn't lost on me that they were both eyeing me suspiciously. But that was their problem, not mine. I had stuff to do, and I was still focused on my plan: Get in and get out. I went right back to typing, and they eventually left.

After an hour of undisturbed work, my cell rang. It was Gary calling. He said he had pulled paperwork to transfer my mother's cash assets into my account and needed me to sign a few papers. Also, he mentioned that he had overlooked another account my mother had that contained a quarter of a million dollars.

"You're coming into a lot of money, Addie. You might want to think about hiring an asset manager. I'm not suggesting myself or someone I know. I'm just putting it out there. At the very minimum, see an accountant so you can fully understand the tax implications."

"That's good advice."

"What time shall I expect you today?"

"Gary, is there any way I can sign them electronically? I'm a little busy now, and I don't think I can make it to your office today."

"Unfortunately, I need to witness you signing the forms. But it's no rush. We can do this anytime. Just let me know when you have a free moment."

After hanging up with Gary, I kept my head buried in my laptop, coming up occasionally for a coffee refill downstairs. Before I knew it, it was a little after seven in the evening. You'd think I'd take a break and kick back after finding out I was now a millionaire. Nope. I loved my online businesses and had no intention of shutting them down.

I rubbed my eyes and leaned back in my chair, wondering what I would do with all that money. I wasn't Virgie, so buying every luxury brand item I could get my hands on didn't interest me. I'd lived a simple life over the past decade and liked it. Even buying a house or property didn't interest me. Planting roots wasn't me. I was a free spirit and loved being able to pick up and go.

Creating a foundation that could help people less fortunate than myself did interest me, however. Throughout my travels, I had met a lot of disadvantaged and displaced women and children. I'd like to help them with the basics: food, shelter, and health care. I'd also want to teach those women skills they could use to improve their lives.

My bladder urged me to visit the restroom. On the way there, I saw that all the offices on my floor were empty.

Where did everyone go?

I remembered then it was a Friday. After using the bathroom, I headed downstairs, hoping the barista was still around. She wasn't. In fact, I didn't see anyone.

Am I the only person here?

I checked to see if Virgie or Felisa were around, but their offices were empty. It felt strange being alone in the building, like I was trespassing. A chill ran through my body, the same coldness I had felt when I stood over Kam's grave.

I don't know why I got spooked, but I hurried to my office, collected my belongings, and left. There was a small parking lot for Cubbyhole members, but it was always filled. I had parked my car in the public parking structure, a few minutes' walk away. Before I reached my car, I could smell it: bananas. Someone had smeared some across my windshield. Tucked under the windshield wiper was a note that read: *It was a mistake to come back.* It had been written in blood.

FIFTEEN

It was just bananas, but it still got under my skin. This was the type of crap that had been dished out to me throughout my teen years, except the razor blades and the blood-written message upped it a notch. It also didn't help that someone continued to trespass on my property. I wasn't necessarily afraid of anyone in the bully group. I just didn't want my progress slowed by this crap. A flood of anger rushed through me as I sat in the car in my driveway.

I climbed out of my car and stomped my way into the house. I was pissed that I had let that banana and note stunt unhinge me. That's precisely what they wanted to happen. If I got riled up, they won. I headed into the kitchen, pulled a frozen pizza out of the freezer, and placed it in the oven.

While the pizza baked, I changed into something more comfortable (aka stretchy clothes made for pizza eating). The smell of cheesy, tomatoey goodness when I came back downstairs caused my stomach to growl. I peeked into the oven. The cheese had already started to melt, and an oily shine had formed on the pepperoni slices. My plan for the night was to reread an old vampire book I had in my bedroom while stuffing my face.

I was so rushed to get the pizza started that the only light I'd switched on in the house was the one in the kitchen. The rest of the first floor was completely dark. I went into the living room to switch on a floor lamp when a floorboard on the porch squeaked. I tiptoed back to the kitchen, grabbed my trusty knife, and peeked out one of the front windows. Someone was definitely on my porch.

I got you now, you piece of crap.

I slowly unlatched the deadbolt and grabbed hold of the doorknob.

On the count of three...

I adjusted my grip on the knife handle.

One.

Someone will lose.

Two.

And it's not going to be me.

Three!

I pulled open the door and screamed as I lunged forward.

The man on my porch jumped back, throwing his hands up defensively. "Whoa, whoa, whoa! It's me, Addie. Don't kill me!"

I flipped the switch for the porch light. "Spencer?"

"Yes, Addie. It's me." He stood at a half crouch, peering at me through his crossed arms.

I shook my head in disbelief. He looked nothing like the Spencer I remembered. He was taller, looked muscular under his T-shirt, and had a five o'clock shadow covering his jawline. I didn't remember him *having* a jawline.

"I know, I know," he said as he slowly straightened up. "I've changed over the years," he said. "So, are you inviting me in or what?"

"Spence, what the hell are you doing sneaking around my house?" Spencer was the last person I had thought I would run into. I motioned for him to come inside.

"You look different, too. I wasn't sure if it was you, so I wanted to make sure. You know, this is the first time I ever set foot in your house," he said as he looked around. He turned around to face me with his arms open. "Can I get a hug? Maybe put the knife down first."

"Sorry." I placed the knife on the coffee table. "I'm just...I can't believe it's really you."

I moved in and gave him a long hug. "I'm sorry," I said.

"For what?"

"You know...for essentially ghosting you all these years."

He pulled away and looked down at me. "I thought you were dead, Addie."

"I know. I don't have a good answer for you. I just wanted to get out of this town, and I felt like to save my sanity, it had to be a clean break. I didn't even tell Netty I was leaving, and my mother only learned of my decision the night before I left."

"I get it, Addie. I'm just thrilled you're not dead," he said with the same crooked smile he had as a kid. "I really missed you. A lot."

"I missed you, too." I hugged Spencer again, because I didn't want him to see me cry. The floodgates had opened.

"Hey, hey. It's okay," he said as he rubbed my back. "This is a good time. A happy time for us."

"I know. I just feel so bad. I didn't even try to look you up when I came back."

"Yeah, you didn't. By the way, is that food I smell?"

I wiped my nose with the back of my hand as I laughed. "Yes, I'm making a pizza."

I handed Spencer a dishtowel in the kitchen so he could wipe the drizzle off his hair and face. We spent the next hour or so in the kitchen, eating pizza and catching up.

"You look good, Addie. You're beautiful."

"Thank you. You glowed up well, too."

"Where were you this entire time?" he asked.

"Mostly traveling. I mean, sometimes I'd stay in a place for a bit, like six months, but then I'd pick up and go. Forty countries so far."

"That's incredible, Addie. You certainly carved out an enviable life."

"And what about you? Have you been in Danville all this time?"

"Sadly, I have. I wish now I did what you did. I own a bookstore in town."

"A bookstore? No way. That totally suits you."

"Yeah, you should stop by and hang out. It's called the Tingling Spine. I specialize in mystery, thriller, and suspense titles. But I do have a small section dedicated to dark fantasy."

"Perfect. I would love to hang out there."

We spent the rest of the night on the couch, telling each other about our lives. I loved hearing everything Spencer had to say. He also made me feel at home for the first time since I'd been back. Don't get me wrong, I loved Netty like family, but Spencer and I had been inseparable as kids. Seeing him again filled a hole in my heart I'd had no idea was there.

I knew I had done Spencer wrong by leaving town the way I did. And it didn't help that I made no effort to contact him when I returned. I could see the hurt in his eyes. It also hurt me, but I had to do what I did, and I did my best to explain that to him.

"Shhh," he said. "I'm not angry at you, Addie. You know I would never have stopped you from doing what you felt needed to be done. You had to leave. It made complete sense. In fact, if you had told me about your plans, I would have encouraged you to go."

"What did I do to deserve such a great friend like you?"

"The feeling's mutual... I'm sorry about your mother," he said.

Spencer had eventually met my mother, when we were in high school. He'd walk me home almost every day. Sometimes my mother would be sitting outside on the porch. She'd always ask him to stay for dinner, but Spencer politely declined each time. We both knew our friendship worked well the way it was. It was the same with his parents. I'd only met them a few times. I didn't think my mother or his parents fully understood how close Spencer and I had become. We were essentially each other's shadows all the way up until I left.

"How are your parents?" I asked.

"Older but doing well. Thanks for asking."

Spencer let out a yawn, causing me to glance at the clock. It was past midnight.

"It's late," he said. "I should let you go to bed."

"No, don't go. Stay the night. I have plenty of room here, in case you haven't noticed."

"Not only is this the first time I've been inside your house, but I'm also being invited to sleep here. We're breaking new ground, Addie."

I laughed. "I know. This is the new and improved Addie."

"If that's the case, I approve."

I set Spencer up in the guest room. I'm not sure what time of the night I migrated, but I ended up leaving my room and crawling into bed with him. It was like old times when we would nap side by side at the creek. It felt comforting to hear his soft breaths next to me. Spencer had always made me feel safe, from the day we first met. It was no different that night.

SIXTEEN

THE SUMMER WHEN I WAS 13

I CREDIT SPENCER for upping my reading game. I had always read because of my mother, but my reading list was limited to popular books for kids. I only bothered to explore what my mother or the librarian recommended. Spencer showed me entire worlds within the fantasy realm I had had no idea existed. He helped me move on from cute fairies to vampires, werewolves, and other fantastical beasts of the underworld. At the same time, Spencer got into crime, mainly true crime. I started visiting the library with Spencer instead of my mother. We'd go there on Saturday afternoons to avoid my mother, who occasionally went on Saturday mornings.

One Saturday afternoon at the library, I was sitting between two bookshelves and flipping through an illustrated book about vampires that terrorized a village when Spencer plopped down next to me with a devious smile.

"What?" I asked.

Spencer looked around before showing me a book. "Look what I found. A book on Jack the Ripper. It even has photos from the crime scenes and the bodies." He quickly flipped to the page and showed me the Ripper's victims.

"Are you borrowing that?" I asked.

"Yeah, it's so awesome."

I didn't find the book sick or anything like that. It was just that I'd never seen any book with graphic pictures of actual dead people.

"Will they let you check it out?"

"I think so. It's not like I'm borrowing a *Playboy* magazine. Plus, I have a couple of books about dragons and warlocks I can mix it in with. Did you find anything good?"

"Yeah, I found a ton of books, and I can't wait to get started on them."

I checked out first and then waited for Spencer by the door. He put down his stack of books and smiled as he presented his library card to the librarian. She gave him a concerned look when she came to the book about Jack the Ripper. But he just smiled as if nothing was wrong, and she let him check out the book without any problem.

Spencer had become obsessed with true crime books and started reading about famous serial killers like Ted Bundy, John Wayne Gacy, and David Berkowitz, aka the Son of Sam.

We'd be lying on the flat rocks near the creek reading, and Spencer would often read entire chapters to me. It didn't bother me that much. It felt like I was listening to a newscast or something.

One day, he was reading about the Zodiac Killer, who was the only one that caught my attention, mainly because he had operated in the Bay Area and was never caught.

I was lying on my back with my hands behind my head and my eyes closed, listening to Spencer read to me. He had a calm voice that easily drew me in and sometimes lulled me to sleep. That afternoon, I wasn't really paying attention to what he was saying. His voice was more or less like white noise. I don't know how long I had been zoning out before I realized he'd gone quiet.

"Spence? Are you okay?"

That wasn't the first time I'd caught Spencer crushing on me. He looked at me the same way I saw boys looking at the popular girls in school. I figured Spencer had a crush on me. I liked him, too, but I didn't want to be his girlfriend. I enjoyed being his friend too much to risk it. Every couple I saw in school always broke up in three months and never spoke to each other again.

He eyed me for a moment longer before answering me. "I'm sorry. I was thinking about how people make fun of you. It's not fair."

"It's not a big deal, Spence."

"I don't see anything wrong with you, so I don't know why Virgie and the others keep doing it."

"Uh, excuse me, Spence the Dense, they also make fun of you."

"I know." He chuckled. "I guess we can suffer in silence together."

"Yeah," I laughed along with him. "Now finish reading to me, okay?"

I tried to stay strong in front of Spencer, because I knew it bothered him that I was being bullied. Sure, Virgie and the others teased Spencer, but nothing like what they did to me. I had become their pet project.

And I absolutely hated it when they called me Addie the Maddy. My biggest mistake was letting them know that. It became a tool for them. I learned to keep them from knowing if what they were doing bothered me.

There were times they convinced me I'd gone mad. I'd be listening to a lecture in class, and when it was over, I couldn't recall a single thing because I had been so preoccupied with ignoring them. It was like that time frame had been completely erased from my memory. Plus, I noticed all my pencils were starting to have bite marks on them. I definitely didn't remember chewing on them.

I started to think I might be doing crazy things and simply not recalling them. If that was the case, maybe I *was* Addie the Maddy.

SEVENTEEN

THE SUNLIGHT HAD FOUND a tiny crack in the drapes and hit me right in the eye, forcing me to wake up. I was on my side with my back facing Spencer. I rolled over to look at him, and to my surprise, he was smiling at me.

"You're up," I said.

"Yeah, I woke a few minutes before you did. Your snoring made it impossible to sleep."

I elbowed him. "Shut up. I don't snore," I whined.

"Yeah, keep clinging to that life raft if you want, sweetheart."

"'Sweetheart'?" I pretended to hold a phone against my ear. "Hey, it's James Cagney calling. He wants his vocabulary back."

"You're silly."

Spencer wrapped his arms around me and snuggled his face into my hair. "You smell good."

"It's pheromones."

"You think?"

"Yeah, because I didn't shower yesterday. I'm a ripe one."

"A ripe banana."

I straightened up. "Oh, my God, speaking of ripe bananas, were you the one who left them on my front porch?"

Spencer gave me a funny look. "Someone left bananas on your porch?"

"Yes, rotten bananas. They also smeared some on my car window when I was in town."

"No, I didn't...but why would you think I did that?"

"Forget what I said. It has to be the bully group up to their old tricks, but this time they've upped the ante."

"What do you mean?" Spencer propped himself up on his elbow.

"The bananas had razor blades stuck inside, so I would cut myself if I grabbed them. Thankfully I didn't, because I spotted them first."

"Crap! That's totally messed up."

"That's not all. There was a message written in blood."

"In blood? Are you sure?"

"Well, it looked and smelled like it. I could be wrong. But it said 'We haven't forgotten about you.' I mean, who else could be behind that?"

Spence lay back down and ran his hand through his hair. "You'd think after all these years they'd grow up. What a bunch of assholes."

I realized I hadn't told Spencer anything about my encounter with the bullies since returning to town. We'd gotten so caught up with telling each other about our lives since high school that it had slipped my mind.

"That's not all, though. I had dinner with the bully group," I said.

"Wait, when did you have dinner with them, and why?"

I explained to Spencer how I had bumped into Virgie and that she'd invited me to work at the Cubbyhole.

"You're actually working there?"

"Yeah. She apologized, and it seemed like a genuine offer, so I decided to take advantage. Anyway, she and Felisa invited me to dinner on my first day there. She's also part owner of the Cubbyhole."

"Yeah, I know. They made such a big deal of it when they first opened. So, what happened at this dinner?"

"When I showed up, Reed was there. And it was being held at Jude's restaurant. They didn't mention any of that when they invited me."

"She set you up. She wanted to put you on display for everyone to see."

"I kind of figured, but I was curious to see if Virgie and Felisa were being sincere or not. What do you think of them? Do you interact with them at all?"

"Not really. I totally ignore them whenever I see them around town. But to answer your other question, I'd be wary of their intentions for now."

"I've been on the fence with Virgie and Felisa. Reed straight up still hates me. He made it very clear during that dinner. He ignored me most of the night, except when he wanted to brag or talk down to me."

"Reed grew into a much bigger dick, especially after he started managing his father's businesses. How did Jude treat you?"

"He seemed the most genuine of them all, but he was also working that night. He was equally nice to every customer in the restaurant."

"I'm telling you, Addie, forget about them. They're not important, and you can't trust them."

Spencer climbed over me and got out of bed. "Hope you're hungry, because I'm cooking you an amazing breakfast."

Thirty minutes later, Spencer placed a plate in front of me with a veggie and cheese omelet, crispy bacon, and a side of French toast.

"When did you learn to cook?"

"Life happened. I moved out of my parents' home and had no choice." Spencer took a seat at the table. "What are your plans today?"

"I think I'll spend the morning working on the house. I haven't decided on the afternoon. I might head to the Cubbyhole. I'm not sure."

"Do you need help?" Spencer asked as he munched on a strip of bacon.

"What about your shop?"

"I have a woman that works part-time for me. She can open the shop today."

"Well, I do need help moving stuff out of the basement."

"I can help with that. Also, if you don't go to the Cubbyhole this afternoon, you should come to hang out at my shop. I'm dying to show it to you."

"Then it's decided. We're spending the entire day together."

"Just like old times."

After breakfast, Spencer and I headed down to the basement. I recounted to him my experience with the water heater when I was a child.

"Sounds spooky," he said. "Maybe a ghost from the past was trying to speak to you."

"I can get around okay with Spanish and Italian, but I never learned to speak water heater, so they're SOL."

"Was it easy to pick up those languages?"

"It was, because I lived in Spain and Italy long enough that I was forced to learn or continue looking like a dumb American."

Spencer looked at the tools and shelving. "You know, you could sell all this stuff and make some nice coin."

"I know, but I don't want to have a garage sale. I'm either donating or trashing. That's it. If you see something you like, feel free to take it."

"I can cook, but I'm not a handyman. I know my limits."

With Spence helping out, we were able to transfer everything out of the basement and up to the living room and front porch by noon.

"You should get a dumpster delivered here. That way, you can toss all your trash inside, and when you're done, the company will come and haul it away. It's easier than bringing this stuff to a landfill. The weekly garbage pickup won't even take the furniture."

"That's a good idea."

After a quick call, I had a delivery scheduled for the following day.

"You hungry?" I asked Spencer. "I'll make us a couple of sandwiches. After, we can head into town, and you can show me the Tingling Spine."

"Sounds good."

After three, we finally made our way to Spencer's bookstore.

"Wow, there are so many books," I said as I looked at the tall shelving in the store that created a maze of narrow passages.

"It's not that big of a space, so I had to be creative to stock the books I wanted. I quite like the labyrinthine feel to it."

"Yes. It's perfect."

"Go on, explore," Spencer said.

Just as I stepped forward, the front door opened, and in walked Mrs. McDermitt.

"You!" she said with a curling lip. "How dare you show your

face? You don't deserve to walk around free." She pointed her umbrella at me.

Spencer and I stood frozen as she stepped into the store, her eyes drilling into me with hate. I didn't dare take a step back, not even a tiny one, out of fear she would lunge at me with her umbrella. Mrs. McDermitt stopped a foot and a half away from me. She looked older than when I had last seen her. The wrinkles on her forehead, especially the two vertical ones between her eyebrows, had deepened, making her look as if she was in a constant state of rage.

"You should be rotting in jail right now." Her voice was a low rumble. "I don't know how you fooled the police, but I know the truth. I know you killed Kam."

"I'm sorry about your daughter, Mrs. McDermitt," I finally managed, "but I had nothing to do with her death."

"You lie." Spittle bubbled onto her lip as she pointed her finger at me, chipped nail polish glinting in the sun.

"Mrs. McDermitt, I think you should leave," Spencer said as he approached her.

She slashed at him with her umbrella as if it were a sword. "You are just as guilty, harboring this fugitive."

"Mrs. McDermitt, please," Spencer said with a raised voice. "I'm asking you to leave right this second."

She shot me a look. "You won't get away with it this time."

"Mrs. McDermitt. I'm no longer asking. Get out of my store right now!"

Spencer grabbed Mrs. McDermitt by the arm and dragged her to the door. He shut the door behind her just as she started to shout again. He locked it and flipped the open sign to closed.

"I'm sorry, Spence," I said. "You don't have to close your store. I'll leave."

"No. You'll stay here, where it's safe. She'll get tired and leave, and then I'll reopen."

"She's much worse now," I said. "She didn't seem this hateful twelve years ago."

Spencer shrugged. "Time has a way of twisting the mind around until a new reality emerges."

"She lost her daughter. I get it. She's angry and wants someone to blame. But if she knew that her daughter wasn't a perfect angel, she might have a change of heart."

"I doubt it. Rarely do parents see the bad in their children. Look, Addie, I can see the old you bubbling to the surface here. Stop making excuses. I'm sorry her daughter is dead, too, but that doesn't mean she gets to take it out on you. And she especially isn't doing it in my store. Nope. I will not have that crap. We dealt with enough of this bullshit when we were kids."

This was a side of Spencer I'd never seen: Bold. Unapologetic. Brave. He was nothing like the little boy I had known. He'd grown mentally as well as physically.

"You're right. I don't know what it is about this place that makes me act this way. I haven't been this person for the past twelve years."

"It's probably because you associate Danville with bad memories."

"What about Mr. McDermitt?" I asked. "Is he unhinged, too? I'd like to know if I have to worry about him."

"I seldom see him. Mrs. McDermitt's store is only ten minutes away, so I see her more often than I'd care to. But I've never seen her lash out like this."

"That's because I wasn't around until now."

Spencer rested his hands on his waist. "I think you should file a complaint with the police."

"Really? Don't you think that's a little overboard?"

"Don't forget the way Kam treated you when we were younger. She wasn't innocent."

Spencer had a point there. She might not have been the

worst of the group, but she was a part of it. She contributed. She could have stopped or even told the others to lay off me if she thought it was wrong. But she didn't.

"I'm serious, Addie. Chief Abbott won't stand for it. Dredging up the past isn't something he wants."

Because Chief Abbott was the one who had headed up the investigation into Kam's death, all eyes had been on him, and he'd failed to solve the case. Not the kind of blemish anyone wants on a resume, but he'd bounced back from it—he was the Chief. So perhaps he preferred the past to stay in the past. But I always had the feeling he still suspected me. Even when I saw him outside the coffee shop, he gave the same vibe.

I glanced out the front windows of the shop. Mrs. McDermitt was still outside, shouting about her daughter's death to anyone who would listen.

"That's exactly what she's doing right now," Spencer said, "shedding light on this town's dark past. If you were hoping to keep a low profile while you're back in town, she's ruining that right now."

Listening to Spencer and watching Mrs. McDermitt only reinforced my initial thought about coming home: Get in and get out.

EIGHTEEN

For the remainder of the week, Spencer came over in the mornings to help me with the house. We spent half of that time working and the other half reminiscing about the past. Even though we made progress, it would have been the same amount had I been working by myself. Hanging out with Spencer was too much fun. In the afternoons, we'd go to his store. I'd either browse the books, or if I had work to do, I'd plop down with my laptop on an old couch he kept in the back. Sometimes I'd head over to the co-working space if the store traffic picked up. I kept expecting Virgie to rescind her offer of free membership. She never did, though when I did bump into her, she wasn't nearly as cheerful as when I'd first arrived.

Spencer always called in the morning to let me know he was on his way, and there was always a pang of guilt after I hung up. I felt like I was monopolizing his mornings. He did have a business to run, even though he said it was no problem.

"I'm worried I'm taking advantage of our friendship and using you for cheap labor," I said one morning when he called.

"Addie, I told you it's not a problem. The store is always slow in the mornings, and I have help."

"You know how you can overstay your welcome at a friend's place? Well, I don't want to overadvantage your physicality."

"First off, 'overadvantage' isn't even a word. And second, why are you using big words like 'physicality' when you talk to me?"

I laughed. "Shut up, Spence. You know what I mean."

"I have an idea. Let's take the day off and hang out near the creek. I'll pack a picnic, and we can just chill and read and whatever, just like we used to. How does that sound?"

"I don't know, Spence, it's cloudy outside."

"Yeah, but it's not raining. Come on, don't be an old maid. Get ready. I'll be over in thirty minutes or so. Okay?"

"Okay."

———

Spencer picked me up as planned, and we drove to the creek with our picnic basket, blankets, a bag of books, and a couple of umbrellas, just in case.

"Do you still hang out at the creek?" I asked.

Spencer shook his head as he parked his car. "The last time I came here was with you. I don't think it would be the same if I came alone."

"I wonder if it still looks the same. It will be a bummer if it's totally changed, or if it's not even there anymore."

"Yeah, that would suck."

The trail didn't look the way I remembered it. I couldn't tell if it was because nature had changed it or because my memory had been watered down. It was probably a little of both.

When we finally popped out at the creek, my initial reaction was that the creek and the large rocks looked much smaller.

"Are you sure this is it?" I asked Spencer.

"Yeah, see that rock? That's the one you used to like lying on."

"It looks so small now."

"Well, you were shorter when I first brought you here. That's probably what you're remembering."

"Yeah, I guess."

We settled down on the rock and stared out at the creek. It was nice being there with Spencer, but it didn't feel the same as it had during those glorious summers. I glanced over at Spencer, and déjà vu hit me. He had that same look on his face from when we were kids. Did Spencer still have a crush on me?

The next thing I knew, he'd leaned over and kissed me. Not on my forehead, not on my cheeks, but right on my lips. And it wasn't a quick peck. To my surprise, I kissed him right back.

When we finally broke away for air, Spencer smiled, like he'd just done something he shouldn't have but liked it anyway. And to be honest, I felt the same way. It was strange—it was *Spencer*, and we had been friends since we were ten. This time, I leaned in and kissed him. I needed to know if I would feel the same if I initiated the kiss. I did, and we kept kissing. After a few minutes, Spencer pulled away.

"What's the matter?" I asked.

"Nothing. Addie, I just want to get this out in the open right now. I like you. I've always liked you, I mean as more than a friend. But I want you to know I'm not expecting anything because we're kissing. And I don't want to put all this pressure on what we're doing here and complicate things between us. I'm not expecting—"

I put my finger against his lips. "Shhhh. I agree. Let's both not overthink this."

"Oh, okay, that's good. I value our friendship more than anything, and I don't want to screw that up, but..."

"But what?"

"I love kissing you."

"And I love kissing you, too."

Before taking a break, we made out for a bit longer, like two teenagers in a basement. I still couldn't believe Spencer and I were doing that. Growing up, he was always Spencer, my partner in crime. I never really saw him as my boyfriend; I didn't want to screw up our friendship, so any thought I might have had of that I'd always pushed out of my mind.

"What are your plans after you get your mother's estate squared away?" he asked as he lay next to me. "I'm just asking for conversation."

"It's fine, Spence. I won't read into anything you say. But to answer your question, I'm not sure. My lawyer is moving faster on the paperwork than he'd anticipated, but the house is the big question."

"Why?"

"Selling it might take a while. He said I might get pushback from buyers in the area because it's my house... It's got history. It might be an easier sell to an outsider."

"That's dumb. It's a great house. Plus, the property is huge."

"He said the property would be the main selling point. Two houses could fit on it, or one mega-mansion."

"That's true. So, assume you sell it without any problems. Then what? And just know, I'm not expecting you to change whatever plans you had because we kissed. I want an honest answer."

"I planned to do what needed to be done as quickly as possible and then leave. I honestly thought I could be in and out within a week."

"Really?"

"Yeah. I hate to say this, but because of the way I left this town, especially with you, I didn't want to dredge up any more problems. I didn't know how you would feel seeing me again. I had just assumed you would hate me for what I did."

Spencer sat up. "Come on, Addie, I could never hate you. Be annoyed with you? Yes. But not hate," he said with a goofy smile. "I told you already. I understand why you did what you did. Not everything we do in life needs to be explained. Our decisions are our own, and we don't owe explanations to others for why we make them."

"Do you mean that, or are you saying that to make me feel better?"

"I mean it. Really. Neither of us owes the other an explanation. We should just accept. That's true friendship."

"Thanks, Spence. I really needed to hear that from you."

"No problem, love."

I shot Spencer a confused look.

"I'm kidding." He held up both hands. "I'll wait until we're married to call you that."

My eyes popped, and my jaw dropped. Spencer laughed as he pointed at me.

"You should see your face. It's like you saw a ghost. I'm joking. Calm down, will you?"

Spencer dug into the picnic basket and took out two sandwiches and a large bag of chips.

"You ever thought of just keeping the house?" He handed me a sandwich.

"I did, but I would never use it. I didn't even visit while my mother lived there. Plus, there's the hassle of maintenance. It's just easier if I sell it."

Spencer nodded as he chewed. "Makes sense. Plus, you'll get a nice chunk of money from it. That'll be nice."

Only Gary and I knew about the money I would be inheriting. I never mentioned it to Netty, and I wondered if she knew how much money my mother had stashed away. I thought briefly about telling Spencer, but decided to keep it to myself. It might come across as bragging.

"You said earlier you wanted to get in and get out," he said. "Where would you go? Back to traveling around the world?"

"I'm not sure. I spent the last twelve years doing just that. I really like the freedom, and the experiences are incredible."

"It sounds like it. Do you miss it now?"

I thought about his question for a moment. "I do. But I think it has a lot to do with being back in Danville. And the stuff with the bananas and Mrs. McDermitt doesn't help matters."

"Did you file a complaint with the police like I told you to?"

"No. I don't want to cause more friction. And she's easily avoidable."

"But that's my point. What Mrs. McDermitt is doing is bullying. Avoiding her while you're in town is the result of it. You shouldn't have to go out of your way to avoid her."

"The truth is, if it weren't for you, I wouldn't ever leave the house except for groceries. Netty is a blessing, but other than you two, there is nothing about this town that I like or need to experience. I hate to admit it, but it's still the same town that chased me away twelve years ago."

NINETEEN

SPENCER GOT a call that the store was getting busy, so we cut our day at the creek short, which was fine by me. Plus, a light rain had started.

"Hey, Spence, you don't have to drive me back home. I know you're in a hurry to get back to the store. I'll just go into town with you. I can get work done at the Cubbyhole."

"Are you sure?"

"Yeah, I'm fine. I brought my laptop with me just in case, anyway."

On the ride into town, thoughts of kissing Spencer filled my head. I was still taken aback by making out with my childhood friend. I liked it. I really did. But there was guilt. I knew I was leaving. There was no way I would stay in Danville, no matter how much fun I was having with Spencer.

If I continued to hook up with him, was that selfish? Was I just serving my own needs while I was in town, and as soon as I was ready to go, I'd hug Spencer and say 'Adios'? I really didn't want to lead him on. I knew he had said there was no pressure, but still. The crazy part about all of this was that I couldn't deny my romantic feelings for him. Maybe I got caught up in the moment, or maybe I'd always had them and suppressed them all these years. I needed clarification. I definitely found him attractive, and he was a good kisser. The fact that we were such good friends made it really easy to fall into his arms.

During my travels, I'd had other relationships, if you could call them that. Most were flings, as I was constantly on the move. The longest I'd dated someone was in Spain, and that was only for three months before I packed up and took off. I rarely kept in contact with these men; if I did, it was on a surface level. Honestly, I'd never had a real, meaningful relationship. Spencer was the only man I'd ever truly had a friendship with. I never felt the same connection with those other men. Sexually, it was fulfilling, but none of them could offer anything beyond that. So what did that mean? Had Spencer always been destined to be my soulmate?

A short ride later, Spencer dropped me off at the Cubbyhole. "Let me know if you want a ride home later, okay?"

"I will. Thanks, Spence."

I headed inside and up the stairs to my office. No sooner had I tucked myself behind my desk and opened up my laptop than I heard a throat clear. Standing in the doorway were Virgie and Felisa, and they didn't look happy.

Not again.

"Hey, what's up?" I asked, ignoring their frowns.

"We're trying to be cool to you. We're literally letting you work here for free."

"Uh, yes, I know that. Thank you."

"So then, why are you starting up stuff?"

"Excuse me?"

"Oh please, Addie. You know exactly what we're talking about."

"Actually, I don't. Could you elaborate?"

"Someone smeared rotten bananas all over my and Felisa's cars this morning."

Bananas? Really?

"Wait, you think *I* did it?"

"I don't know. Why don't you tell us?"

"Uh, not to bring up the past, but you two threw bananas at me when we were little. So I'm guessing you think this is my way of getting back at you. Do you honestly think I came back after being gone for twelve years just to smear a banana on your car?"

"We found this note on my car." Virgie placed a piece of paper down on my desk. I turned it around to read it: I haven't forgotten.

"This note is why you think I smeared bananas on your car?"

"It kind of looks that way. It says, 'I haven't forgotten.'"

"It wasn't me. In fact, I was with Spencer all day. You can ask him. Secondly, I'll remind you again that *you two* threw rotten bananas at *me*."

"Oh, come on, Addie. That was years ago, and Felisa and I have already apologized for that. We're serious businesswomen now, and we don't have time for these childish games."

If you have to tell someone you're a serious businesswoman...

"I agree. I don't, either. Just so you know, someone left rotten bananas on my porch and smeared them on my car's windshield. Did I come here and accuse you two? No, I did not. Did I think it was you two? Of course, that thought popped into my head. And there was a note on my car, too. It said, '*We* haven't forgotten;' emphasis on 'we.' So I'm not sure what games you two want to play, but please leave me out of it."

"Why on earth would we leave rotten bananas at your house and on your car, only to smear some on our own cars and blame you?" Felisa said. "That makes no sense. We would just do it to you and not deface our own cars."

I could tell by the look on Felisa's face that she really believed she'd just made a compelling rebuttal.

I shrugged. "I'm telling you, I had nothing to do with your tires being slashed or bananas smeared on your cars. And if you deny that you did the same to me, then it's someone else doing it to cause a problem between us."

Virgie let out a defeated breath. "Maybe. Look, I'm sorry. It's just that this isn't the only time it's happened. I've had some threatening messages taped to my car before."

"Really?" Felisa asked. "You didn't tell me about that. I've also had messages left on my car."

And just like that, they both forgot about me and walked off as they compared what had happened to each other.

There was still a good chance Virgie and Felisa's intentions to make amends were the real deal. My thoughts on Reed stayed the same. Maybe he was trying to stir the pot between Virgie, Felisa, and me. It definitely seemed like something he would do for kicks. I called Spencer to tell him what had just happened.

"Wait, they accused you of smearing rotten bananas on their cars?" he asked. "That makes no sense. They were the ones who used to throw bananas at you when we were younger."

"I know, but then Virgie admitted that there were other threatening messages left on her car that she never told Felisa about. Felisa said she'd gotten messages, too."

"What did these threatening messages say?"

"I don't know. They didn't tell me."

"Seriously, Addie, these girls are playing you. Don't fall for it."

"You think? I'm starting to think they're telling the truth and that Reed could be the one causing trouble."

"It's all of them. They were a tight friend group back then, and they're a tight friend group now. Don't fall for it. Hey, look, it's busy here. Can we talk later?"

"Yeah, sure."

Spencer had made a good point about the bully group. They really could all be in on it, trying to bully me by making it look like I was the one who came back to town to cause trouble. I had no proof that someone had smeared rotten bananas all over their cars except for their word. And that message Virgie showed me? She could have easily printed it out before they came into my office. It wasn't written in blood like the one I got. I also couldn't be sure their tires had actually been slashed. It could have all been a lie. But I knew I'd found bananas on my car and on my front porch. Someone was behind this.

TWENTY

THE SUMMER WHEN I WAS 14

THIS WAS GOING to be a great summer. I knew it would be because my mother had finally broken down and bought me an SLR camera. I'd been begging her for one for nearly a year.

"Why do you need a camera, and why does it have to be one of those expensive ones professionals use? How about I buy you a disposable one from the drugstore in town?" she said whenever I brought it up.

My answer was always the same: "Because."

Two days after the school year ended and summer had officially started, she surprised me with a present at breakfast.

"Go on, open it," she said.

"But mom, it's not even my birthday."

"It doesn't need to be your birthday for me to want to give you a present."

I tore the wrapper off, revealing an old shoebox.

"You bought me shoes?"

"Open it, Addie."

I tore the lid off.

"No way!"

Inside was an SLR camera with three lenses: a normal, a

telephoto, and a wide angle. She'd also bought me five rolls of film.

"Thank you so much!" I hugged my mom before running to my room to play with my camera.

"Be careful about using that film," she called out. "It's not cheap!"

I took dozens of fake photos in my room, pretending I was a famous photographer. I didn't want to waste a roll of film until I knew everything about operating my camera. I already had a stack of photography books I'd borrowed from the library that I'd been reading.

Digital cameras were starting to become popular, but I wanted a film camera because of the books I'd read, and because I found out the high school had a darkroom. Once I realized I could develop my own film, I was sold.

Like my mom said, the film was expensive, and I didn't want to hear her complaining about the costs. Developing my own film would save her money. But first, I had to learn how to operate my camera and shoot great photos. I spent the next week holed up in the house reading books on photography. Spencer complained every day, because I kept telling him "No" when he came over asking to go to the creek.

I practiced taking photos inside the house and outside. When I finally felt like I had a handle on things, I loaded a roll of film into the camera and started shooting.

I blew through all five rolls in one day, and I had yet to learn if any of my photos were good until I developed them. I asked my mother to drop off four rolls at the drugstore for developing, and I kept one for practice in the darkroom. The only problem was that I wouldn't officially be enrolled in high school until the fall. But I didn't want to wait that long.

The library kept copies of the yearbooks, so I knew which teacher oversaw the school's photography club and the darkroom. It was Mr. Clark, and he liked to hang out at a coffee shop near the library.

So, when Saturday came around, I agreed to go to the library with Spencer.

"I can't believe the hermit has finally come out of her cave," he said.

"Come on, Spence. It's only been a week."

"Feels like a year. Summer is our time. You know that."

"I know, but I really want to learn photography. Mr. Clark is a high school teacher and he's also in charge of the darkroom. I want to see if he'll give me early access."

When we got to the library, I spied Mr. Clark across the street, sitting in the coffee shop.

"Hey, Spence, I'll meet up with you later. I'm going to talk to Mr. Clark."

"Okay, but just don't take forever."

I crossed to the other side of the street and went inside, just as it looked like Mr. Clark was getting ready to leave.

"Excuse me, Mr. Clark. Hi, my name is Addie."

"Hello, Addie. Do I know you?"

"No, but you will when I start high school in the fall. I love photography."

"Is that so? Then you know the school has a photography club."

"Yeah, I know. I'm joining as soon as school starts. But I also know there's a darkroom."

"Ah, so you're interested in learning how to develop film?"

"Yes, I really want to learn."

"Not every student in the club is into it. A lot of them are converting to digital cameras."

"Not me. I have an SLR, and I'm a film diehard. Um, is there a way I can practice in the darkroom during the summer? I promise I won't break anything."

"Well, it's only for students, but I can make an exception. Students who are members of the photography club have access to it during the summer. But you have to follow all the rules. Can you do that?"

"Yes, absolutely."

"I'm heading there right now. Care to join me?"

"Um," I looked back over my shoulder at the library. "Yeah, sure I can."

I figured I'd just go there and check it out and then head back to the library. I didn't have my film on me anyway.

Mr. Clark and I walked there, which took fifteen minutes. The darkroom was housed in a tiny building at the rear of the school, near the cafeteria. He taught me the password for the keypad and then took me on a tour of the darkroom.

"There are two doors. There's the outer door to come inside and the inner door for the actual darkroom. Make sure the first door is closed first before you open the second door." Mr. Clark moved a black curtain to the side and opened the second door. On the other side of the door was a second black curtain we had to pass through. Once we were past it, I entered a room lit by a red light.

"Hi, Mr. Clark," a girl's voice said.

"Addie, I want you to meet another soon-to-be freshman at Danville High School, Kam McDermitt," Mr. Clark said. He leaned in to me. "You weren't the only eager beaver to want early access. Anyway, I have other business to attend to. Addie, on the wall are instructions on how to develop your film. I'm sure Kam can answer any questions you might have."

I smiled at Kam. I didn't know it then, but she would befriend Virgie and Felisa at the start of school and become my fifth bully.

TWENTY-ONE

THE NEXT DAY, I had an early morning visitor at the house. I thought it must be Spencer, but when I opened the door, I was greeted by Chief Abbott. From the look on his face, it didn't appear to be a friendly call.

"Good morning, Chief Abbott. This is a surprise," I said.

"Good morning, Addie. I'm sorry to bother you so early in the morning, but I need to speak with you."

I stepped out onto the porch. "What's on your mind?"

"Virgie Gillis had her garage door vandalized last night."

"That's terrible," I said, even though I knew eventually we'd get to the part where I was suspected of doing it.

"A perpetrator spray-painted graffiti across the door."

Chief Abbott showed me a photo on his phone. In big red letters were the words, *I haven't forgotten – Addie the Maddy.*

"I see. We've reached the part where I get blamed, right?"

"Nobody is blaming you, Addie, but I have a duty to investigate."

Really? The chief of police suddenly decides to handle a simple vandalism complaint himself instead of letting one of his officers do it?

"I didn't do it. Now what?"

"I know this isn't pleasant, Addie, but I gotta ask the questions. Where were you between midnight and six o'clock this morning?"

"I was here in my home, sleeping."

"You didn't leave, not even a quick trip to a convenience store?"

"No, I did not."

"Virgie has also reported that she's had a tire on her car slashed and rotten bananas smeared on her windshield."

"Yes, I'm aware. She's already accused me of that. Look, Chief Abbott, I know how this looks, like I'm a bitter person who's decided to come back and get revenge on my bullies."

"I won't argue that, but I want you to know I don't share those views. You are innocent unless there is evidence showing that you committed these acts, which I don't see. Now, some people won't look at this objectively because of your history."

"I appreciate your vote of confidence."

"I heard about your run-in with Mrs. McDermitt. Just so you know, I spoke with her and told her to leave you alone."

"Thank you, but you didn't need to do that."

"Oh yes, I did. If I don't nip it in the bud right now, rumors will start to spread, and soon, everyone will have misinformation running around in their heads. Not on my watch. It ain't happening again. If anyone in this town threatens you or accuses you of wrongdoing, I want you to let me know. And I mean it, Addie."

"Well then, I should tell you it's already happening. I mean, besides what you already know. I had someone leave rotten bananas on my porch, except these bananas had razor blades buried in them. There was also a note that read, 'We haven't forgotten.'"

Chief Abbott frowned. "Why didn't you report this? Bananas booby-trapped with razor blades isn't a game. You could have seriously hurt yourself."

"I know. And I think the message was written in blood."

"Are you sure?"

"It looked like it to me. It's still in the trash can over on the side of the house."

I walked over to the trash container and retrieved it for Chief Abbott.

"Here you go. Maybe you can analyze it to see if it really is blood."

"I will. Addie, this is serious. This is what I'm talking about. Whoever did this might be laughing, but I'm not. What else has happened?"

"I've had bananas smeared on the windshield of my car with another note written in what appeared to be blood. I don't have that one. It took place when I was parked in one of the public parking structures in town."

"Sounds like someone is following you."

"Probably. Honestly, I didn't take this that seriously because Virgie and the others used to throw rotten bananas at me. If I were you, I'd question them again. Especially Reed."

"Why is that?"

"Because Reed hated me when we were younger, and he still hates me now. To try to put the past behind us, Virgie and Felisa apologized and invited me to dinner. Reed was there, and he made it clear that he still didn't like me. He either talked down to me or ignored me throughout the dinner. I suspect he might be responsible, but I wouldn't discount that they all could be in on it." I shrugged. "They're bullies."

"I appreciate your candor. This is exactly why I'm here. To gain insight and hear all sides of the story."

I decided not to mention the trespasser on my property, since I knew it was Spencer, but the car following me after my dinner with Virgie and the others was definitely not Spencer's car. In fact, I hadn't even mentioned that to Spencer.

"Addie? Is there anything else?"

I snapped out of my train of thought and back to the present moment. "That's it. All I want is to be left alone. When I'm done dealing with my mother's estate, I'll be gone."

"And that's your choice, but it's my job to make sure you're safe while you're here. You will let me know if anything like this happens again, right?"

"I will."

Chief Abbott motioned to the dumpster on the front lawn. "Looks like you're making progress."

"Things are moving faster than I expected. Spencer has been helping me."

"Spencer, as in the owner of the Tingling Spine?"

"That would be him. We were close friends as kids."

"Yes, I believe I recall seeing you two together back then. Well, I don't want to take up any more of your time. Have a good day."

The rain started to come down again as Chief Abbott drove off. A gust of wind blew rain droplets against me, and I quickly slipped inside, shutting the door behind me. It seemed like a good day to stay put at the house.

I fixed myself a cup of coffee and sat on the sofa in the living room. Now that Chief Abbott was officially involved in this nonsense, I hoped he would be able to do something. He couldn't do much when he was an officer, but he was the chief of police now. Surely he was capable of more.

Something Netty had mentioned over our dinner popped back into my mind. She'd told me to never stop facing my fears. Spencer had also told me not to revert to behaving like the old

Addie. So, what was I to do? Find out who was really causing the trouble?

Yes, Addie. That's precisely what you should do. This town already ran your name through the mud once. Are you going to let them do it again?

TWENTY-TWO

I SPENT the rest of the morning doing laundry to keep my mind off what I really wanted to do: find the person who was causing the trouble. I could sit it out again and hope Chief Abbott got it right this time, or I could give him a helping hand. It was time the new Addie Baxley took control.

Mrs. McDermitt deserved answers, and so did I. That was precisely why I drove to her shop for a mature, woman-to-woman discussion.

She was sitting on a stool behind the cash register when I walked through the door. There were no customers in the shop. She looked up from her phone with a smile on her face. It disappeared the second she recognized me.

"What the hell are you doing here?"

She gripped the counter with her hands as she slipped off the stool. It was a classic case of Dr. Jekyll and Mr. Hyde. I wondered if she would have reacted similarly if other shoppers had been around.

"I'm here to see you. It's time you and I have a real conversation."

"What's there to talk about?"

"Someone in this town is trying to cause trouble between Virgie, Felisa, and me. As you may or may not know, they bullied me for eight years. Your daughter was a part of that bully group in high school."

"How dare you speak ill of her!"

"I know you don't want to hear it, but Kam bullied me in high school. There are a lot of people who can attest to that. Go ask Chief Abbott if you don't believe me."

"So you're the one who sent him here."

"I did not, but it's no secret that you cursed me out a few days ago. You made a spectacle of yourself. So if someone wants to stir up trouble, you're painting a target on your back as the main culprit."

Mrs. McDermitt reached under the counter and felt for something. A beat later, I heard something click behind me.

Did she just remotely lock the door?

A devilish smile appeared on her face. "You think I'm the one causing trouble?"

"That's why I'm here, to find out if you have anything to do with the rotten bananas left on my front porch. Razor blades were embedded in them so I would cut my hand. There was also a message written in blood that said, 'We haven't forgotten.' Did you do that?"

"I want to see you in jail, not with a cut on your hand."

"Someone has also been leaving threatening notes on Virgie's and Felisa's cars. In fact, someone defaced Virgie's garage last night and made it look like it was done by me."

"Because it *was* you. You never belonged here, and you resent others for their happiness."

"It was not me. And what do you mean, I don't belong here? That makes no sense. I caused no trouble for your daughter. I tried to be her friend, but she decided to join Virgie's gang of bullies. Look, I know you can't stand the sight of me, but I promise you, I had nothing to do with your daughter's death. Whoever killed her is still walking around freely."

"Get out of my shop!" she shouted. "Get out!"

"Fine. I tried to make peace with you, but if this is how you want it, so be it. Go ahead and live your miserable life."

I turned around and pushed the door open, but it was locked. I looked back and saw Mrs. McDermitt quietly snickering. She reached under the counter and unlocked the door.

I swear, the people in this town are crazy. How I got stuck with the nickname Addie the Maddy is beyond me.

When I left Mrs. McDermitt's shop, I was pretty wound up. So far, my hunt for the troublemaker wasn't producing the desired results. Reed was the other person I suspected, but my gut told me approaching him the same way I did Mrs. McDermitt wouldn't go very well. Mrs. McDermitt was angry about her daughter's death and would probably always feel that way until there was justice. I could understand her attitude toward me. She needed someone to blame, and I was an easy target.

As for Reed, he was just an asshole. He'd always been a mean person. I didn't know how he remained friends with Virgie and Felisa, or even Jude, who had always been and probably still was his best friend.

You need allies, Addie. Not more enemies.

The Cubbyhole wasn't far. So I decided to talk to Virgie. We had common ground—someone was messing with both of us. Maybe we could do something if we worked together.

The receptionist at the Cubbyhole always smiled at me, which was nice, even though I knew that was her job. "Hi, is Virgie around today?"

"Yeah, she's in her office."

"Great. Thanks."

I arrived at the front of Virgie's office and knocked on the doorframe. "Hi."

"Now, you are the last person I expected to see here," she said with a look tilted toward disgust.

"Um, I heard what happened. Chief Abbott told me. I wanted to tell you in person that I wasn't the one who defaced your garage door."

"The note was signed by 'Addie the Maddy.' If you have some vendetta against us, I suggest you drop it. We're trying really hard to be cool to you, and I know we mistreated you before, but that's in the past. And we were just kids. Kids do dumb things."

"That's so not it," I said, raising my voice. "So stop trying to make this about revenge. I stayed away from this godforsaken town for twelve years, and the only reason I came back was to handle my mother's estate. Trust me, I didn't fly back here to paint a message on your garage door or throw bananas on your car. Someone is making it look like we're attacking each other."

"Is that what you really think?"

"I do. Do you have enemies in town?"

"No."

"Okay, well, I do, and it makes complete sense to assume that these people who don't like me could be the ones doing these things."

"Like who?"

"Mrs. McDermitt, for one."

"But Kam was our close friend. Why would her mother spray-paint my garage door?"

"Like I just said: to cause problems. Mrs. McDermitt loathes me. She thinks I killed Kam and can't be convinced otherwise. And if I'm being honest, losing her daughter has put her mental health in a bad state."

"I don't think she spray-painted my garage. She's, like, sixty-five."

"She could have hired someone to do it."

Virgie shrugged. She wasn't buying it.

"I have one more suggestion, but you might feel the same about this person."

"And who's that?"

"Reed."

"Oh, my God, Addie. Reed would never slash my tire only to have to fix it later."

"Why not? If he knew he could fix it easily, why not slash it? It's a great way to make me look bad. It's the same with the graffiti on your garage door. Did he offer to clean it for you?"

Virgie kept her mouth shut.

"He did, didn't he?"

"He's painting over it. And anyway, I know Reed. He wouldn't do that. Plus, he's super busy."

"That may be true, but he doesn't like me. You saw the way he acted at that dinner party. And he was the only one who didn't apologize for his past behavior. I believed you, Felisa, and Jude when you did."

"You spoke to Jude? When did you talk to Jude?"

"It's not what you're thinking. He spoke to me the same night we had dinner at his restaurant. Did you tell him to apologize to me?"

"No."

"What about Reed or Felisa? Did you ask them to apologize?"

"I told Felisa what I had done, and she agreed it was the right thing to do. I never mentioned anything to Reed."

"So you three all made up your own minds to apologize. Reed is the only one who hasn't. He didn't even say anything about my mother's passing."

"But that's Reed. He can be like that sometimes."

"I'm just saying, whoever is doing this wants you and me to fight. They don't want us to get along. It very well could be

Reed. Maybe he wants everything to be exactly how it was when we were younger."

"Someone left a box of rotten bananas outside Jude's place," Virgie said. "The same message was left."

"Did he also think it was me?"

"Of course, because he knows about everything that's happened to Felisa and me."

"You, Felisa, and now Jude. The odd man out is Reed."

TWENTY-THREE

SHORTLY AFTER MY conversation with Virgie, I left the Cubby-hole and drove home. At that point, I was sure Reed was behind everything. If I could see it, clearly Chief Abbott could, as well. I just hoped he had the will and capability to end it. In the back of my mind, I knew this was petty stuff the police shouldn't be involved in. Sure, there was some property damage at Virgie's, but leaving rotten bananas around, even with razor blades, didn't seem to rank very high on the violent crime meter. Deep down inside, I didn't think anything would be resolved unless Reed escalated from bananas to something else. In the meantime, I just needed to focus on getting out of town as quickly as possible.

When I returned home, I saw Netty's car in my driveway. She waved at me from the front porch.

"Hi, Netty," I said as I got out of my car. "What brings you here?"

"Oh, I just thought I'd check in on you and see how things are coming along with the house. The dumpster is filling up."

"Yeah, I'm making progress. Spencer has been helping out on some mornings."

"That's nice of him. You know, I can always help out. It's not a problem."

I unlocked the front door, and we both headed inside.

"I already feel guilty about Spencer helping. Really, it's not that big of a deal. I can handle things. Would you like some coffee?"

"Sure, that would be nice."

I headed into the kitchen to get the coffee maker started. When I came back out, Netty was poking around the wall cabinets in the living room.

"Whatcha looking for? Mice?" I asked.

"I'm sorry. I just wondered what one keeps in wall cabinets like this."

"You don't know? I assumed you would know everything about my mother."

"I know she was a bit of a pack rat." Netty took a seat on the sofa.

"That's for sure. There are so many things I haven't gone through—for instance, those wall cabinets. I'm sure they're stuffed to the brim."

"That was your mother."

I sat down beside her. "Netty, I want to ask you something. While I was cleaning out the basement, I came across boxes of baby items—there were clothes, toys, blankets, and even a crib. Did you know about that stuff?"

Netty nodded. "It's time you knew the truth. Your mother never wanted you to know this, but she was expecting a baby before they adopted you. She miscarried and never quite recovered from it. She fell into a depression, and to be honest, I'm not sure she ever got over that."

"Why did she keep this from me?"

"She didn't want you to feel like you weren't important or that you were a second choice. I want you to understand something. Your mother loved you very much. Boxing these items up and putting them out of sight was a way for her to focus on you."

"Is the miscarriage why she adopted me?"

"The adoption was your father's idea. He was afraid he was losing her to depression. You coming into her life saved her. It gave her a reason to keep living, even though she was still troubled. I met your mother shortly after she married your father, and we were good friends ever since. Your mother was always the life of any party...bubbly, with an infectious laugh. She loved introducing herself to people. She would stick her hand out confidently and say, 'Wendy Baxley. It's a pleasure to meet you.'"

"Really?"

"It's the truth. I know you never got to see this side of her, and this is exactly why it was kept from you. Your mother made me promise never to say this to you. I think in her head, she knew she would never be the old Wendy again." Netty grabbed hold of my hand and squeezed it gently. "I'm not telling you this to make you feel bad, so don't fill your head with bad thoughts."

"I'm fine. Please don't stop. I want to hear this."

Netty drew a deep breath and let it out slowly. "All right. Well, no one ever thought a miscarriage would happen the way it did. Not your mother, not your father, and not even the doctor. Your father thought your mother needed time to grieve, and she'd slowly return to her old self. But she didn't. She fell deeper and deeper into this dark hole. Losing that baby had taken a toll on her. But it all changed on the day she received notice that the adoption was approved—your adoption, Addie. Bits and pieces of the old Wendy resurfaced. I remember talking to her on the phone when they picked you up. She sounded so happy."

I grabbed a nearby tissue box and dried my eyes.

"Are you okay?"

"I'm fine." I sniffed. "I just had no idea about this."

"You coming into her life saved her. I honestly believe that, had that not happened, we would have lost Wendy long ago."

Netty patted me on the back as she gave me a hug. "I think that's enough talk about that for now."

A loud crashing noise jolted Netty and me apart. An object had crashed through the window and rolled across the area rug.

"My dear!" Netty said as she pressed a hand against her chest. "What is that?"

It looked like a rock to me. I stood and started toward it when Netty grabbed me by my arm, stopping me.

"Wait, whoever threw it might still be outside."

With Netty huddled next to me and her nails dug into my arm, we quietly made our way to one of the front windows and peeked out. We didn't see anyone on the porch or in the front yard, but I heard Netty breathe a sigh of relief.

"It's a rock," I said after picking it up.

"Who goes around throwing rocks through windows?" Netty said. "We could have been hurt!"

"There's a note wrapped around it."

Netty moved up beside me as I unwrapped the paper from the rock. "'We haven't forgotten,'" she read.

I sat Netty down and told her about the razor blades and the messages written in blood.

"Oh, you poor girl," Netty said. "What kind of person does such a thing?"

"It's not just me. Virgie and Felisa have also received threats. Rotten bananas were smeared on their cars, as well. They even had their tires slashed, and just last night, someone spray-painted a message across Virgie's garage door. It said, 'I haven't forgotten, and it was signed, 'Addie the Maddy.' Before I came home, I spoke to Virgie about it. Someone is trying to create a problem between us by making it look like we're both doing something."

"I had no idea this had happened."

"Well, Chief Abbott knows about those things because of what happened to Virgie's garage."

"What will he do?"

I shrugged. "I already told him I thought it was Reed Holland. He's the only person from the old bully group who hasn't apologized to me for his past behavior, and he treated me badly during the dinner party. Remember, I told you I was meeting them?"

"You did, but you never told me how that went."

"It was uneventful. Jude Akers, remember him? He was the bright spot. He also apologized."

"This Reed boy is a little troublemaker who never grew up. I always thought his eyes made him look like a weasel."

"Don't worry about it, Netty. I've got things under control. I'm not letting any of this get to me."

"I'm glad to hear that. You keep your head up. A bully doesn't like that. They only get joy when they see you cower and back away. But I do think Chief Abbott needs to know about this rock. Report this as soon as possible."

Netty retrieved a broom and a dustpan from the kitchen and swept up the broken glass on the floor. She told me I should take pictures of the window for the homeowner's insurance, just in case the damage couldn't be pinned on Reed.

"There's a hardware store in town that can fix the window if you don't want to wait for the insurance to deal with it," Netty said.

"I think I'll do that."

"Do you want me to stay the night?" Netty asked.

"I'll be fine, Netty. I appreciate your concern."

Just then, a knock at the front door caught our attention. It was Spencer.

"Hey there," he said with a smile. "I parked in your driveway. I hope that's not a problem. Hi Netty, how are you?"

"Hello, Spencer. I'm doing fine, but Addie had a little problem here." Netty pointed at the broken window. "Someone threw a rock through the window."

"You're kidding!"

"The rock's right there." Netty pointed at the coffee table. "Addie, show Spencer the note."

Spencer read the note. "This is really getting out of hand, Addie."

"I told her she needs to tell Chief Abbott about this," Netty said.

"I agree." Spencer walked over to examine the window. "I think I can put a temporary fix on this."

I saw Netty off while Spencer went to work on the window. He dug around the furniture that we'd thrown into the dumpster and was able to disassemble enough end tables and chair backs to cover the hole in the window. He went to work nailing them into place.

"This should hold until you can get the window repaired."

"Thanks, Spence."

"I'm sure this is retaliation for the garage door," he said. "Yeah, I already heard about it."

"But that's the thing, Spence. It would only be retaliation if I had done it. I didn't."

I brought Spencer up to speed on what had happened that day.

"I hope the chief talks to Reed and sets him straight," he said. "This can easily spiral out of control. Surely, Virgie and Felisa don't see the humor in this if it is him."

"So you've moved away from the idea that they're all in on it?" I asked.

"I think so. Spray painting the garage door and throwing rocks through windows is a step up from bananas."

"Well, we're in agreement. I definitely don't think Mrs. McDermitt is behind any of this. I could tell she was still just a hurt and angry mother during my conversation with her. Stirring up this mess doesn't achieve anything for her."

"You're right about that."

Spencer moved in and gave me a kiss. "I've been wanting to do that all day."

I knew Spencer wanted to take things to the next level. It's not that I wasn't interested in sex. I definitely was, but I kept thinking I didn't want to lead him on. I knew I would leave Danville eventually. I didn't want to break his heart if he fell for me. Or the opposite could happen: I could fall hard for Spencer and decide to stay. But I had to admit, watching him break the furniture apart and then nail it over the window was a turn-on—my own personal handyman.

Since neither of us had eaten, I fixed us dinner. Over the meal, I told Spencer about the boxes of baby items and my conversation with Netty before he'd come over.

"Would you have wanted to talk about that with your mother?"

"That's a good question. Maybe... Yeah, I think I would have. It would have helped me better understand her mood swings."

"Is the peeled paint still in your bedroom?"

"It is, actually."

"Does it creep you out?"

"Not really. It's not that big. Maybe this size." I held up my hand and formed a circle with my thumb and forefinger.

"I wonder if it's just a blue wall or if dinosaurs or racing cars are painted on the wall as well."

"Good question. Let's have a look."

When we were done eating, we headed upstairs to my bedroom, and as soon as we stepped inside, I pushed Spencer down onto my bed and started pulling off his shirt. So much for not leading him on.

TWENTY-FOUR
THE SUMMER WHEN I WAS 15

My first year at Danville High School was similar to my years at middle school. Everyone I went to middle school with had transferred into the same high school, so my bullies continued to be right there with me. The only salvation I had was the darkroom. Spencer was still around, but we didn't have a lot of classes together, so we didn't see each other as much during school as we used to.

I began spending more of my time in the darkroom. It was an escape from my bullies, and I was also having a blast developing my photographs. I'd seen Kam a few times in the darkroom at the beginning of the school year before she was initiated into the bully group. It seemed like we were on the way to friendship. I swear, it was like Virgie could sense happiness inside me and knew exactly how to target it. Before I knew it, Kam was hanging out with Virgie and Felisa and calling me Addie the Maddy.

Everyone in Danville was fake except for Spencer. I still saw Kam every now and then inside the darkroom, but she never bothered me during that time, or when the rest of the group wasn't around. Sometimes she even said "Hi."

My afternoons after school were always spent in the darkroom and Spencer began to complain. Eventually, I told him the
password so he could hang out with me while I developed
prints.

"It's cool inside here; I like the red light. But do you have to
come here every day?" he asked one afternoon.

"I don't have to. I just like it." I dropped a print into the
wash. "Don't you find it peaceful?"

"I guess, but the creek is peaceful, too. Are you bored with
that place?"

"No, I still like it. We can go there on the weekends."

"I know."

"Come on, I'll teach you how to develop photographs. That
way, you're not just sitting there twiddling your thumbs."

But photography wasn't something that would hold
Spencer's interest. We looked for other ways to spend time
together at school. He wasn't much of a fan of organized sports,
and neither was I. We considered the school clubs and settled
on one: the book club. But they only met once a month. It was
inevitable that we'd develop separate interests. Spencer joined
the debate club, and I would always make time to see him
compete. I accepted that this was the way it would be. We eventually made it through our freshman year and got back into
summer mode.

As usual, we spent a lot of time at the creek—not as much as
before, but enough that Spencer didn't complain as much about
my darkroom visits. (Mr. Clark always allowed photography
club members to use it during the summer.) Because I wanted to
photograph something other than what was around my home or
at the creek, I started making trips into town. I could take
photographs of anything that struck my fancy: buildings, people,
or even stray cats and dogs.

I'd imagine I was a private eye and was hired to photograph

people for my clients. I'd gotten pretty good at being invisible, which was useful, because Virgie and Felisa were always in town. They didn't go away to summer camp or have summer jobs. Sometimes I'd see Kam helping her mother at the shop. Rarely did I see Jude or Reed; their parents made them work the entire summer. Reed worked at his father's car dealerships, and Jude put in hours at his father's insurance company. Spencer and I were lucky to have our summer to ourselves.

The bullying during the summers when we were older was different, mainly because we often hung out at the creek, not the park. Jude and Reed were too busy to bully us, so we only had to deal with Virgie, Felisa, and Kam. And Kam wasn't always around.

Whenever I was in town, I'd always search out Virgie and Felisa and sneak photos of them. I wanted to be like one of those paparazzi who took unflattering photos of celebrities. I'd always have a good laugh in the darkroom. It was like an Easter egg, a special hidden treat just for me. I never knew what I'd end up with until I developed the film.

One day, I was laughing at the photo I'd taken of Virgie stuffing her face with a sandwich. Kam happened to walk into the darkroom right then. I couldn't hide the photographs of Virgie, as they were hanging to dry. She looked at them and laughed a little. Then she ignored me and went about her business.

I kept waiting for Virgie to confront me about the photographs, but she never did. I thought for sure Kam would have told her what I had done. But nothing happened. Summer came and went without a peep from Virgie.

TWENTY-FIVE

AFTER ANOTHER ROUND of lovemaking in the morning, Spencer showered and left. His assistant had requested the morning off, and he needed to open the shop. I couldn't help but notice his extra-chipper mood. He'd started whistling in the shower and kept it up until he walked out the front door.

I was sexually active with my childhood friend. That was what went through my mind that morning. Sure, I enjoyed it, but it still worried me that a line might have been crossed that shouldn't have been.

Roll with it, Addie. You're both adults, and no one's arm was twisted.

I poured myself a cup of coffee, sat in the living room, and started thinking about how to break out the day. It took a hot minute before my mind focused on the drama between my bullies and me.

It was one thing to tease me, but to make it look like I had gone on the offensive was new. There had to be an endgame in mind. Paint me as a vengeful bitch? Was that the goal? Only a few people in town liked me anyway, so what more would that achieve? There had to be another reason to make it look like I was starting trouble.

Lots of people believed I had killed Kam, even after the police cleared me. If someone couldn't prove that I might have been responsible, what would be the next best thing? Making it look like I was after the others would make sense. Was that the goal? Defacing property with a can of spray paint and rotten bananas is a far cry from murder, though. I didn't think anyone, even Chief Abbott, was particularly bothered by that mischief. And that's precisely what it was. The townsfolk weren't staying inside with their doors locked in fear of being the next victim of Addie the Maddy and her rotten bananas.

On top of everything else, there was absolutely no evidence that I'd killed Kam. The police questioned me because they were questioning a lot of people. Everyone just assumed I had wanted revenge for the bullying.

The only connection I had to Kam's death was that we'd both signed into the darkroom on the day she was murdered. My fingerprints were all over the crime scene, but that was because I had been there developing my film. There were other fingerprints from other students, as well. The only difference was that they weren't being bullied. I remembered the box of newspaper clippings my mother had kept. I hadn't yet tossed it into the dumpster. It was in the corner of the living room with a few other items from her room.

I grabbed the box and began looking through the news clippings, but I didn't see anything that sparked any new ideas. The only thought I had was to do a deep dive into the people the police had questioned—in particular, Kam's parents. I didn't really know much about their backgrounds. They'd moved to Danville shortly before Kam was set to begin high school, so it wasn't like they had all this known history in town. What did people really know about the McDermitts?

The landline rang, and I figured it was Netty, so I answered.

"Addie, it's Chief Abbott calling."

"Please don't tell me something else happened to Virgie."

"No, nothing like that. But I did have that note you gave me analyzed. I thought you'd want to know the results."

"Is it blood?"

"It's deer blood."

"So whoever wrote it hunts?"

"That's a strong possibility."

"I don't think Virgie or Felisa hunts. Does Reed?"

"He does, and I've already questioned him about this. He denies writing it and states he hasn't been hunting lately. Because I have no evidence that he wrote the note, I have to take his word for it."

"I see. Then there's not much you can do about this problem."

"I advise you to continue reporting any problems you might have while you're still in town. I'm afraid that's all I can tell you for now."

As I hung up, I started to think that maybe I'd had the right idea when I first arrived in town: My best recourse was to settle my mother's estate as quickly as possible and move on with my life. Of course, I was still intrigued by the McDermitts.

I took a shower and got ready to drive into town. I wanted a fast internet connection, and the Cubbyhole could deliver that. I just hoped I was still welcomed there.

It was noon when I arrived in town. Before heading inside the Cubbyhole, I checked to see if Virgie's and Felisa's cars were parked behind the building. Their cars weren't there, so I ran inside and hurried up the stairs to my office.

Mrs. McDermitt was my first search. Most of the initial stuff I came across had to do with her store in town. Sherry was her first name. She wasn't active on social media, which made finding information on her difficult. But I continued looking through the pages of search results and eventually found an old photograph. It was a group of male and female bowlers at a bowling alley—probably members of a bowling league, since they wore matching shirts. The quality of the photo was poor, so I didn't recognize her. Plus, it could have been someone else who had the same name.

I clicked the photo and ended up on someone's blog. There was a caption below it that read, "The Seattle Strikes take first place in the Spare Ball Bowling League." The date was thirty years ago. There was a list of names below the photo. I didn't see Sherry McDermitt's name, but I did see a Sherry Bowman.

Why did Google flag this photo for Sherry McDermitt?

I scanned the post attached to the photo and saw "McDermitt" in parentheses next to the name Sherry Bowman, and it all clicked. When the photo was taken, she had been Sherry Bowman. She must have married later, and the blog owner had included her maiden name as well as her married name.

In the photo, Sherry Bowman was standing on the right side of the group. I enlarged the photo, and I thought it looked like her, but I couldn't be positive. A little boy stood next to her, clasping her hand, but his name wasn't mentioned in the post. I'd always thought Kam was Mrs. McDermitt's only child.

I changed my search to "Sherry Bowman" and got a bunch more hits, but they were all connected to the bowling blog. But there was one result for a marriage announcement in *The Seattle Times* archives. Sherry Brady had married Jeremy Bowman. It looked like the same woman from the blog. Mrs. McDermitt appeared to have been born Sherry Brady, who married Jeremy Bowman and later remarried, making her Sherry McDermitt. The little boy holding her hand in the bowling photo could very well have been her son from the first marriage. Did her son pass away? Had she lost him in a custody battle? He looked to be about two years old in the picture.

I searched for an announcement for Mrs. McDermitt's second marriage but couldn't find any. Still, I was sure I had discovered vital information about her past. And if she had a son and he was alive today, he wouldn't be that much older than me.

Learning more about Reed was easy. He regularly posted on social media and didn't keep his settings private. He published numerous photos of him camping, hunting, and fishing. Many of the pictures included Jude. His most recent hunting post was two weeks ago, and he'd killed a deer. I took a screenshot of the post to send to Chief Abbott. If he wanted proof, there it was: Reed had killed a deer not too long ago. Had he lied to the chief?

The only other thing to come from my background check of Reed was his car. There were plenty of pictures of him with a white Porsche. The car that had followed me wasn't white and appeared to be a much older model, but Reed might have had access to vehicles other than his Porsche. His father owned two dealerships, and they sold both new and used cars.

The other thought that occurred to me was that Reed and Jude were working together. It could have been Jude who followed me that night. But would he really have left during the dinner service at his restaurant just to try and scare me? It didn't seem likely. I hopped over to Jude's social media, but he kept it private. Did Jude even own a car similar to the one that had followed me? I could swing by the restaurant and see if any vehicles in the parking lot looked familiar.

So far, I hadn't discovered a smoking gun. The closest I came was the recent deer post. And the date he posted the photo didn't mean he bagged the deer then. It could have been from weeks ago. I also didn't have anything pinning Reed to the car that followed me.

I leaned back in my chair with a better understanding of the position Chief Abbott was in. He could have also looked at Reed's social media and drawn the same conclusion. No solid evidence, just my gut instinct.

The sun had set by the time I stood to stretch my legs. I used the bathroom and on the way back to my office realized the entire top floor was empty. There were people in these offices when I arrived. Where did everyone go?

Since I was already at the office, I spent a couple more hours managing my businesses. When I was finished, my stomach growled.

I didn't feel like eating alone in a restaurant, so I packed up and headed home. Plus, it had started to rain again. I had just left the downtown area when I noticed a car coming up on me quickly with its high beams on.

I swear, if this is Reed...

I switched lanes, and the car behind me did the same. I got off the highway, and it followed. I made random lefts and rights, and it mimicked every move I made. I approached a traffic light and saw that we were the only two vehicles on the road. The light changed to red, and I stopped. The other car stopped a bit farther behind me. By then, I was more than irritated, so I put the Honda in park and climbed out.

"What do you want, Reed? I'm not afraid of you!" I shouted with raised arms as drizzle fell on me.

The car sat there, idling. I wanted to walk up to it, but my smart side said not to poke the bear. I took my cell phone out of my jacket pocket and called the police.

Right then, the driver revved the engine and, a moment later, did a screeching U-turn and sped away. I couldn't make out the license plate, but I got a good enough look to know it was definitely an American muscle car.

"You've reached 911. What is your emergency?" the operator said.

"I'm sorry, I made a mistake."

I disconnected the call, wishing I had used my phone to make a video of the car instead of puffing out my chest. I could have shown that to Chief Abbott.

The rain had started to come down harder, and I switched my windshield wipers to a faster speed as I pulled out into the intersection. Not more than five minutes later, the mystery car appeared from a side street and came up on me fast, slamming into the rear of my car.

Holy crap!

I steadied my car and stepped on the gas, but my Honda was no match for that car. It quickly caught up and hit me once more, sending my car swerving on the slippery road. As I fought to regain control, the car hit me again, sending me into a three-hundred-and-sixty-degree spin. I stopped on the side of the road, facing the opposite direction and just a few feet from a large ditch. The other car also came to a stop, with its headlights blinding me. It was just the two of us on that road, facing each other.

What are you doing?

The driver revved the engine while my wipers swished back and forth across my windshield. I fumbled to retrieve my phone from my pocket.

Come on! Come on!

As I pulled it out, it slipped from my hand, falling into the crack between the seat and the center console. I shoved my hand into the narrow space, feeling for my phone.

The car mock-charged me.

Crap! Come on, Addie, find the damn phone before you end up as roadkill.

Again the car pretended to charge toward me.

Finally, the tips of my fingers brushed against the phone. I secured a tight enough grip on the phone to fish it out and dialed 911.

"Help, someone's trying to kill me!"

TWENTY-SIX

AFTER I CALLED 911, another car appeared further down the road, scaring off my attacker with the threat of being seen—which was a relief, because it took ten minutes for a police officer to arrive. While I was speaking with the officer, Chief Abbott pulled up.

"It's Reed!" I shouted as he approached. "I know it's him!"

"Calm down, Addie. Tell me what happened."

I reiterated what I'd just gotten done telling the other officer. After I finished, Chief Abbott told his man to go to Reed's home and see what he could find out.

"I'm telling you, Chief Abbot. I know it's him. It has to be."

"But you said it wasn't a white Porsche."

"I know, but his dad owns two dealerships. He has access to other cars."

"I promise you, Addie, we'll get to the bottom of this. What happened here is serious."

"Of course it is. I really think he wanted to kill me. Maybe it's payback for Kam. I know everyone in this town still thinks I killed her."

"I don't think that, and that's what's important."

Chief Abbott looked at the damage at the back of my car. "Do you think you're able to drive it home?"

"Yeah, I think so."

"Tomorrow, I want you to swing by the station, and I'll take some photos in the daylight for the report."

Chief Abbott followed me home to make sure nothing else happened. When we got there, he walked the property. I told him it wasn't necessary to come to look inside the house, and thanked him. I stood on the front porch and watched him drive away. Only when the taillights of his police cruiser were out of sight did I head inside. That was when I noticed a piece of wood used to cover the broken window had been pushed in, creating an opening.

Shit!

I kicked myself for not letting Chief Abbott check out the house. The other pieces of wood and chair backs were still nailed in along the bottom and left side. Someone might have tried to reach in and unlock the door. But that space was tight; even my arm couldn't fit through it.

I unlocked the door and pushed it open, remaining in the doorway. I didn't see anyone or hear anything. I leaned in and flipped the switch for a nearby lamp, lighting up the room. After a moment or so, I went inside. I searched the entire house from top to bottom, carrying a knife, but saw no signs of anyone being inside. The windows and back door were still locked. If someone had wanted to scare me by pushing that piece of wood back and letting me think someone had broken in, they'd succeeded. I took the hammer and nailed the wood back into place, and this time I set a reminder on my phone to touch base with the hardware store the next day and get that window replaced.

I didn't sleep very well that night. I thought every single noise I heard was someone in the house. I must have peeked out the window half a dozen times to see if anyone was roaming around the property. I finally crawled out of bed a little after six, when the sun first appeared over the horizon. On the bedside table, I kept a knife, and leaning against it was one of my mother's golf clubs. I remembered when she bought the set, intent on learning the game. She played twice and never touched them again.

After filling myself up with buttered toast and coffee, I called the hardware store, and they said they could fix the window the next day. I would have preferred that they come that same day, but after looking at the photo of the window I had sent him, the man on the phone explained he had to order a part.

With that settled, I took a shower, dressed, and drove into town. First stop: the police station, so I could finalize my report with Chief Abbott.

The desk officer had me sit and wait for the chief. When he finally appeared, he was walking Jude out. Jude didn't notice me, as I was tucked away in the corner. But Chief Abbott gave me the side eye. He said goodbye to Jude and then turned to me.

"Good morning, Chief Abbott," I said as I stood. "My car is just outside. Do you want me to take you to it?"

"Good morning, Addie. Let's talk in my office first."

I followed him down the hall and took a seat in front of his desk. "Is there a problem?"

"As you saw, Jude was just here. He came to report that his restaurant had been vandalized. Someone spray-painted 'I'm a bully' on the side of the building."

"Let me guess. He said it was me."

"Not in those exact words, but he did allude to it. You all have history."

"Yes, and I was the victim for eight years."

"He knows that, and that's why when I asked him who he thought might have done it, he spoke about you. He admitted that he and the others had bullied you, but they all apologized."

"Everyone except Reed," I interjected.

He nodded. "That said, he also mentioned that the trouble only started once you returned."

"Of course he'd say that. Does Jude have security cameras outside his restaurant?"

"He does, but not in that area. Seems as though whoever did it thought that part through. Do you still think Reed is your guilty party? He and Jude are best friends."

"I do. That message can easily be painted over. Graffiti is all over this town on buildings. This is nothing new. But trying to deliberately run someone off the road is on a whole other level."

"I get your point. Let's take a better look at the damage to your vehicle."

We headed outside to my car, and Chief Abbott looked at the damage.

"It looked worse last night."

What was that supposed to mean?

"I advise you to have an auto shop look it over to make sure there's no hidden damage. Your insurance should cover it."

"I'm sure it will, but since I don't plan on keeping it, I might just use it until I leave and get rid of it then."

While the chief took photos, I walked around to the car's front passenger side.

"Chief Abbott, come look at this."

Scratched into the paint of my car were the words, "We haven't forgotten."

"This was just done," I said.

"I can see that. There are paint shavings still hanging from the scratch."

"This is total bullshit. There's got to be something..."

"What is it?" Chief Abbott asked me.

I was looking beyond him, into the distance. "That car on the side of the road. That's the car that tried to run me off the road last night."

"Are you sure?"

"Absolutely."

Chief Abbott ran inside and reappeared a few seconds later with another officer.

"He just left," I said. "He turned left at the intersection. Do you want me to come?"

"Let us handle this, Addie," Chief Abbott said.

Before I could respond, Chief Abbott and the other officer jumped into separate vehicles and went after the car.

TWENTY-SEVEN

I took Chief Abbott's advice and let him and his men deal with my stalker. I snapped a photo of the scratched message on my car before climbing inside and driving to Spencer's store. I was irritated and wanted to vent. Plus, his store was a safe space for me in town. The Cubbyhole was iffy, considering what was happening between Virgie and me.

Seeing Spencer inside his shop instantly made me feel better. I had been thinking that, with my luck, I'd arrive and he'd be out running errands or something.

"Hey, Addie," he said as I entered. "This is a nice surprise. How is everything?"

"Not good. I think someone tried to break into my home last night."

I brought Spencer up to speed on everything that had happened since we last spoke.

"Geez, Addie. This is getting out of control. It's been like a day and a half since I last saw you. You're telling me someone tried to run you off the road last night and break into your house. Then you find out that Jude had a message spray-painted across his restaurant to make it look like you did it, and to top it off, that crazy driver is still following you."

When Spencer put it that way, the situation had definitely worsened. Everything I just told him about had happened in less than twenty-four hours.

"I can't believe Chief Abbott is taking this so lightly."

"He went after that car," I said.

"But he did essentially nothing last night. It's bullshit, Addie. You could have died."

"I know."

"I think the reason you're not taking it seriously is that no one else is. I'm, like, the only one who seems to be worried here."

"I *am* taking it seriously, but what should I do? The best plan is to do what I need to get done and get out of town as quickly as possible."

"And they'll win if you do that. Because that's exactly what they want."

"So what?"

"So what? Addie, they've gotten away with this crap ever since we were ten. They'll keep getting away with it if we don't stand up to them."

"'We'? Spencer, they're not doing anything to you."

"I know, but you know what I mean. They might as well be doing it to me because you're my best friend. So, of course, it affects me."

"I'm still your best friend?" I asked with a smile. "Even after all these years?"

"Yes, even after all these years. We're friends forever, and friends back each other up."

I gave Spencer a big hug. "I'm so glad you're back in my life."

"Me, too."

"Look, I'm getting worried about your safety. I think I should stay at your place until you can get that window fixed, but even then, it's not that hard to get into your house. It would be easy to break another window."

"The hardware store is fixing the window tomorrow."

"Okay, but still. I'm worried about this person who's following you. Were you able to see who the driver was, even just a little?"

"No, the headlights kept me blind. But it was a muscle car, an older model. I got a better look at it this morning. I think it was either an old Mustang or a Charger. It was far enough away that I couldn't tell. Maybe Chief Abbott will know."

"Well, Reed is always driving around in that stupid new Porsche that he bought, and it's white."

"I know. Everything inside me believes it's him, but then there's the car. My only thought is that it's a used car from the dealership."

"It could be. Well, Chief Abbott saw that car. Common sense says to go talk to Reed and take a look around the dealership. Are you supposed to check back in with the chief?"

"I'm not sure. He told me to let him deal with it. He'll let me know if he finds the person, but I'm not holding my breath. So far, nothing positive has come out of his involvement."

I took a seat on a stool. "Spence, what if it's not Reed? I mean, could it really be one of the others?"

"It's possible. I still haven't ruled out that they're all in on it. It would definitely make it easier to terrorize you and harder to pin it on any one of them. Maybe it's Jude chasing you, and Reed's writing the messages."

"What kind of car does Jude drive?"

"He has a black SUV."

"Well, I know the difference between an SUV and a muscle car. Virgie has a BMW, and Felisa drives an Audi."

"I see what you're getting at."

"Also, it's not like nobody knows what they did to me as a kid. Everyone in town was aware of the bullying. What if it's someone else? Someone who wasn't a part of the bully group."

"Just someone random? I guess it could be. Anyone who went to school with us would know."

Just then, the bell on the door rang, and in walked Reed. He didn't look happy.

"What the hell, Addie? Why are you telling Chief Abbott that I'm making trouble? I just got an earful at the dealership. They accused me of stalking you and leaving you messages written in blood. My father was there. Do you know how embarrassed I was?"

"Oh, come on, Reed. You don't like me. You never did."

"Yeah, so what? So you blame me for the shit that you're doing?" He took a step closer.

"Me? I haven't done anything. You're the big-time hunter, right? Didn't you just shoot a deer? Chief Abbott said deer blood was used to write those notes."

"Screw you, Addie. It's not me, but I'm glad someone's messing with you. You should have never come back to town."

"Leave, Reed! Now!" Spencer stepped between Reed and me.

"Watch your back, Addie," Reed said.

Spencer shoved Reed out of the shop and slammed the door shut. "Man, I can't believe he came over here after Chief Abbott talked to him."

"It's this town, Spence. It just doesn't favor me."

"Don't say that, Addie. None of this is your fault. I think the best thing is to follow Chief Abbott's advice. Stay away from them, especially Reed. Are you still working at the Cubbyhole?"

"I am. I mean, I was there last night. Virgie and Felisa

haven't kicked me out. I'm sure they would have if they didn't want me there."

"It's probably best that you stay away. Whoever's making it look like you're causing trouble can use that to their advantage. If you're at the co-working space and something happens there, it'll be difficult to say it wasn't you."

"I know what you mean."

A knock on the front door grabbed our attention. It was Spencer's assistant.

"Sorry!" Spencer called out as he walked to the door and unlocked it.

"It's fine." Spencer's assistant handed him a flyer. "I ran into Felisa on the way here. She wanted to know if we could hang this flyer in the store. Her dog is missing."

"Great." I threw my hands up. "Ten bucks says I get blamed for that."

TWENTY-EIGHT

SPENCER'S ASSISTANT had spoken with Felisa when she got the flyer. According to her, Felisa said she let her dog out so it could relieve itself. After fifteen minutes, Felisa called for the dog, but it didn't respond. She went looking but couldn't find it. Was the dog taken, or did it just run off? I guess that depended on who you asked.

Instead of heading to the Cubbyhole, I camped out on the sofa inside Spencer's bookstore. Considering Felisa's missing dog, I didn't get the feeling that I would be welcomed there. I spent the rest of the morning on my laptop, working. Chief Abbott hadn't called about the car he went after, unless he tried calling the landline at the house. I'd given him my cell number several times, but he continued to call the house.

"Hey, Addie. How about getting some food?"

I glanced at my watch. It was a little after one. "Yeah, I'm a little hungry. But can we go someplace that's not around here? I just feel like there'll be a lot of staring."

"No problem. I know of a pizza parlor outside of town. It's actually in the next town over."

The pizza place was north of Danville in a town called Walnut Creek. Spencer opted to drive since he knew where it was. Leaving the city limits changed my mood instantly.

"The rain stopped, and the skies are blue again," I said as we drove down the highway.

"Yeah, looks like the rest of the day might be nice for a change."

"I know I've been gone for a while, but I don't remember it raining so much when I lived in Danville."

"It doesn't. I'm not sure what's up with the weather."

"Ever since I came back home, it's been drizzling nonstop. This is the first time I'm seeing the sun."

"Maybe it's a sign that things will get better." Spencer gave my thigh a comforting squeeze.

When we reached the pizza shop, we were both starved. We ordered a large sausage and mushroom pizza with side salads and buffalo chicken wings.

"Mmm, the sauce on the pizza is so good," I said.

"I love this place. I wish they delivered to Danville."

"How did you find it? It seems so random."

"Dumb luck. I was on my way back from San Francisco when I saw it. I gave it a try and instantly fell in love with the pizza. Whenever I get a chance, I make the drive here." Spencer stopped chewing. "I know that look on your face, Addie. Try not to let what's happening get to you."

"Easy for you to say. You're not being targeted. You know what I just can't wrap my mind around?"

"What's that?"

"It's like it's a no-brainer to accuse the bully group, but nothing quite adds up."

"I know, but who else could it be?"

"You've been here for the last twelve years. Is Reed really capable of doing any of this stuff?"

Spencer bit into the crust of his pizza slice. "Reed has always been an asshole. Of the four, I would say he's changed the least since high school. He definitely hasn't matured one bit."

"And yet he and Jude still appear to be best friends."

"Yeah, there's some weird bond between them. If the four of them aren't working together, I don't see Virgie or Felisa doing any of this on their own."

"Exactly. Felisa is such a ditz. No way she's capable of planning this. Jude seems to have calmed the most since high school. Virgie has matured, but she still reeks of fake."

"That puts us right back at Reed."

"You know what else is weird?"

"What?" Spencer said as he munched on a chicken wing.

"I get how they would try to make it look like I'm the one causing the trouble, as if I wanted revenge. But why would they also torment me at the same time? If I were doing this, I'd make it look like I was a troublemaker doing stuff to them and leave it at that. Don't you agree?"

"Totally, but maybe making you look bad wasn't enough for them. Maybe they missed bullying you."

"But making it look like I'm doing all this bullying, and at the same time nearly running me off the road last night... That doesn't make any sense. It makes me look like a victim."

"That's true. It doesn't make any sense when you put it that way."

"That's why my plan to come here and leave as quickly as possible is valid. That town is messed up. It's never changing."

"Speaking of leaving, I've been giving it some thought—how and why you first left, I mean."

"And?"

"I'm impressed. You didn't know anyone and didn't have a job, but you didn't let that stop you. You didn't play it safe like I did by staying here."

"It's different for you, Spence. You weren't bullied the way I was. And being accused of Kam's murder was the final straw. I had no choice."

"You're right. But what you did is still impressive, and it's made me think a lot."

"About what?"

"About doing what you did and getting out of this town. Twelve years have gone by, and I haven't achieved much of anything."

"What are you talking about? You have your own thriving business."

"Yeah, I know, but it was still the safe route. My parents gave me the money to start that place. If they hadn't, I'd be working at some dead-end job. Anyway, that's not what I want to talk about. I think I want to do what you're doing. You know, take off and see what comes of it."

"Are you serious?"

"One hundred percent. I'd love to come with you—and before you say anything, there is no pressure relationship-wise. We've been getting along so well, I'd hate to lose you again, but I know you're leaving. I'd love to come with you and learn how to do what you do. It doesn't mean our relationship has to change or evolve. If we end up being just travel buddies, I'd be down for that. You've inspired me, Addie."

My face was flushed with heat, and I couldn't maintain eye contact with Spencer. I had never had anyone tell me I was inspirational.

"Do you really mean that?"

"The inspiration part? Absolutely. You did something amazing, Addie. Most people think their life is what it is and accept it. You didn't do that. You changed it to what you wanted it to be."

"Thanks, Spence. That's probably one of the nicest things anyone has ever said to me." I wiped a tear away from my eye. "But what about your store?"

He shrugged. "I can find someone to manage it, I can sell it, or I can focus on online sales and manage it from the road like you do with your businesses. That's doable, right?"

"Yeah, it is... I don't know what to say." I sniffed.

"Don't say anything. It wasn't a yes-or-no question. It's a discussion. We can keep talking and see where it goes, okay?"

"Okay."

Spencer and I ended up hanging out at the pizza parlor for nearly two hours. After, we headed into the downtown area for ice cream. During that time, I opened up about my travels in ways only my mother had been privy to before that. I told Spencer about all my different experiences and how they put life into perspective for me.

Traveling had opened my eyes to so much. Even with the bullying I had experienced while growing up, my problems paled in comparison to what so many people around the world faced. I learned not to take life for granted and not to waste a single day. Life was a one-time opportunity with no do-overs.

"Wait, you helped rescue trafficked children?" Spencer's mouth hung slightly open. "Like, rescue them from the traffickers?"

"I did. Sometimes we snatched them in the middle of the night. Other times, we used decoys to get the children to safety. We tried to avoid confronting the traffickers directly, leaving that to the police. They're a nasty group of people."

"Not only are you amazing, but you're also a badass. I'm serious, Addie. No one in Danville does stuff like that. If the bully group knew about the stuff you did—wait, if the *town* knew about the stuff you did, I bet people would treat you differently."

"Not a word to anyone, Spence. I didn't do any of this to curry favor with the residents of this town. I did it for those who needed my help. Promise me, Spence."

"I promise. Not a single word."

———

By the time we got back to Danville, I was beat. I had no energy to drive, and I asked Spencer if he could just drop me off at home. I could pick up my car the following day. By the time we had pulled into my driveway, the sun had set.

"Are you sure you don't want me to sleep at your place tonight?" he asked. "I'm here."

"Maybe tomorrow night we can have a sleepover." I winked at him. "I'm just really tired today."

I knew Spencer worried about me, but I also knew he was eager for seconds. I wasn't against sleeping with him, but I just wanted some alone time that night.

"Call me if you change your mind."

"Bye, Spence."

I already knew how I wanted to spend the evening: a long soak in the tub, then some reading, and call it an early night. I watched Spencer drive off before I turned and headed toward the porch steps. I considered walking around the property, knowing I could use my phone's flashlight.

Just do it, Addie. You'll feel better after.

I took a quick walk around the property and saw nothing out of place. All the lower-level windows on the house appeared intact. I hurried back to the porch steps and made my way up. I nearly tripped over something at the top of the steps, something soft with a bit of weight to it. I thought some junk from the stack on the porch had toppled. I tried moving the object off with a slight kick but slipped on something wet. I took out my phone, switched the flashlight back on, and pointed it down.

I screamed and jumped back, slamming into the porch railing. A sharp pain shot up my back, causing me to wince, but my eyes remained focused on the porch. Blood was everywhere, and a small white dog was in the middle of it.

TWENTY-NINE

"Reed's a hunter," I said.

Chief Abbott nodded. "I hear you. I know you're upset, but many people in this town hunt."

"That may be true, but not all of them tormented me when I was a kid," I said. "Chief Abbott, a dead dog was left on my porch, Felisa's dog."

The chief sat opposite me in my living room. He appeared lost in thought as he stared at the rug. He'd arrived fifteen minutes after I made the call to 911. He had recognized the dog immediately, just like I had.

"Chief Abbott?" I waved a hand to grab his attention.

"I'm sorry. I was thinking." He straightened up. "If Reed was responsible, and he wanted it to look like you were out for revenge, leaving the dog on your porch with a note saying 'I haven't forgotten' doesn't make sense. It should have been left at Felisa's place with that note, right?"

"Well, yeah. That would make more sense, but we're talking about Reed here. He's not the sharpest tool in the shed."

"I agree with you there, but still..."

"What's with this doubt?"

"What do you mean?" he said as his eyes narrowed.

"I feel like you don't believe that I'm innocent."

"That's not true. I'm here now trying to figure out what happened, aren't I?"

"Reed kidnapped Felisa's dog, gutted it, and left it on my porch so I would be blamed."

"I have a problem with that explanation, as I stated earlier. It makes no sense to leave the dog on your porch. But maybe it does if you want me to believe Reed did it."

"Wait, are you saying I'm responsible for this? You think I'm trying to set Reed up?"

"You had a difficult childhood, Addie. I can understand how coming back home might mess with your head."

"I can't believe you're saying this. You think I'm sabotaging myself?"

Chief Abbott held my gaze for what seemed like an eternity, until the sound of a car pulling up outside broke the stalemate.

"That must be Animal Control." Chief Abbott stood and walked outside.

I watched through the window as he spoke to the man who'd come to collect the dog. He'd mentioned earlier that he would tell Felisa what happened to her dog, which was fine with me; I wasn't volunteering to do that.

When I first heard Felisa's dog had gone missing, I'd just assumed it was another stupid trick to make it look like I was trying to get revenge. I even thought the dog must not have been taken, but rather was being kept hidden in her house or something. Everything that had happened up until now seemed petty. A kidnapped dog seemed to fit into that mold.

But that wasn't what happened.

Killing Felisa's dog took things to a whole new level. And I had to admit, I was thinking the exact same thing as Chief Abbot. If Reed did want to set me up, why leave the dog on my porch? He should have left it at Felisa's place. And Felisa would never agree to have her dog killed. It wasn't adding up. Someone had killed her dog, but it most likely wasn't Reed. So who was it?

Chief Abbott and the Animal Control officer were talking in hushed voices, and I couldn't make out what they were saying. I could have gone outside and stood on the porch while he collected the dog, but I'd already stepped in the sticky red stuff once, and I wasn't keen to do it a second time. Instead, I filled a bucket with warm water and soap and waited. As soon as I got the okay, I wanted to clean the porch. I still couldn't believe what had happened to Felisa's dog. I felt terrible for her, even though I knew she would lash out at me when she found out. She'd act like Mrs. McDermitt and blame me because she needed someone to blame.

After Animal Control left, Chief Abbott helped me clean the blood off my porch, even though I told him it wasn't necessary.

"It's faster and easier if we both attack it," he said.

After we finished swabbing the porch, he walked around the property and checked that all the windows were securely shut.

"Are you okay staying here alone?" he asked. "Maybe you should call someone."

"I'm fine. Whoever is behind this wants me to cower. I won't do that."

He nodded. "I'll order extra patrols in the neighborhood. Call if you need me."

THIRTY

THE SUMMER WHEN I WAS 16

WE WERE two days into summer when Spencer got his driver's license. I still hadn't gotten my learner's permit, but that didn't matter, because Spencer had wheels. His parents had purchased a junker for him. It had rust spots and a few dents, and the paint had dulled, but I didn't care. To me, it meant freedom. We could branch out from the creek and go to the skating rink or the cinema whenever we wanted—but more importantly, we could get out of Danville and visit the neighboring towns, where no one knew us or our nicknames.

The downside—and there was a downside—was that Virgie and her gang of bullies also had driver's licenses and their own cars. We expected to see them at the fairgrounds or the lake, but we never expected to see them on our trip to San Francisco.

That day, Spencer and I had planned to tour Alcatraz Island. Spencer had never been, and kept telling me throughout the school year that we would make the trip as soon as he got his license.

"Look at it. It's beautiful," Spencer said as he stared at the island off in the distance.

"It's a prison, Spence. Murderers were kept there."

"Al Capone was imprisoned here. Did you know it was escape-proof because of the strong currents and the sharks that swim in the bay?"

"But didn't some people escape? I think there was a movie about it with Clint Eastwood."

"Yeah, but they don't know if they survived the swim to shore. That's really what made it escape-proof."

We were standing on the pier waiting to catch the next ferry to the island. When the double-decker boat docked, we were both surprised to see Virgie and her gang disembark.

"Oh look, it's Addie the Maddy and Spence the Dense," she said. "Are you guys on your way to meet your relatives?" She cackled.

"Forget them," Spencer said as he led the way to the ferry's upper deck.

"How is it that we have such rotten luck? Of all the days to come into the city and take the Alcatraz tour, we had to do it on the same day as them."

"It could have been worse. We could have bought tickets for the same time slot."

"Yeah, that would have been the worst."

"I can imagine them walking behind us and providing commentary," Spencer said. "Remember at the skating rink when Jude taped those pieces of paper to our backs? 'Mr. and Mrs. Loser'?"

"How could I forget? We didn't even know the signs were there until we were out in the parking lot."

"Yeah, we thought everyone was watching us because we were skating so well."

We made our way to the front of the ferry, where we would have a fantastic view of the bay during the trip. That day's weather was classic San Francisco: sunny blue skies and crisp air. There were a ton of sailboats cutting through the bay's glassy waters. The seagulls squawked noisily above, and the air smelled perfectly salty. I took photos of everything, ripping through my first roll of film in seconds.

"I didn't see Kam with them. That's weird, right?" Spencer said. "Come to think of it, I don't see Kam hanging around them much anymore. Do you?"

I was trying to capture photos of the seagulls flying above the boat when Spencer elbowed me in the arm.

"Hey, are you listening to me?" he asked. "Earth to Addy the Maddy."

"Sorry, I was busy taking a Pulitzer Prize–winning photo."

"Okay, whatever. Did you hear what I said?"

"I did, and no, I don't see them together much. But I do see Kam. Sometimes I run into her in the darkroom."

"Really? That must suck."

"Eh, she tends to mind her own business when she's in there. I do the same. It's like neither of us exists to the other."

"I wonder if they're not getting along? Before, it was five peas in a pod. Now it's four."

"Why do you care? The less of them, the better."

"I'm looking out for us. I don't want to get flanked. It would be just like Virgie to devise a plan where it looks like Kam isn't friends with them."

"And what would that accomplish?"

"Maybe her job is to infiltrate and spy. Maybe that's why she's in the darkroom. She wants to set you up."

"I don't think so. She's developing film while she's there."

"That's my whole point. She learned how to develop the film so she can sell the role."

"Spence, I think you're reading too much true crime."

"Hey, I'm just looking out for us. I don't trust anyone in that group."

I shrugged and went back to taking photos. Spencer had a

point. I had also wondered why Kam wasn't hanging out with Virgie and the others as much as she used to. During my reconnaissance missions into town for photos, I'd begun to see Kam at her mother's shop more often. I figured her mother was making her work there, so she just didn't have enough time for Virgie and the others.

One afternoon, I showed up in the darkroom just as Kam was leaving. I noticed a print on the floor next to the trash can. It was of Kam and some other person who I couldn't recognize; that part of the print was overdeveloped. She'd obviously meant to toss it into the trash but missed. I studied the photo of Kam and the mystery person. Kam had a giant smile, something I never saw much of when she was at school. The person she was sitting next to was a boy, so I ruled out Virgie and Felisa. It didn't look like Jude, and this person had brown hair, so I could also rule out redheaded Reed. He had his arm slung around Kam's neck. Did she have a secret boyfriend?

I thought briefly of keeping the print and showing it to Spencer, but in the end, I tossed it into the trash. I wouldn't have wanted her to show off a print of mine to somebody else without my permission. If the photos I had of Spencer and me got out, that would be the end. We'd be labeled as the weird couple. We were already odd on our own; we didn't need to do it as a couple.

THIRTY-ONE

IT WAS another sleepless night where it seemed like I woke up
every hour on the hour. I kept having mini-dreams where I
would continuously come home to a dead dog on my porch.
While sitting on the toilet at three in the morning, I thought I
heard a noise outside, like two people having a muffled conversation. But when I peeked out the window from the bathroom, I
didn't see anyone and the noise had disappeared. Either I was
turning into a nut job, or the shock of finding Felisa's dog on my
porch had finally settled in.

I crawled back into bed, but the image that had popped into
my head kept me awake. It was the little boy holding Mrs.
McDermitt's hand in that bowling photo. I switched on my
bedside lamp, got out of bed, and lay flat on the floor to look
underneath my bed. If memory served, I would find a shoebox
filled with old photographs. It was still there.

I pulled it out and started going through the photos. Most of
them were of stupid things around and in my home, but I
remembered there were also photos I'd taken from my trips into
town.

Come on. Please be here. Please be here.

I found what I'd been looking for near the bottom of the box. I'd taken some photos of Kam inside her mother's store. I remembered a teen boy being there with her, laughing and talking. I snapped the picture, thinking he might be Kam's boyfriend. I didn't recognize him and knew he didn't go to the same high school as me. I never did anything with the photos after developing them, and I had forgotten all about them until a few seconds ago.

I went through the series of photos I took of the two until I found one that gave me a clear look at the boy's face.

Could this be the little boy who held Mrs. McDermitt's hand in that bowling picture? If it was, then he was Kam's older brother and had grown up. He was at least two or three years older than her, which fit, because he looked to be about two or three in that bowling picture.

I hurried downstairs to my laptop. The connection to the hotspot on my phone was incredibly slow in the house, but I powered through. After ages of loading search results, I found the photo of Mrs. McDermitt and the little boy again. I enlarged the photo and compared it to the one I'd taken.

This has got to be him. They look the same, especially the eyes.

He was definitely the little boy in the photo. Mrs. McDermitt must have had Kam not long after that bowling photo had been taken.

There was a large box in the attic—the one place in the house I still needed to venture into—that should be full of photos I had taken during my high school years. There might be more photos of this boy. I wasn't exactly sure what I was after, but my gut told me to keep digging. I hadn't been in the attic since I lived with my mother. I wasn't even sure if the box was still there.

A retractable stairway leading up to the attic was located in the second-floor hallway ceiling. The attic was quite big, as it ran the length of the house. Before I left, I'd moved many of my belongings up there.

I used a chair from my bedroom to reach up to the latch in the ceiling and pulled the stairs down. The sun had already started to rise at that point, so light flowed in through the attic window at the front of the house. Thanks to the exposed beams, the space smelled like old wood. At least it wasn't chilly like the basement. There were a bunch of portable clothes racks filled with my mother's clothing. *They weren't there before...* I slipped around them, looking for my box, which I found toward the rear, under a stack of old suitcases.

I opened it up and found all the old pictures I had taken and developed in the darkroom back in high school. It wasn't long before I found some of Kam and that boy, who I now thought had to be her brother. I assumed his last name was likely Mrs. McDermitt's previous surname, Bowman.

And then I stumbled across a photo of them wearing matching shirts. Printed on the front of Kam's shirt in scripted lettering was her name: Kam. And on his shirt, in the same scripted lettering, was his name: Lane. They were leaning against a dark-colored muscle car similar to the one that had been following me, except in the picture, it looked brand new.

Hello, Lane Bowman. Nice muscle car you got there.

As I climbed back down the retractable stairs with the photo, I heard a noise. And it wasn't coming from outside the house. It was inside.

THIRTY-TWO

IT'S TOO EARLY in the morning for me to be Addie the Maddy. I know I heard something.

I heard the noise again. Someone was definitely in my home. I quietly returned to my bedroom and grabbed the golf club.

This will split someone's head open just fine.

I headed to the top of the stairs. Whoever was in my house wasn't concerned about making any noise, because they'd gotten louder. I heard a cabinet door shut, and then footsteps, followed by rustling.

I tiptoed down the stairs, club ready to strike whoever had broken inside. The person sounded like they were in the living room. I stepped off the last stair and paused. All I had to do was round the corner into the living room, and I'd come face to face with the intruder.

You can do it, Addie. Go out swinging.

I tightened my grip, drew a deep breath, and raised the club. I moved swiftly into the living room, screaming like a crazed woman. The person was bent over, with their back facing me. As I was about to strike, they turned and jumped back.

"Netty!" I said.

"Arrgghh!" she screamed, raising both hands to protect herself. "Don't kill me!"

"Sheesh, Netty. You scared me half to death." I lowered the club.

"Same here." She pressed a hand against her chest as she drew heavy breaths. "You nearly gave me a heart attack. What are you doing with that club?"

"I thought someone had broken into the house."

"Well, I did do that..." She moved over to the couch and fell back into it. "I'm sorry, Addie. I didn't see your car outside and assumed you spent the night at Spencer's."

"How did you get inside?" I asked before glancing over at the open cabinet. "And what are you looking for?"

"I'm so embarrassed. I have a key to the house. Your mother gave me one in case of emergencies. I meant to take it before you came back. I would have told you, too, but before I could, Gary had put that lock on the door, and I couldn't get inside."

"Take what?"

"Remember that porcelain doll your mother had?"

"Of course. Netty, you could have told me you wanted it. I don't want anything here. It's all going to charity or to the dump."

"I don't know, I thought you'd think it was silly. I'm sorry. I've always loved that doll and thought it would be a nice thing to keep and remember your mother by."

I realized then that I wasn't the only person who'd lost someone important. Netty had lost her best friend. Of course, she would want something to remember her by. I sat down beside her and gave her a hug.

"Netty, I'm the one who needs to apologize. I should have told you from the minute I arrived that you could have anything you want in the house. My mother was just as important to you as she was to me. It was selfish of me not to consider your feelings. I'm sorry."

Netty waved off my remark. "I'm just a silly old woman."

"That's not true, Netty. I know you and my mother were very close."

"Like two peas in a pod." She chuckled.

"Netty, I know."

She crinkled her brow as she looked at me.

"We may not have discussed it, but I know. I've seen how you two looked at each other and cared about each other when I was younger. I might not have understood everything then, but I did later, after I had left. I know you and my mother were more than just friends."

Tears welled in her eyes as she stared at me, her mouth slightly agape. "I don't know what to say."

"Say nothing. I don't need an explanation."

"Your mother never wanted to mention it to you and insisted that we keep it a secret. She feared if people in town found out about us, it would make things harder for you. Every decision she made, she considered you first and whether or not it would affect you. All she wanted was for you to be happy. That mattered the most to her, and she'd sacrifice even her own happiness to ensure you were okay."

Now I was the one bawling. There we were, two women hugging and crying on a couch at seven in the morning. Hearing from Netty how much my mother had sacrificed saddened me and left me feeling guilty.

"I should have visited," I said. "It was selfish of me not to."

"Your mother would have been the first to tell you to stay away—not because she didn't want to see you, but because she loved you so much. She couldn't bear to see the people in this town hurt you again. She'd always told me she wished she could have done more to protect you when you were younger. She always thought she failed you as a mother."

"That's impossible. She was the best mother ever. She allowed me to grow and be me."

Netty hugged me harder as I cried harder.

"That's it. It's time you finally had yourself a good cry and mourned your mother's passing. It's important. Let it out."

I did exactly what she asked. I couldn't have stopped, even if I wanted to. The walls I had put up around me before coming back home had come crashing down that morning. Trying to treat this trip like it was a business trip was absolutely ridiculous. I had come home to lay my mother to rest, not to settle an estate.

"I feel like an ungrateful, spoiled little girl," I said between sniffs.

"You did what you did because you had to. Your mother had always told me that if she passed, I was to handle everything. She didn't want you to have to come back. You got out of this town intact. She wanted you to stay that way. I hate to say it, but it would have broken her heart if she knew what was happening now."

I pulled away from Netty.

"What is it, dear?"

"Oh, my God, I need to tell you. I've been doing a little digging. Did you know Kam had a half-brother? I think he's the one who's been following me."

"Following you?" Her face looked as if she'd just caught a whiff of something smelly.

With all that had happened in the past few days, I hadn't had a chance to tell Netty about almost being run off the road. I quickly brought her up to speed.

"You're kidding, aren't you?"

"I'm not. I honestly thought he'd run straight into me.

Thankfully, another car appeared, and he left. I had assumed it was Reed causing all of this trouble."

"And why wouldn't you? The bananas and the messages written in blood—it sounds like him."

"I know, but the car never matched up. Reed drives a white Porsche. The only explanation I could think of was that he had used one of the cars from his dad's dealerships. Chief Abbott questioned him about it. Of course, nothing came out of it except that it made Reed angry."

"But how does Kam's half-brother fit into the equation?"

I ran upstairs, grabbed the photos, and then quickly explained everything I had uncovered about Mrs. McDermitt's past.

"You see this picture?" I showed her the photo of Kam and Lane leaning against the car. "That's how I figured out his name. It's written on his shirt. But that car—that's the car that's been following me."

"It's an old Ford Mustang," Netty said as she took the photo from me and examined it. "Exact same model as in that old Steve McQueen movie, *Bullitt*. When I was in my early twenties, a friend had one just like this." She handed the photo back to me. "It's possible that, with care, it's still running perfectly fine now. But what are you trying to say, Addie?"

"I think maybe Lane is somehow involved."

"But why would he be involved? He doesn't live in Danville, nor did he grow up here."

"I don't know, but I'm positive that's the car that tried to run me off the road."

THIRTY-THREE

Later over breakfast, Netty continued to urge me to report what I had discovered to the police. I initially wasn't going to, only because I didn't think they would do much about it except go through the motions.

"Addie, you need to do your part. Never mind if you don't think anything good will come out of it," Netty said. "At least you'll be on the record as having reported it."

"Yeah, you're right. I need to go into town anyway to get my car."

"I can come with you to the police station, if you want."

"Thanks, Netty, but that's not necessary."

"Well, let me give you a ride to your car."

"I'll be fine. I'll just call a rideshare service to take me into town. It's not a big deal. And plus, there are some things I want to do around the house first."

"Well, all right. You let me know what comes out of your conversation with the police."

Netty gave me a hug. I walked her to her car and watched her drive off before heading back inside. Part of my hesitation, which I knew was stupid, was that everything else I reported to the chief had fizzled out. The most action he had taken was when he went after that car outside the police station. And that had turned into a whole bunch of nothing. I wanted to make sure that the car in the picture was the same one that was following me. I wasn't sure how I would do it, but I felt like I needed something more than "it looks similar."

I spent another hour looking through my photos for something more telling, but the photo of Kam and Lane leaning against the car with those T-shirts on was the best I had. I searched online for Lane Bowman and got a hit for a person living in Oakland. The birth year was around the correct time frame, but I couldn't be sure if this was the Lane I was looking for. That photo of Lane and Mrs. McDermitt had been taken in Seattle, but I got no hits in Seattle, or elsewhere in Washington. Social media wasn't helpful, either. I found a couple of other Lane Bowmans who lived out of state, but they looked nothing like the Lane in the picture I had taken. In the end, I couldn't come up with anything more. Netty was right, though. I needed to do my part and bring this information to Chief Abbott.

After a quick shower, I tried booking a taxi from a rideshare service, but either I kept getting canceled, or I would get a message that no cars were available in my area. I couldn't help but think it was my home address turning drivers off.

I should have let Netty drive me into town.

I thought briefly of calling Spencer but assumed he was already at the bookstore. I'd often walked into town from home when I was a kid. It was about a forty-five-minute walk. It was drizzling, of course.

Suck it up, Addie.

I put on a coat, grabbed an umbrella, and headed out. The quickest route from home into town had me walking past my old high school. I hadn't been there since I was a student, nor had I thought of it since coming home. I stopped out front and stared at the buildings from the sidewalk. The sight brought back a wave of memories, mostly terrible. It hadn't changed much from what I remembered. The murals on the main building had been updated, but aside from that, it was the same drab school I'd attended. The last time I'd set foot on campus was at my graduation.

The school year hadn't started yet, so the place was deserted —not a single car in the parking lot. The campus wasn't gated, so I was able to walk around with no problem. I glanced at my watch. I had some time to kill.

The main building, where the classrooms were located, was three stories and designed in such a way that the inside of the building was all classrooms. They were accessible through doors that surrounded the exterior of the building, with no passage-ways between rooms. In other words, it wasn't possible to walk inside it.

I headed to one side of the building, where I remembered all the science and math classrooms being. Between each classroom were lockers stacked five high against the wall. I stopped in front of my old locker. They were still the same putty color, but the graffiti and stickers were different. Visions of kids walking around me filled my head. They were laughing and talking, something I hardly ever did at school. It felt like being back in school twelve years ago. I hoped the person who had my old locker had a better time in school than I did.

At the rear of the building, there was a walkway leading from the library to the cafeteria. The library was a familiar place for me back then. The cafeteria was a war zone, and I avoided it as much as possible. But if I continued past the cafeteria, I knew I'd find the darkroom. That was perhaps the only place on campus I had reasonably fond memories of. I was curious to know if it was still standing, so I walked ahead. It was.

The darkroom was a small building made from concrete

blocks. No windows, just a single door, with no signage. It looked exactly the same as I had remembered it. It even had the same security keypad on the door.

The passcode was burned into my brain. Even after all these years, I could easily recall it. Just for giggles, I punched it into the keypad, and to my surprise, the door unlocked. I couldn't believe the school had not changed the passcode once in the past twelve years.

Should I take a peek?

I looked back over my shoulder and didn't see anyone, so I slipped inside. The entrance was the same, a narrow area that led to the second door. A tiny light bulb was on the wall, and I flipped the switch. Even the sign-in sheet hung in the exact same spot. There were names on the list; evidently the darkroom was operational. It made me happy to know others were getting some use out of it. The last student to sign in had been earlier in the week.

I turned the light off and entered the darkroom through the second door. After feeling around on the wall, I flipped the switch, and red light filled the room. My eyes filled with delight. I drew a deep breath.

Ahh, this smells how I remembered it, like chemicals.

I'd had so many good times in the small space. Photography and processing had become a source of comfort and sanity for me. The darkroom had been my oasis on campus, a place where I could be myself and feel safe.

I ran my hand along the counter where I had spent so much time developing my prints. Even the same trays that held the developer, fixer, and stop bath were still in use. Wooden tongs and film clips were lying around. During my time, we would have put everything away neatly after we were done. I wondered if Mr. Clark was still employed at the school and oversaw the photography club and darkroom.

Someone's prints were still hanging. I moved in for a closer look. The first photos included students in the cafeteria and hanging out near their lockers. The next batch was of a girl posing next to a car. When I reached the last photograph, I did a double take. I detached the photo from the clip for a closer look. As much as I had hoped I'd been mistaken, I wasn't. It was a picture of my house—with me standing at the front door.

THIRTY-FOUR

SOMEONE WAS DEFINITELY FOLLOWING me around. I rechecked the sign-in sheet. The last sign-in had been days ago. How did this person know I would be in the darkroom? Was the photo left by chance? Even I hadn't thought I would visit it until that day.

They're following me right now.

That was a strong possibility. The thought that someone could be waiting outside had me worried. I folded the photo and stuffed it into my purse. I needed to tell Chief Abbott what was happening.

But what if this person is literally waiting outside?

I took a look at my umbrella. It was one of those big ones that didn't fold up, and the handle was solid wood. It had some weight, and I felt I could swing it like a bat if need be.

Before I left the darkroom, I made sure to book a car from the rideshare app and checked to see that it was already on the way, just in case I had to run. Not surprisingly, it was easy to get a driver when the pickup address wasn't my home. I remained inside the darkroom until I got a notification that the driver had arrived in front of the school. Only then did I crack the door open, looking for someone. The coast looked clear, and I took off running.

My blouse was drenched in nervous sweat, but I made it into the car without having to beat anyone back and was safely on the way into town. I called Chief Abbott to let him know it was vital that I speak with him.

"You're speaking to me right now," he said on our call.

"I'm aware, but this conversation needs to happen in person. I'm on my way into town now. Do you have time to meet with me?"

"I'll fit you in when you get here."

Ten minutes later, I was sitting in a chair in front of Chief Abbott's desk.

"Okay, Addie. What's so important that you had to come here and tell me in person?"

"This." I placed the photograph on his desk. "Today, I found it in the darkroom at Danville High School."

He examined the photograph briefly. "You mind telling me what you were doing in the school's darkroom?"

"What was I doing there? You're focusing on the wrong thing. Look at the photograph. Don't you see it? That's a photo of my house with me on the front porch. It was hanging in the darkroom, being developed."

"Yes, I can see that, Addie. But you still didn't answer my question."

"Someone is stalking me. They left that picture in the darkroom to taunt me."

"First off, there's nothing illegal about photographing your house from the street. Secondly, your home is unique, one of the few Victorians in the area. Has it ever occurred to you that maybe it was a school assignment, or just someone admiring your home?"

"Under normal circumstances I could think that, yes. But

these are not normal circumstances. I think I know who tried to run me off the road a few nights ago."

Chief Abbott leaned back in his chair. "I'm still interested in how you got into the school's darkroom, being that you're not a student and haven't been one for over a decade."

"I was on the way into town when I decided to walk around the campus—you know, to reminisce and see if it changed at all. Is that a problem?"

"Continue."

"I was into photography big time when I went to school there. I spent many hours in that darkroom, so I wanted to see if it was still around. The school hasn't changed the passcode to the keypad. That's how I got in. I swear it was just a look around for old times' sake. That's it. And then I found the photograph."

I took out my phone, pulled up a photo I'd taken of the sign-in sheet, and showed it to Chief Abbott.

"Those are the students who signed into the darkroom. You could ask them if they took the photo, if you believe it was a school assignment. Or you can listen to my theory."

"What's your theory, Addie?"

"Kam had a half-brother. His name is Lane Bowman. This is a photograph I took when I was in high school." I scrolled through the pictures on my phone until I reached the one I had taken earlier of Kam and Lane and showed it to Chief Abbott. "The boy leaning against the car with Kam is Lane. It says so on his shirt. But more importantly, that car they were leaning against was the same one that tried to run me off the road. It's also the one I saw the last time we spoke, the one that you followed. You can't deny it's the same car, a Mustang. I know you can see it."

"They are the same car, but it doesn't mean it was the car that tried running you off the road. This is not the only car of this make and model in the wild."

"I realize that. But what if that was Lane's car back then, and he still owns it now?"

"And what? He decided to come to Danville so he could stalk and taunt you?"

"Yes, that's exactly it. I'm starting to think he might also be the one causing the trouble between the bully group and me... you know, Virgie and the others."

"I know who you're talking about. I'm also aware of Lane Bowman."

"You are?" I pulled my head back in surprise. "Why didn't you say anything, especially since he has the same car?"

"I didn't see a need to mention him to you. I only know about him because Mrs. McDermitt mentioned Lane when I questioned her about Kam's death. He grew up in Seattle because his father had custody of him, but he would occasionally visit during the summer—which explains that photograph you took. As for the car, there's no proof that his Mustang chased you down."

"I can't believe you're blowing this off."

"I'm not blowing it off, Addie, but I must do things according to the law. You know, it was only a few days ago that you were sure Reed Holland was causing all this trouble."

"I know, and everything points to him, besides the car. He's always driving around in his white Porsche, but Lane has the same car that tried to run me off the road. Look, Chief Abbott, everyone in this town thinks I killed Kam. That's no secret. To this day, Mrs. McDermitt still believes I'm responsible and should be locked up. So it's no stretch to think Lane shares her views. And what about Felisa's dog and that car running me off the road? You can't deny that the situation is escalating. Do I need to end up in the hospital before you take action?"

The lines on Chief Abbott's forehead deepened. "You make it sound like I haven't done anything. I have. I just haven't found any evidence to support your accusations. I'm not denying that someone is stirring up the hornet's nest. And I agree, things have escalated, but—"

"Look into Lane, Chief Abbott. Ever since Mrs. McDermitt yelled at me, things have gotten worse."

Chief Abbott didn't say anything, but I could tell the wheels in his head were spinning.

"I'll talk to Mrs. McDermitt and see if Lane owns a Mustang and if he's been in town lately. Will that satisfy you?"

"Yes, it would. Thank you."

"But promise me one thing: Stop playing amateur sleuth. And don't trespass in the darkroom again. Do I have your word on that?"

"You do."

THIRTY-FIVE

AFTER SPEAKING TO CHIEF ABBOTT, I headed to the parking structure where I had left my car. I half expected to find it broken into, or damaged even more, but it wasn't. Something went my way, finally. I thought briefly about stopping by the Tingling Spine and saying hi to Spencer, but decided to return home and continue working on the house. In my mind, getting out of town would end any and all problems, especially the stalker one.

I still couldn't believe how lackadaisical Chief Abbott was toward my findings. He seemed more concerned by my trespassing than by my violent stalker. Technically, I *had* broken into school property. And yes, I'd stupidly admitted that to a police officer. He had every right to focus on that. It could have been worse. He could have charged me. I wasn't thinking straight; I was so focused on Lane Bowman and the picture of my house that I thought that would trump the trespassing.

What did I expect? Chief Abbott wasn't a private investigator working for me. But at the very least, some concern was in order. Maybe he *was* concerned and just expressed it differently. But he already knew about Lane Bowman. Why did it have to take me bringing it up for him to connect the dots?

On the way back home, my curiosity started to itch again. I'd made a couple of lefts and rights and was driving down the street where the McDermitts lived.

What are you doing, Addie?

I wasn't sure, but there was nothing illegal about driving past their house. I slowed as I approached. The two-story home looked exactly how I had remembered it. The landscaping looked the same, except for the pine tree in the front yard. It was gone, and more importantly, there was no Mustang in the driveway. However, there was a garage.

I drove to the end of the block and parked my car. I knew I was about to do exactly what I had just promised Chief Abbott I wouldn't do. But hey, that's life, right? We don't always keep our promises. And anyway, I had a stalker. I needed to look out for myself. I grabbed my umbrella and got out.

As I approached the house, I kept the umbrella low, just above my head. I glanced around to see if any nosy neighbors were watching me. The left side of the garage had two windows. I could peek inside and see if the garage was empty. Even if someone was home, they wouldn't be able to see me. A narrow pathway and a tall hedge separated the McDermitts' property from their neighbor's, so I'd be hidden from view.

I looked around one last time as I approached the driveway. With the coast clear, I darted into the pathway and crouched. My heart raced as slickness developed across my face and neck.

Why am I so nervous?

Because you're trespassing. Again.

I closed my umbrella and inched my way forward until I was under the first window. Raindrops were still finding their way into the partially sheltered pathway, so I didn't want to stay too long. I slowly stood until I could see inside the garage and saw a dark-colored car parked inside. A tingling sensation rippled through my entire body. Was it a Mustang? It looked like one from behind, but I would know for sure if I could see the front grille. I would need to look inside from the other window to do that.

I crouched back down and moved forward on my tippy toes. My thighs burned from holding this position. As soon as I reached the second window, I stood. Goose pimples erupted across my body. It was a Mustang. I was positive it was the one from that picture I'd taken years ago.

Was Lane staying with the McDermitts? Or worse, was the person driving the car Mrs. McDermitt? The thought that she could really be the one had me second-guessing everything. I'd never suspected that it could be her, but one never knows what another person is fully capable of.

Just then, the door from the house into the garage opened. I lowered my head until my eyes were near the bottom sill of the window. In walked a man talking on his cell phone.

Oh my, God. Is that Lane?

I knew it wasn't Mr. McDermitt. This guy looked just a few years older than me. I couldn't see his face clearly, as he was looking down and standing at the opposite side of the car.

"I know. I know," he said. "Don't worry. I'm leaving now, and I'll lie low for a while."

I gasped, triggering him to look over in my direction. I dropped down and scooted up against the side of the garage.

Please don't see me. Please don't see me.

"I said I'm leaving now. Chill."

His voice was much clearer and louder. He had to have been standing just on the other side of the wall. I did my best to make myself tiny, but all he had to do was look down, and I was sure he'd see me.

A moment later, I heard the car door close and the garage

door open. I quickly scooted into the hedge, causing the rain-water that had collected on it to thoroughly soak me. I could still see down the narrow pathway, so I pulled out my phone and started recording. A few seconds later, the Mustang drove past. It was only a blip, but I still captured it. Lane Bowman was back in town. And he was stalking me.

THIRTY-SIX

I FINALLY HAD proof that Lane was in town and that he drove a Mustang. The only problem was that Lane appeared to be heading into hiding. I hurried back to my car.

Do I show the footage to Chief Abbott? If I did that, it would be a slap in the face, because I clearly hadn't kept my promise. He'd know I went to the McDermitts' home with one intention: snooping around.

But I couldn't just sit on what I'd seen. I had to do something. I decided to drive back into town and bounce the situation off Spencer. The rain started to come down harder, and as much as I wanted to hurry, I felt the tires slipping on the road, forcing me to drive slower than I wanted.

Spencer was stocking books on a shelf when I arrived at his store.

"Hey, Addie," he said with a smile as I walked inside.

"Hey, Spencer. Is your assistant here?"

"No, she's off today. It's just me holding down the fort."

"Good. I need to talk to you about something important."

"Is everything okay? You look a little frazzled...and wet." He handed me a box of tissues.

"Did you know Kam had a brother?"

"Um, no, I didn't. Why?"

"She does. I mean, she did. He's her half-brother. Mrs. McDermitt was married before and had a child in that marriage. His name is Lane Bowman. He lived with his father in Seattle."

"Uh, okay, but I'm not sure why you're telling me all this."

I quickly brought Spencer up to speed on the car and the photos I'd taken as a teenager.

"I'm positive this boy in the photo is Lane," I said as we looked at the picture on my phone. "It says 'Lane' on his T-shirt, and this car is the one that's been following me."

"The one that tried to run you off the road?"

"Yes. Netty said it's a 1968 Mustang."

"Yeah, it's a popular model. It was in a famous Steve McQueen movie. So what are you getting at?"

"There's more. After I talked to Netty about this last night, she said I should tell Chief Abbott."

"And what did he say?"

"He found out about Lane while investigating Kam's murder. He already knew about him."

"And he never thought to explore that?" Spencer shook his head in disappointment.

"I know, right?"

"I really feel for you, Addie. This stuff only started when you came home. Clearly, it's all intentional and aimed at you."

I shrugged. "There's still more. Before I went to see the chief, I stopped by the high school."

"The high school? Why would you ever want to go back there?"

"Why I went there isn't important. What is important is that the passcode to the darkroom was the exact same passcode from when we were students."

"Really? You'd think they'd change it every year."

"Listen, Spencer. I found this in the darkroom."

I pulled out the photo from my purse.

"That's your house. Wait, is that you?" he asked as he leaned in for a closer look.

"It is, and it was taken recently."

"What did the chief say about it?"

"He didn't say much. He was more focused on the fact that I trespassed on school property and broke into the darkroom. He thinks there's a reasonable explanation. You know, because my home is an old Victorian, maybe someone took a photo of it for the architecture or something."

"Sure, but that doesn't consider what's happened thus far. Is he living in a cave? A statement like that only makes sense if you're completely unaware of everything else that's been happening."

"That's exactly what I'm saying. And I tried to tell him that, but he got more irritated. He made me promise to stop trying to be an amateur sleuth and not trespass anymore."

"Well, *someone* has to do his job."

"He did agree to talk to Mrs. McDermitt, though. He said he would see if Lane was in town and whether or not he owns a Mustang."

"Like she'll admit to that if it's true."

"That's why I stopped by the McDermitts' house after meeting the chief."

"And?"

"I peeked inside the garage. Well, let me just show you the video footage I captured."

"No way. That's a 1968 Mustang."

"Yep, and it was parked in the garage. Not only that, but I also saw Lane. He came into the garage while he was talking on his phone with someone. His exact words were. 'I'm leaving now. I'll lie low.'"

"Are you serious? Did you get that on video, too?"

"No, I just have the footage of him driving away, but anyone can put two and two together. I came here right after. I'm not sure what to do with this, Spence. If I show this to Chief Abbott, I'll have to admit that I broke my promise to him and trespassed on private property again."

"But you have evidence that it's Lane. He needs to know about this."

"I know, but how do I do that without getting myself into trouble? The last thing I want is for Chief Abbott to dismiss it all because of how I acquired it. That's why I came here. We've always been able to figure things out together."

Before Spencer could answer, Virgie stormed into the shop.

"Where is she, Addie?" she said as she eyed me.

"Where is who?"

The first thing that popped into my head was Felisa's dog. But I was positive Chief Abbott had said he would give her the bad news. Did he not do that?

"Oh, don't play stupid with me. Where the hell is Felisa?"

"Felisa? How would I know?" Spencer looked just as confused as I did.

"Virgie, you'll need to expand," he said.

"She's missing. Like, as in gone. She hasn't returned any of my phone calls or texts from last night, and her family hasn't heard from her either."

Spencer and I both shook our heads, at a loss for words.

"I really don't know where she is," I said.

"Did you try her place?" Spencer asked.

"Don't play Spence the Dense now. Of course I did. She's not answering."

"Maybe she wants to be alone and away from you," Spencer said.

"Why would she want to stay away from me?"

I can run down the list if you'd like.

"Virgie, I have no idea where Felisa is. She and I are not friends. I don't know why you'd think I would know where... Oh, I get it." I started to nod upon realization. "You think I have something to do with her disappearance. I see what's happening here. Well, I'm not involved, so why don't you turn around and leave?"

"It wasn't enough to kill her dog. You had to do something to her, too? What has Felisa ever done to you?"

Is she serious?

"Virgie, neither of us knows where Felisa is," Spencer said. "Please get out of my store."

Virgie removed a piece of paper from her pocket. "I found this at her place."

I took the paper from her. It was a printed note that read: *I haven't forgotten. Payback's a bitch!*

"Virgie, I didn't write this note, and I have no idea where Felisa is. For all I know, this is some sick joke you guys are playing on me."

"You just can't get beyond it, can you, Addie? You'll live your whole life with a grudge because of some silly teasing while we were in high school."

"'Silly teasing'? Are you fricking kidding me? You and the others made my life a living hell!" I shouted. "Why do you think I got out of this town as soon as possible?"

Virgie's eyes widened, and she backed off. "You're a crazy woman. Stay away from me."

"What? I am not a 'crazy woman.' Stop gaslighting me."

"Hey Virgie, I don't know what's happening, but if Felisa really is missing, you need to report it to the police, not come here and accuse people." Spencer opened the door. "Now get the hell out of my shop."

Virgie spun on her heels and left just as quickly as she had arrived. I looked over at Spencer, at a loss for words. Could Felisa really be missing?

THIRTY-SEVEN

Spencer would not take no for an answer. He insisted on spending the night at my place. I didn't really fight him on it this time. The company was welcome, and I didn't feel like being alone with everything that was going on. I spent the rest of the day at his shop. He also closed up early.

"Do you want to grab dinner before we head back?" he asked as he turned the key in the door.

"I just want to get home. I don't feel like being in town any longer."

"Well, since we have to drive separately, I can swing by a fried chicken joint I know of and pick up some food. It's awesome chicken. I'll also get coleslaw, corn on the cob, and fries."

"That does sound delicious."

"It's settled. I'll pick up the food and head to your place after."

Spencer had parked in the same parking structure I had, so we walked there together. Neither of us talked about the events of the day. Instead, Spencer revisited the idea of him leaving town with me.

"I've been really thinking about it, and it's something I want to do," he said.

"Are you sure? Do you think it's about moving on or just wanting a break? You really haven't had a proper vacation since we graduated."

"I know, and I have considered that. I think it's a combination of both things. But it's something I want to do. I just don't want to be a burden to you. If you don't think you want me tagging along, it's fine to say that."

"That's the thing, Spence. I don't want you 'tagging along.' I want you to come because you want to do something for yourself. Following me around isn't a good enough reason. Does that make sense?"

"Totally. 'Tagging along' is probably the wrong way to phrase it. I want to do something different with my life. I realize staying here in Danville is like keeping one foot in the grave. It's not like I have fond memories of this place, and all it really feels like is the same old shit, but I'm older. I would like to learn from you on how to become a seasoned traveler; I want to watch someone who's a pro at it. There must be things you know now that you wish you knew back then."

"Hundreds. Some of it made me a better, stronger person. Some of it made my life harder, and I wish someone would have taught it to me from the get-go...This is me," I said as we reached my car. "We'll continue this conversation later, over fried chicken."

"Deal. See you in a bit."

Traffic was light on the roads, so I got home pretty quick. I parked my car off to the left of the driveway. That way, Spencer would have room to park beside my car. I headed up the porch stairs, and just as I put my key into the lock, I noticed one of the chair backs used to cover the window had been pushed back again.

I remembered I was supposed to be around for the hardware store to fix the window. I'd totally forgotten.

Did they try to fix it and give up? But why take it off halfway and then just leave? I also remembered I'd given them the landline number, not my cell, so they had probably tried to reach me, failed, and called it a day. But what if it wasn't them? My arm fit through the opening, but I couldn't quite reach the doorknob to let myself in. If someone had a longer arm, they could have gained entry.

I stepped inside carefully and quietly, listening for the slightest noise. The wind blew behind me, sprinkling me with rain, and I quickly shut the door. My gut told me to wait in my car until Spencer arrived. But I was stubborn and fed up with walking on eggshells. I wasn't that girl anymore. I flipped on lights as I walked through the living room, dining room, and kitchen, where I grabbed a knife. Before checking the bedrooms, I lit up the hallway, the stairway, and the second floor. I didn't see any signs of someone being inside. Just then, I heard a car outside. I looked out from my bedroom window. Spencer's car was parked next to mine, and he was climbing out. He saw me in the window and waved as he shut the door to his car. My gaze moved away from him to the bushes near the edge of the property, where I saw the familiar outline of a person.

"Spence!"

I spun on my heels and hurried down the stairs, tripping on the last step and careening into the wall. How long had he been watching? Had he been in the house? I ran as fast as I could toward the front door.

"Spence!" I pulled the door open, and Spencer was standing there holding a large takeout bag.

"Whoa! I didn't realize you were that hungry."

"He's here." I stepped around Spencer and onto the porch. "Where is he? He was just there a few seconds ago."

"Who, Addie?" Spencer turned and looked in the same direction I'd been focused on.

"He was standing right there, watching the house."

"I don't see anyone. Are you sure?"

"It's not the first time, Spence. And when I came home, the chair back was pried off the windowsill. Look at it."

Spencer tested the strength. "I can fix it." He looked back at me. "Didn't you call the hardware store?"

"They were supposed to come today, but I totally blanked. I wasn't here. I thought it might have been them. And then I saw the person standing at the edge of my property, and—"

"Hey, calm down. Everything's okay." Spencer put an arm around me and guided me back into the house.

"I'm not imagining things. I saw someone just now. I think it's Lane."

"You think he knows you were at the McDermitts' house today?"

"I'm not sure. I don't think it matters. If he's the one trying to run me off the road, he doesn't need any more motivation to come after me."

Spencer put the takeout bag down on the coffee table. "You got a flashlight? We'll walk the property and check the outside of the house."

A few minutes later, we were outside in the rain. I led Spencer over to the spot where I'd seen the person standing.

"He's always here, in this spot," I said.

"Well, he's gone now."

We made a loop around the property and then headed back inside. I grabbed a couple of plates and a few utensils and brought them to the living room.

"This chicken is the best," Spencer said. "So addictive."

I must have had a sourpuss because Spencer's smile disappeared. "Addie, I know you're worried about Lane. I mean, having someone on your property is scary. Do you want to call Chief Abbott?"

"I should let him know, but we don't need to do it now."

"Are you sure?"

"Positive. Let's eat before the food gets cold."

We spent the next hour eating and talking more about Spencer packing up and hitting the road. It helped to take my mind off my stalker.

"You definitely don't want to bring anything more than one piece of luggage," I explained to him.

"Are you serious?"

"Yes. That's all I did. You just need to make tough decisions about what you really need. You'll be surprised that most of the stuff you own is just that: stuff. It's replaceable. Anything you need, you can buy as you go."

"Wow, talk about minimizing my life. I didn't think about that."

"You're not moving from one apartment into another. It's about mobility at this point."

"Where do you keep your stuff? Don't you acquire items along the way?"

"I do, but I'm careful about it. Sure, there were so many things I saw that I would have loved to have purchased, but I knew I would be packing up my stuff in a few months. After a while, it became a habit. I don't even think about it anymore."

"You see, it's stuff like this that is helpful. I would have left town with a crap load of stuff."

A knock on my front door grabbed our attention. Spencer popped off the couch first.

"Sit. I'll get it."

Spencer opened the door wide enough that I could see Chief Abbott on my front porch.

"Hi, Spencer. Is Addie around?"

"I'm here," I said, walking to the door.

"I know it's a little late, but I need to ask you a few questions."

"Is this about Felisa?"

He nodded. "I'm guessing you heard. You mind if I come in?"

"Not at all. Have a seat."

"Felisa Chu hasn't been heard from since last night."

"Chief Abbott, are you here to tell me I'm the prime suspect?"

"I'm not. I'm talking to everyone who has had contact with her."

"Well, I should be at the bottom of that list. I haven't spoken to or seen her in a while."

"When did you last see her?"

"A while ago...at the Cubbyhole."

"And did you talk to her at all during that time?"

"I wouldn't call it 'talking,' but she and Virgie approached me to tell me about the messages they received. This was around the time Virgie had her garage door vandalized."

Chief Abbott nodded.

"From the looks on their faces and how they were acting, they thought I did it."

"And what came out of that conversation?"

"Nothing, really. I told them I had been receiving threats and had a rock thrown through my window." I pointed at it. "Then Virgie started talking about other things, and she said Jude also received notes. They sort of went into their own world and left me alone. That was literally the last time I saw Felisa. The person you should be talking to is Lane Bowman. I think he's the one behind this."

"I spoke to Mrs. McDermitt. She said Lane isn't in town."

"Of course, she did. But I'm telling you, someone was standing on my property and watching my house."

"It's true," Spencer said.

"You saw this person, too?" Chief Abbott asked.

"Not exactly. But I showed up at the same time as Addie spotted him. I was walking toward the house, so I didn't know there was someone there until she told me."

"I see."

"Chief Abbott, Lane is in town. Mrs. McDermitt is covering for him."

"And what makes you say that?"

I glanced over at Spencer.

"Show him, Addie. He needs to know."

I fetched my cell phone and pulled up the footage of Lane driving away in his Mustang.

"It's really quick, but that's the same car that tried to run me off the road," I said.

"Where is this?" he asked.

"That's the McDermitts' home."

I told Chief Abbott how I saw Lane and overheard him on the phone before he drove off.

"I know what you're going to say, that I trespassed and broke my promise to you, but if I hadn't done that, you would have believed everything Mrs. McDermitt told you. You need to talk to Lane. I think he lives in Oakland. I searched his name, and an address in Oakland popped up."

"Addie, I'm serious when I tell you to stay out of this. You need to let me and my men handle this investigation."

"But I found Lane, and he was driving the car that tried to run me off the road."

"No, you found a car that looks like the one that tried to run you off the road. You have no proof it's the same car, only the same make and model. Unfortunately, I have to follow the law."

Chief Abbott made a phone call, telling his men to check out an address for Lane Bowman in Oakland.

A screeching sound outside caught our attention. We all looked, and at the bottom of my driveway was Reed's Porsche. He and Jude climbed out.

"Addie, you've taken this bullshit far enough!" Reed shouted. "Where's Felisa?"

Both men were coming up my driveway fast.

"Addie!" Jude had spotted me in the doorway. "Get out here now!"

Chief Abbott stopped Spencer and me at the doorway. "Let me handle this."

He met them at the bottom of the porch stairs.

"My advice is for you two to turn around and go home. Right now!"

"Chief, Addie's the one behind all of this," Reed said. "She's been causing trouble since she came back into town."

"Funny, because the same has been said about you."

"That's bullshit!"

"Watch your mouth."

"Felisa's missing," Jude said.

"I had nothing to do with that!" I shouted. "Stop blaming me for this crap. You're the ones who are the bullies."

"For crying out loud, Addie!" Reed shouted. "That was years ago. Get over it!"

"Hey! Both of you go home!" Chief Abbott pointed to Reed's car. "Now!"

"But Felisa's missing," Jude pleaded.

"I'm aware of that, and I'm investigating her disappearance. But I can't have you two walking around and dealing out your own brand of justice. I won't have it, not in this town. Now, go home."

Chief Abbott walked them back to the Porsche. They

exchanged a few more words, but Spencer and I couldn't hear what they were talking about.

"You know, it's looking more and more like Lane is behind all of this," Spencer said. "I don't know what his beef with you is, but it's the only thing that makes sense for why you and the bully group are both having problems. Jude and Reed did look worried about Felisa. That wasn't faked."

"I agree. Maybe now Chief Abbott will make it a priority to find Lane."

THIRTY-EIGHT
THE SUMMER WHEN I WAS 17

I REMEMBER the exact day it happened. The sun had just set, and Spencer was dropping me off at home after we had hung out all day.

"I'll see you tomorrow," I said as I got out of his car.

"See you," he said before driving off.

I made the walk up the driveway. As I hurried up the porch steps, I noticed the front door was open, which was weird because my mom always nagged me about leaving it open. She didn't like flies in the house. I pushed the door open, and I saw the mess before I could call out that I was home.

It looked like someone had terrorized our house. My mother's plants were turned over, and garbage was strewn about among broken plates, bowls, and cups. I couldn't believe what had happened. And then Netty appeared with a broom.

"What happened?" I asked.

"Someone broke into the house and made a mess of things."

"What? Where's mom?"

"She's upstairs."

I hurried up the stairs and found her in the guest room. It was where she kept her collection of porcelain dolls. My mother was sitting on the floor in the middle of the room. She was sniffling as she tried to fix the hair on one of the dolls. Some of them had their faces broken or dresses ripped off. But there were a few that were worse. Those dolls had their mouths covered with silver duct tape, and someone had used a marker to make it look like they had black eyes. Their hands were taped behind their backs, and their ankles were also bound.

"Mom, who did this?"

I sat down next to her.

"I don't know, sweetie. Someone mean."

I helped my mother salvage the dolls worth keeping. We cleaned them up as best we could, and she had to throw the others away. She made me promise not to tell the police. I didn't know why she wanted to keep it from them. But when the police came, I didn't say anything about the dolls. Neither did Netty.

No one brought it up again. The following day, news had already spread that someone had broken into our house. I'd always thought the bullies did it, but we had no proof. It was just my gut instinct and how they'd look at me every time they saw me that summer.

THIRTY-NINE

THE FOLLOWING MORNING, I woke up and found Spencer looking out the window. The morning sun hit his naked body perfectly, and while I wanted him to crawl back into bed, admiring him was just as enjoyable.

"Good morning," I said playfully.

He turned to me. "The police are here."

"What?" I said as I sat up and scooted off the bed.

I stood next to Spencer and peered out the window. A squad car was parked at the bottom of my driveway, and two officers were on their way to my front door. We put on clothes and hurried downstairs.

"Hi, Addie," one of them said as I opened the door. "Sorry about the early call, but we need you to come into the station with us."

"Why? What happened?"

"It's best we talk down there. There have been some new developments."

"Developments?" Spencer said, annoyed.

"Addie, the sooner we leave, the better."

I told them to give me a few minutes and closed the door.

"What do you think happened?" I asked Spencer as we headed back upstairs.

"Maybe they caught Lane?"

"Maybe, but why would they need me to come into the station?"

"Beats me, but we'll find out soon."

I changed into a much more appropriate outfit and met the officers outside. Spencer followed us in his own car. On the drive over, I didn't bother to ask more questions, and the officers kept their lips locked.

At the station, Spencer was told to stay in the waiting area while the officers escorted me to an interview room. I quickly got the feeling that something was wrong. Seriously wrong. The mood was sterile and quiet, and if I'd ever had the opportunity to stand in a morgue, I imagined it would make me feel the way I was feeling now: nervous and sick to my stomach.

The door to the interview room opened, and in walked Chief Abbott.

"Hi, Addie. I appreciate you coming in. I won't beat around the bush. We've had a serious development in investigating Felisa Chu's disappearance. I need to show you something, but I will warn you. It's graphic."

Chief Abbott had brought a manila folder in with him. He removed black and white photographs and laid them on the table.

Goose pimples appeared on both arms as I looked at the photos of Felisa. She had silver duct tape secured around her mouth. Her eyes were swollen shut, and she had dark bruising around parts of her neck. Most of the pictures were close-ups of her face. Only one showed her entire body. She lay on her side with her hands secured behind her back. One sleeve from her blouse was torn and hanging by a few threads.

"Is she dead?" I asked softly, unable to tear my eyes away from the photos.

"It doesn't look good. Addie, these photos were found in the darkroom over at the high school."

The situation made complete sense at that moment. From the early morning visit to the officer's gloomy mood to the staring from others when I entered the station. Lastly, there was the look on the chief's face. It was the same one he'd given me when he interrogated me during Kam's murder investigation.

"You can't be serious," I said, shaking my head.

Chief Abbott's silence gave me my answer.

I felt as if I were living the same nightmare twice. This was supposed to be a simple visit home to take care of my mother's estate. Now I was in an interrogation room and considered a suspect in what appeared to be the abduction and possible death of Felisa Chu. I had admitted to trespassing on the school's property. I had admitted to entering the darkroom. And to make matters worse, I had snuck around the McDermitts' home.

"Surely you don't think I had something to do with what happened to Felisa?" I asked.

"Felisa could very well be dead in these pictures. I have to explore every angle."

"I had nothing to do with this. Yes, I know I went into the darkroom without permission. But do you seriously think I put these pictures in there? I was just there the other day, and I told you I found that photograph of my home."

"These photos were found this morning by a staff member at the school."

"I know what it looks like, Chief Abbott, but you can't be serious. I was at my home last night. You visited me there. Spencer spent the night. Go ask him. And before that, I was at his shop. I went there after seeing you. Come on, Chief

Abbott, do you honestly believe I kidnapped Felisa and beat her?"

A few silent moments passed as we sat still, eyeing each other, waiting for the other to break. The chief finally did by letting out a breath of air.

"I don't, Addie," he said. "Take a closer look at these pictures. Does anything look familiar to you? I know there's not much to see, but we need all the help we can get right now."

I took a closer look at the pictures. Only one thing came to mind: my mother's dolls. Felisa had silver duct tape across her face, and she'd clearly been beaten. Could it really be the same person? Was this a message?

"There's something you should know," I said. "I don't know if it's connected, but it's what popped into my head. Remember when my house was broken into and vandalized?"

"I remember."

"Something happened that my mother didn't want anyone to know about, so we kept it a secret all these years. She had a collection of porcelain dolls. We found them with silver duct tape across their mouths, and a black marker was used to make it look like they had black eyes, like they were beaten. Their outfits were also torn." I pointed at the pictures of Felisa. "They looked like her."

"Are you trying to tell me that the person or persons that broke into your home years ago are behind this?"

"You asked for my thoughts. That's what popped into my head. Maybe if we caught the people who broke into my house, we wouldn't be in this situation."

Chief Abbott shot me a look. Yeah, it was a cheap shot, but I felt like the Danville Police had done nothing but fail me.

After making me account for all my time over the last few days, Chief Abbott ended the interrogation.

"Did you find Lane?" I asked.

"He wasn't at his home in Oakland when my men went there, and the McDermitts claim they don't know where he is, but we are searching for him."

"I'm telling you, Chief Abbott, Lane is the missing link in all this."

He nodded but said nothing as he held the door open for me. "You're free to leave, Addie."

Since Spencer was already at the station, the chief brought him into the room for questioning. While I sat in the waiting area for him, Reed appeared from another interrogation room.

He looked at me with a hardened stare as he walked out. I didn't need to be told what he'd been brought in for. It appeared Chief Abbott really was talking to everyone. The photos of Felisa popped back into my head. I wondered if Lane was responsible. Was he capable of murder?

Spencer didn't spend much time talking to the chief, maybe twenty minutes.

"What did he ask you?" I asked when he appeared.

"He wanted to know what I had been doing for the last three days. I think he's trying to see how strong everyone's alibi is. Come on. Let's get out of here. I'll drive you back home."

"Reed was here," I said as we walked back to his car. "He left while the chief was questioning you."

"I'm guessing Jude and Virgie are also among the people to be questioned. I know you think this is about you, but it's not if he's talking to everyone."

"Hold that thought. Did he show you the pictures?"

Spencer shook his head. "What pictures?"

I shook my head in disappointment. "They found pictures of Felisa in the darkroom this morning." I climbed into Spencer's car. "It's the primary reason they wanted to talk to me. She might be dead, Spence."

He started the engine and started driving.

"Did you hear what I said?"

"I did. I'm processing. What kind of photos?"

"Someone beat her. She had tape over her mouth and was tied up. I don't know if she was dead or unconscious."

"Why would he show those photos to you? Those are, like, crime scene photos."

"He said he wanted to know if I recognized anything."

"If that's the case, he should show everyone those photos."

I shrugged. I debated if I should tell Spencer about the dolls but decided against it. I had told the chief because he'd asked. And honestly, I didn't really believe there was a connection. I'd always thought my bullies were the ones who broke into my house, and they were also under suspicion and being questioned by the chief. But there was no way Virgie would want harm to come to Felisa.

When we got to my house, I asked Spencer if he wanted breakfast, since we hadn't had time for anything before I'd been whisked to the police station.

"Coffee would be nice," he said.

We hung out in the kitchen while the coffee brewed.

"Are you sure you don't want something to eat? I could make you some eggs or even just some toast."

"Nah, I'm good. I don't really have much appetite, but if you're hungry, feel free to make something."

"I'm not hungry, either. This thing with Felisa is terrible. I can't believe she could really be dead. Just yesterday, I thought it was all just something the bullies had cooked up."

"I thought so, too... Did she really look dead?"

"I think she was."

"Why would the person responsible take pictures of it and then hang them in the darkroom, of all places?"

"Are you kidding? To frame me, Spence."

"But then this person would have to have known you went to the darkroom, so they're watching you."

"We've already established that someone is watching me."

"Right. Also, they would need access to the darkroom, meaning they would need to know the password."

"You're right. So, a past student?"

"That's what I'm thinking. Maybe it is one of the bullies. Maybe one of them is deranged and taking this way too far."

"Well, then that would point the finger back at Reed, right?"

"Yeah, I suppose so."

I poured coffee into two mugs and then handed one to Spencer.

"So, Reed wants to make it look like I killed Felisa?"

Spencer shrugged as he took a sip of the brew.

"But where does that leave Lane? I'm positive he was the one who ran me off the road... Wait a minute. Nah, it can't be."

"Can't be what?" Spencer lowered his cup.

"Do you think it's possible that Reed and Lane are working together?"

"That's an interesting thought. But how would they know each other?"

"Reed could have met Lane when he visited Kam."

"I guess. Why do you think Lane has it out for you? Is it purely because he believes you killed Kam?"

"What else could it be? I'm sure he believed everything his mother told him."

"But he only visited periodically, right?"

"Yeah but if he and Kam were close, like they talked daily on the phone, then of course he'd be angry about what happened."

"Yeah, but this is all theory. You have no proof what kind of relationship Lane had with his sister or mother, aside from a summer visit."

"Ugh. None of this makes any sense."

I sat at the small table in the kitchen, lost in my thoughts. Every time I was sure I knew who was responsible, I'd find a hole in my theory. I was starting to understand where Chief Abbott was coming from. Catching the person responsible for this—for the vandalism, for Felisa, for Kam, for all of it—wasn't as black and white as I thought it would be.

"Could you tell where Felisa might be from the photos?" Spencer asked.

"Not really. All of the photos were close-ups of her face, except one. She was lying on a wooden floor. The wall behind her was also wood."

"What kind of wood? Was it nice flooring, like you would find in a house?"

"No, it was old. Remember that abandoned shack near our spot at the creek?"

"Yeah."

"It was that type of wood, weathered and..."

Spencer and I locked eyes. We didn't need to confirm that we were both thinking the same thing; we quickly got into his car and drove down to the creek. We parked near the trail. The drizzle wasn't too bad, but I took an umbrella anyway. Plus, I wanted something to bash someone on the head with if needed.

We took a few wrong turns—it had been a while since either of us had been in that part of the woods, but we eventually located the trail.

"There it is," I said.

The shack looked a lot smaller than I had remembered, but I chalked it up to the fact that I had been a lot smaller back then. We slowed our pace as we neared.

"Wait." Spencer stopped me and looked around.

"What is it?" I whispered.

"Nothing, just being careful."

Spencer moved in front of me, and I followed in his steps. The structure was made entirely of wood and was about ten feet by six feet, maybe a little bigger. There were no windows, just a single door. We'd gone inside it a couple of times. Back then, it had been empty except for a couple of crushed soda cans, scattered paper debris, and a broken bottle. We always thought it must have been a hangout for people to use drugs, though we never saw anyone else there in the daytime.

It was a lot darker in the woods with all the tree coverage, and the cloudy skies didn't help visibility, either. Spencer grabbed the door handle and pushed it, but the door didn't budge.

"Is it locked?" I asked.

"No, I don't think so. Just stuck."

He leaned into it with his shoulder, and the door opened a bit. He gave it another push, and this time it swung open. Spencer used the flashlight on his phone to light the inside. Lying illuminated on the floor was Felisa.

Spencer rushed to her, calling her name, but she was unresponsive. Pinned to her clothing was a handwritten note: *I haven't forgotten what you did*.

FORTY

WITHIN THIRTY MINUTES, Danville Police had arrived. Officers taped off a large area surrounding the shack and waited for crime scene investigators to arrive. The responding officer interviewed Spencer and me, but also asked that we stay put until Chief Abbott arrived. We sat on the ground near a large tree, about twenty yards away from the commotion, and waited.

"How long will they keep her body here?" I asked Spencer.

"Probably until the CSI guys do what they need to do. I know the coroner needs to be the one to move it, and I don't think they're here yet."

"I still can't believe Felisa's dead." I leaned my head against Spencer's shoulder, and he grabbed hold of my hand before giving me a kiss on my forehead.

"This was supposed to be a simple, quick visit home," I said. "I thought I'd sign a few papers and be on my way. Now I'm sitting in the woods where Felisa was murdered."

"I can't believe it either. She might have bullied us, but she didn't deserve this."

"I know everyone will think I was involved once word gets out. But that's not what bothers me the most. It's the fact that

Felisa is dead...well, she was murdered. Some sicko did this just to get to me."

"Stop, Addie. You need to separate yourself from all of this. You said it yourself. You came home to deal with your mother's estate, that's it. As sad as it is, Felisa's death had nothing to do with you or me. If you think about it, we helped Chief Abbott with the investigation. I wish we'd found her alive, but we didn't."

I knew Spencer was right, but it didn't diminish the emptiness growing in my gut. What had started as a bunch of rotten bananas left on my porch had now escalated to murder.

Spencer elbowed me gently in the arm as Chief Abbott approached us.

"Addie. Spencer. I appreciate you two sticking around," he said. "Give me a few moments to talk with my men. I'll be back shortly."

Chief Abbott headed over to the shack and went inside. A few minutes later, he stepped out and spoke to a few officers before taking a walk around the shack and finally making his way back to us.

"I know what you two told my guy earlier, but I'd like to hear it again, in your own words: how you found Felisa," he said as he looked directly at me.

I cleared my throat. "Well, Spencer and I were talking about the situation after we went back home this morning, and he asked about the photos you showed me. When I described the wooden floor Felisa was lying on, it triggered a memory of this place we'd been familiar with since we were kids. I said it looked like the wood in this shack."

"Yeah, and once she said that out loud," Spencer said, "It was like, voilà. We had the exact same thought at the exact same time."

"That she was here?"

"Yes. It was a shot in the dark, but we figured, why not check it out?"

"You said you knew about this shack since you were both kids?"

"That's right," I said. "Spence and I used to hang out at the creek. It was like our private getaway. That spot is not far from here."

"Would you mind showing this spot to me?"

Spencer led the way through the woods until we reached the creek. Chief Abbott spent a moment or two looking around.

"What did you two do here?"

"We'd bring lunch and just hang out," I said. "Sometimes, we'd read or play cards. Other times we'd just talk or take a nap."

"We mostly hung out here during the summer," Spencer said, "to avoid Virgie and the others...because of the bullying."

Chief Abbott nodded. "Anybody else come here?"

"Not that we know of," I said. "At least not when we were coming here."

"And by the time we were seniors, we were hardly spending time here," Spencer added.

"And neither of you has been here since?"

"Well, we did visit once when I first came back to town, just to reminisce," I said.

"I hadn't been here since high school," Spencer said. "I guess other people could have known or discovered the spot during that time. It's public land."

"Are you positive Virgie or her friends didn't know about it?" Chief Abbott asked.

Spencer and I looked at each other and shrugged.

We were both keen on getting out of there. Spencer needed to get to his shop, and I didn't like being in the woods. It was creepy, especially since Felisa's body hadn't been moved yet.

"Now, it's not lost on me that there might be some backlash, Addie," Chief Abbott said as we walked. "I want you to report anything that happens to you, no matter how trivial you might think it is. I do not want the same crap to happen as when Kam McDermitt was found murdered. And trust me, Felisa Chu's death will be big news for this town. We haven't had a single homicide since... Well, anyway, I want both of you to be vigilant and aware of your surroundings. Am I clear?"

We both nodded. I almost asked, "What about Lane?" but held my tongue. I figured the chief already had enough on his mind and didn't need me nagging him about Lane.

"Do you want to hang out at the shop?" Spencer asked as we walked back to his car.

"Could you drive me home instead? I'm feeling tired. Maybe after a nap, I'll stop by."

"Are you sure? We just had a traumatic experience. You're not in shock, are you?"

"No, I think I'm fine. I just want to lie down for a bit."

When we got to my house, Spencer insisted on taking a walk around the property just in case anything had happened there while we were gone.

"We need to be careful," he said. "Whoever killed Felisa could target you or me, but most likely you. Wait. What I mean is, it'll make it look like tit for tat if they go after you. That still sounded bad, but you know what I'm trying to say, right?"

"I know, I know. Don't worry. I'll keep all the doors locked."

"Call me if you need anything."

Spencer gave me a kiss on the forehead and a hug. After he left, I headed to my bedroom, and within seconds of hitting my bed, I was fast asleep.

FORTY-ONE

I SLEPT for the remainder of the day and all through the night. I was completely disoriented when my cell phone started ringing. It was Gary calling, and it was 7:00 a.m.

"Addie, it's Gary. Sorry to call so early, but I heard the news. Do you need me to recommend a defense lawyer?"

"Good morning, Gary." I cleared the frog out of my throat. "Um, do I need a defense lawyer? I'm not a suspect in Felisa's death. At least not according to my last conversation with Chief Abbott."

"I realize that, but I thought you might want to consult with one, considering the situation and your past in Danville."

"I appreciate your concern, Gary, but I'm good now. But the sooner we can wrap up my mother's estate, the better off I'll be."

"I'm working as fast and as diligently as possible. Let me know if there's anything else I can help with. I'm only a phone call away."

"Thank you, Gary."

Now that I was officially up, I crawled out of bed and made my way downstairs for coffee. Once I had a cup of hot brew inside of me, my mind wandered back to the similarities between my mother's dolls and the photos of Felisa. Mentally comparing them to the photos Chief Abbott had shown me, I wondered if there might be a connection. However, there was one problem. If Lane was behind all of this, how would he have known about the dolls?

Your imagination is running wild, and you want to tie it all to Lane.

The only explanation I could conceive of was that the bullies were responsible for the break-in; Kam had participated and mentioned it to Lane. But there was no need to tie Felisa up like the dolls if all he wanted was to frame me for her murder—unless it was totally coincidental. It's not unusual for a kidnapping victim to be tied up like that.

If this really were about revenge, making it look like Virgie and the others were starting trouble with me could demonstrate a motive on my part—to get back at them.

Was Lane really capable of crafting an intricate plan like this? Maybe. I didn't know him. I also supposed Mrs. McDermitt could be involved. She wanted me in jail and probably didn't care how or why I was locked up, only that it was done. She definitely could be the brains and Lane the muscle.

If the end goal was to frame me, they hadn't achieved that; the Chief wasn't buying it. Did it make them that much more dangerous? If they realized killing Felisa hadn't implicated me, what would be next?

I glanced out the kitchen window. The trees rustled from a gust of wind, reminding me that I still needed to fix the front window. I went over to the window and pushed on the wood several times, but it didn't budge. I decided to see if the wood was just as secure from the outside. When I opened the front door, I jumped back in surprise. A man I didn't immediately recognize stood right in front of me.

I sucked in a quick breath as I tried to shut the door, but he threw his shoulder into it, forcing it back open and sending me stumbling backward. He quickly shut the door behind him. It was just him and me, a foot apart. His hair was wet, and bubbled raindrops dotted his face. Several scenarios ran through my head.

Fight?

Scream?

Run?

Reason?

Before I could decide, he snatched my hand by the wrist and yanked me into him. I didn't try to fight it or pull my hand free. I just stood there, staring at him and into his hardened stare as hot breaths bounced off my forehead. Lane had finally caught up with me.

Why was I not screaming?

Why was I not kicking or punching?

Why was I just allowing him to control me?

I was cognizant of what was happening. Why wasn't I doing anything?

"Do you know who I am?" he asked.

I was surprised that I was even able to nod.

"I've heard a lot about you," he said.

How? Why?

"My sister talked about you."

She did?

I managed another nod to let him know I heard him.

"You think I'm here to hurt you, don't you?"

I tugged on my hand, and surprisingly Lane let it go. I took a step back.

"You think I'm responsible for what's happening in town, but I'm not."

Lane took a step forward.

"People always kept their distance from me because they

didn't understand me. They thought I was weird. Kam was the only one who didn't judge me. She treated me like a normal person. Believe me when I tell you, I'm a lot like you, Addie the Maddy."

A cold flash burned across my chest, and I took another step back.

"What do you want?" I asked. "Why are you here?"

"You need my help as much as I need yours."

"I find that hard to believe."

"I know you do. If I were in your position, I'd think the same."

"You tried to run me off the road," I said.

"Yes, I did. My mother believes you were the one who killed Kam. I thought the same."

I took another step back. He followed.

"Don't run, Addie. It won't help."

I glanced at Lane's hands. He wasn't holding any weapons, nor could I see any bulges in his pockets or a sheathed knife hanging from his belt. But he was still physically more significant than me. *He beat Felisa to a pulp. He could do the same to me.*

"I can see it in your eyes. You don't believe a single word coming out of my mouth." His eyes traced my body. "You're shaking."

The sound of a car engine outside caught our attention, causing him to stiffen up and look toward the front door.

Lane grabbed me by my arm as he pressed his finger against his lips. "Shhhh."

A car door slammed shut.

"Trust me, Addie. I'm here to help."

Lane let go of me and ran down the hallway.

"Wait..."

"Figure it out, Addie, because we need each other," he said as he ran out the back door.

A second later, there was a soft knock on my front door.

"Addie, are you home?" Netty called out.

I let Netty inside. She was carrying a bag.

"I brought some food." She looked me up and down as she closed her umbrella. "I wasn't sure if you were eating, with all that's... What's wrong? You look like you've just seen a ghost." Her eyes looked beyond me. "Why do you have the back door wide open? You'll catch a cold with this draft blowing through the house."

I walked to the back door and looked outside. Lane was nowhere to be seen.

"Are you okay, dear?" Netty asked as she followed.

She paused in the hallway, just outside the kitchen. She still had a concerned look on her face. I shut the door and returned to her. She placed a hand on my forehead.

"Are you feeling okay? You don't have a fever."

She placed the bag she'd been carrying on the kitchen counter and started removing plastic food containers. "It's a good thing I came over. I don't think—"

"He was here."

Netty looked back over her shoulder at me. "Who was here?"

"Lane Bowman, Kam's half-brother. He left right as you arrived—out the back door."

"What? Why was he here?" Netty moved away from the counter, concern running the length of her forehead. "Did he try to hurt you? Are you okay?" Netty started to look me over again.

"He wanted to tell me that he's not responsible."

"Was he talking about Felisa?"

"That's the thing. I'm not sure. When we heard your car pull up, he got spooked and ran out the back door."

"Addie, you need to report this to Chief Abbott right away. That man is a maniac. Thank God I showed up when I did. He might have shown up to kill you, Addie."

"That was my initial thought, but the more I think about it... If Lane wanted revenge, and framing me for Felisa's murder was his goal, why come to my house to confront me?"

"Because he's a lunatic. Who knows what's going on in that head of his?" Netty looked me dead in the eyes. "I'm guessing you haven't heard yet."

"Heard what?"

"Jude's dead."

"What? When?"

"This morning. From what I heard, his car ran off the highway straight into a tree. He might have lost control while driving in the rain. It was raining hard."

"An accident? Are you sure?"

"I know what you're thinking. I think everyone in town is thinking it: First Felisa, now Jude."

Is that why Gary called? Was he also aware of both Felisa and Jude?

"Are people blaming me? I've been at home, sleeping since yesterday afternoon." I sat on a chair, my gaze falling to the floor as I processed what Netty had just told me.

"Can anyone vouch for that?" she asked softly as she sat next to me.

I looked at her. "Netty, why would you ask that?"

"Addie, I know you're innocent, but I also know Chief Abbott will eventually find his way here to you and ask that same question."

"Gary called me this morning, asking if I needed him to recommend a defense attorney. I thought it was strange, considering Chief Abbott didn't think I had anything to do with Felisa's death. Gary must have already known about Jude and assumed."

"Most likely. You know how gossip spreads in this town." Netty placed a hand on my shoulder. "Don't worry. Your Aunty Netty doesn't believe any of that crap. From what you've told me, Kam's brother is the guilty party here. The fact that he was here, in your house... Did he threaten you?"

"Not exactly, but it wasn't a social visit."

"You need to tell Chief Abbott so that they find him quickly."

FORTY-TWO

NETTY and I talked for another hour or so about my situation. She believed telling Chief Abbott about Lane was the right thing to do. I didn't necessarily disagree with her, but what Lane had said earlier gave me pause—that thing about us needing each other. I couldn't for the life of me understand what he meant by that.

"I'm worried about you, Addie," Netty said. "But I can see it in your eyes. You believe you need to keep digging into this mess, or you'll always wonder, 'what if.' Regret is like an itch you can't scratch away. It'll always be there, gnawing at you. I don't want that for you, either."

Netty gave me a big hug.

"I'm proud of the woman you've grown up to be. Your mother would have been, too."

"Thank you."

"You remind me a lot of myself when I was your age: Bold. Independent. A little stubborn..." A grin formed on Netty's face. "In other words, keep up your 'I don't take shit from anyone' attitude. It'll serve you well."

"I will. I promise."

"Just be careful."

After seeing Netty off, I was eager to find Lane. I needed to find him before Chief Abbott did. I'd had two encounters with him, which was two more than the chief and his men. Of course, I hadn't planned it that way; it had just happened. If anything, our first run-in at the McDermitts' was pure luck. He had orchestrated the second one at my home. I might have gained more insight if we'd had a few more minutes together.

I assumed Lane had been following me since I arrived in Danville. I thought back to the sightings of a person watching the house, and running past the window while I was in the basement.

People in town knew my mother had died before my return. Mrs. McDermitt could have mentioned it to him. And if Lane truly wanted to hurt me, he had every chance when we were alone in my living room. Instead, he chose to have a conversation. "Figure it out, Addie." That's what he said. Was that an invitation to continue engaging with him?

Stop talking to yourself, Addie. It's not helping. Find Lane and have a talk with him. He's been following you. Where could you go that he would know and be out of sight? The creek?

I hopped into my car and drove straight to the creek. Of course, he would know about it if he followed Spencer and me there. I parked my car on the side of the road, grabbed an umbrella, and walked into the woods. A few steps later, I reached the section of the trail where I could continue to my secret spot or veer off and make my way to the shack where Felisa was killed.

There was a tiny chance that Lane could be lying to me, that he really had killed Felisa. Was this a trap? Did he want to lure me there so he could also kill me? Was I about to do something incredibly stupid?

Coldness settled on my body as I suddenly became aware of

the dampness on my clothes, the drizzle. I kept my umbrella closed, only because if push came to shove, I could beat someone away with it closed. I started toward my secret spot, but then stopped and headed toward the shack.

The woods were quiet except for the occasional flutter of bird wings above. As I approached, I slowed my steps and crouched. My eyes scanned the area ahead until I spotted the yellow crime scene tape. I wiped a few raindrops off my face as I observed the shack for a few moments.

I moved forward to the small clearing surrounding the shack. The front door was closed. I stepped under the crime scene tape and walked over to the door. I quickly looked around before placing a hand on the door handle. Tightness formed across my chest.

The body isn't there, Addie. You know that.

I did, but I also knew I was looking for Lane. Was he inside, waiting for me?

I gently placed my ear against the door and listened for a moment. I didn't hear anything, so I pushed the door open. The shack was empty.

I made my way out of the area as quickly as possible; it creeped me out. It wasn't until I had the secret spot in sight that I started to calm down. Familiar grounds. But Lane wasn't there.

Maybe finding him isn't what he meant by 'figure it out.'

I had one more place I could check, but I wasn't looking forward to it. I'd already visited the darkroom at the school and had to admit to Chief Abbott that I'd trespassed on private property. I wasn't sure he'd be polite the second time around. But I went there anyway.

Instead of parking at the school parking lot, I parked across the street on the side of the road. I made my way on foot to a small access road used for deliveries to the cafeteria. I knew there was a chance the school had changed the passcode because of the photos of Felisa that had been left there. Indeed, Chief Abbott would have told them to do it. Surprisingly, they hadn't, and I walked right in like I had the last time.

I checked the sign-in sheet. No one had visited that day, and it didn't indicate that someone was using the darkroom currently. I pushed the inner door open and entered the darkroom. I slid my hand up the wall, searching for the light switch. A second later, the glowing red light came on, and Lane appeared.

No sooner had I drawn a breath than his hand had slapped down over my mouth and muffled my scream. His other arm wrapped around me and held me tightly against his body so I couldn't escape.

I struggled to free myself, hitting him once with a balled fist before he drove me back into the wall.

"Stop," he said. "Don't make this difficult."

Lane was too strong for me to escape his grasp. I stopped fighting.

My chest heaved sharply with each breath I drew into my nostrils. My eyes remained transfixed by his.

What now?

Lane removed his hand from my mouth, and I breathed much easier.

"Stop looking at me like I'm going to kill you," he said. "I'm not; you need to trust me."

"That's going to be hard, considering your actions," I said.

Lane released me and stepped to the side, purposely blocking the way out.

"I didn't kill your sister," I said. "If you want me to trust you, you must do the same."

"I already know you didn't kill her."

"You do? But your mother's convinced I did. So are a lot of people in town, even after all these years."

"My mother will never get over Kam's death. She'll live with the pain until she dies."

"I'm confused."

"For years, she talked about how you were responsible, that you were the one who killed Kam. I accepted that it was true—so yes, I did believe, at one point, you had killed my sister. I was hurt. Kam was my best friend, and losing her took a piece of me away."

"I'm sorry...but I'm still confused."

"There's one thing I know about Kam that other people don't. She wasn't a bully."

"Easy for you to say. You didn't grow up here. But I did, and I was on the receiving end of her bullying."

"I know you were. She told me about it, but you don't realize that she was bullied. Kam isn't a bully, but her so-called 'friends' put her in that situation. I know it's not a valid excuse, but it's true. Kam was bullied at her previous school, so much so that my mother insisted they move for a fresh start. They came to Danville. Kam had an opportunity to start over, but then she met Virgie and Felisa."

"Wait, are you saying they bullied her?"

"No, but she recognized the type of people they were. They were like her bullies at her old school. So she became friends with Virgie and Felisa, made them think she was like them."

"She told you this?"

"She did. She told me how she bullied you, and she hated it but didn't know how to stop it. She wanted to be left alone and graduate high school unscathed."

"So why did she play along? Do you know how hellish my life was back then?"

"I know what I'm telling you won't change things, and you'll always view Kam as your bully, but she wasn't that kind of person. She hated pretending to hate you."

Hearing Lane's words brought back memories of all the instances when I'd found myself alone with Kam in the darkroom, or even in the hallways outside the classrooms. She never bothered me during those times. In fact, she mostly ignored me.

"She bullied me only when Virgie or Felisa was around. I'd always found that strange."

"You see, I'm telling you the truth. Kam hated seeing you bullied. She would tell me about it all the time. She knew how you felt but was too afraid to do something. She was afraid of being bullied again. It's a messed-up situation. I wish I had known how to stop it. The thing with Reed also didn't help matters."

"What thing with Reed?"

"He had a crush on Kam. At first, she liked the attention but never took him seriously. But pretty soon, he started obsessing over her. I remember Kam telling me that he thought they were boyfriend and girlfriend and became super possessive. She had never agreed to that and had no idea where he got that idea. When she told him she wasn't interested, he got angry. She worried he could turn the others against her, so she told me she did her best to manage Reed, but it was difficult. I could hear the stress in her voice when we'd talk on the phone. She was reverting back to her old self, and that..."

"And what?"

"She tried once before to kill herself. That's what prompted my mother to move to a new city. I'm sure Kam would have tried again and succeeded if they didn't move. But life has a way of being cruel. Kam stepped out of one hell and into another."

"So you..." I took a step away from Lane, raising the umbrella I still had clutched in my hand. "None of this makes any sense. How do I know you're not lying? You tried to run me off the road, Lane!"

"I did. I'm sorry. My mother's constant nagging got me all twisted. It's stupid. And I regret it. But I can't ignore what Kam told me. When I remember what she said, the way she would talk about Virgie and her friends... I knew you couldn't have killed Kam."

"You think they're responsible for Kam's death?"

"I do. But you have to believe me, I had nothing to do with Felisa's death. I did not kill her, but thanks to you, the police think I did. That's why I decided to confront you. That's why I told you we need each other."

"Need each other for what? Why do I need you?"

"We both need our names cleared. We can do that for each other."

I took another step away from Lane. I still couldn't tell if he was lying or not. If he honestly believed someone in the bully group had killed his sister, that was motive for revenge.

"I know it looks bad," Lane said as he took a step toward me, "but just listen to what I have to say."

"You're scaring me, Lane."

"I'm sorry, but I need you to know I didn't kill her."

"Then who did, Lane? If it wasn't you and it wasn't me, who killed Felisa?"

"I think Reed did."

"Reed? They were all friends. Why would Reed kill Felisa?"

"Because I think he killed Kam. I don't think he ever got over the rejection. And I think he's the one that's making all this trouble now."

I couldn't believe what I was hearing. We were back to Reed? Could he really be the guilty one? If he did kill Kam, was he unstable enough to kill Felisa just to get back at me?

"I don't know what to believe, Lane."

"Believe me, Addie. As I said before, we need each other. Clear my name, and I'll help clear yours."

He turned and left the darkroom, leaving me believing that I had been right from the very beginning. Reed *was* responsible.

FORTY-THREE

I LEFT THE DARKROOM SHAKEN, confused, and wondering what my next step should be. If I asked the people I trusted, Spencer and Netty, they'd say I should report my encounters with Lane to Chief Abbott and stay out of it. But what would Chief Abbott do with that information that he wasn't already doing?

Number of times I've run into Lane: three.

Number of times Chief Abbott has run into Lane: zero.

Seemed like I was winning a game I had no interest in winning. So if I ignored Spencer and Netty, the option I was left with was trusting Lane—a wild card.

Addie, don't forget your original plan. Get in and get out.

I hadn't. But the situation had drastically changed. Two members of the bully group were dead. Was Virgie next? Would this somehow end up being pinned on me? Even worse, could I also be a victim? Not to mention, at the rate Gary was moving with my mother's estate, getting in and out was proving difficult.

And if that dilemma wasn't enough, when I reached my car, I found my left front tire had been slashed. There was a note tucked under the windshield wiper. It was hard to read because of the rain, but I could make out enough to know what it said: *We haven't forgotten.*

Who the hell was "we"? Was it really Lane screwing with me? Was this nothing but a game to him? I had almost started to believe him. I spun around, searching for him, but I didn't see him anywhere.

He's probably laughing as he pats himself on the back, that asshole.

The rain started coming down harder, and I had to make a decision. I knew Spencer was working at his shop. Netty didn't like driving in the rain, so I hesitated to call her. I tried booking a car through the rideshare app, but I kept getting a message that their drivers were busy. My last option was to walk into town. There was a shortcut through a wooded area; if I went that way, it would only take twenty minutes. Plus, I could go to Spencer's bookshop once I got there. I opened my umbrella and started walking.

The shortcut was a single-lane road that wasn't heavily trafficked by cars. When I was in high school, I would always take that route to get to town faster; all the students did. It was a peaceful walk that I had always enjoyed. Birds often sang, and a scurry of squirrels roamed. I recalled taking a lot of photos of them back in my school photography club days. But that day, there were no birds or squirrels. Just ugly gloom.

As I walked, minding my own business, the sound of tires on the gravel road caught my attention; a car was coming up behind me. I kept waiting for the driver to go around me with each step I took.

What's the holdup? Just pass already.

I finally looked over my shoulder to find out what was causing the delay. My stomach sank as I saw the car. It was a white Porsche.

Reed!

I could see his smug grin as he drove slowly behind me, about twenty yards back.

Look at the bully, so proud of himself for picking on a woman half his size.

I stopped walking and threw my arms up. "What do you want, Reed?" I shouted.

The Porsche's engine revved twice before the wheels screeched and the car rocketed straight toward me. I quickly moved behind a large pine tree. If Reed wanted to run me over, he'd have to get through that tree first.

The Porsche swerved as it skidded to a stop, and Reed climbed out of the driver's seat.

"You bitch!" he shouted as he headed toward me.

I wasn't about to find out why he was so angry. I ran.

"Get back here!"

Reed chased after me.

"Leave me alone, Reed. I didn't do anything to you."

"You did to Jude."

"I had nothing to do with that."

The thumping of his footsteps grew louder.

"Leave me alone!" I screamed at the top of my lungs as I tried to run faster. But Reed slammed into me from behind, flying through the air before we both hit the ground hard. I pushed up with my arms to get to my feet, but Reed's crushing weight fell on me and flattened me back against the ground, forcing the air from my lungs.

For a moment, I thought Reed would suffocate me to death. Instead, he flipped me over and straddled me, pinning my arms down with his knees. I tried to move, but it was like I'd been glued to the ground. He raised a balled fist, and I knew what was coming next. I shut my eyes and braced for impact.

The murmur of voices drifted in and out of my ears. They were soft enough that I could hear them but not loud enough to make any sense of them. The voices were male. I could tell that much.

"Addie?"

Did he say my name?

"Addie, can you hear me?"

I think he's calling me, but I can't be sure.

I opened my eyes briefly before shutting them. The sting of the light hurt. After a few seconds, I tried again and saw shapes that resembled people. After a few blinks, my eyes focused and I recognized Chief Abbott. He was standing next to one of his men.

"Addie?" he said as he took a step toward me. "How are you feeling?"

I tried to sit up, but he gently pushed me back down.

"The doc says you got a nasty bump at the back of your head, but other than that, you're okay."

"Am I at the hospital?" I said in a hoarse voice.

"Yes. Addie, if you feel up to it, could you answer some questions for me?"

I nodded.

"Do you remember being in the woods just outside of town?"

I thought briefly and was about to shake my head when my memory started returning. Images of me staring at my feet as I walked, the white Porsche screeching to a stop, running in the woods, and...Reed.

"I remember. Reed was angry. He chased me in his car. I think he was the one who slashed my tire."

"We found your car. It's been disabled, as you said. What else can you tell me?"

"He was very angry. I tried to get away."

"He came after you?"

I nodded.

"What happened then? I know everything is foggy right now, but I need you to try and remember. What happened when he chased you?"

"He tackled me."

"Okay, and what happened next?"

"He attacked me. I must have blacked out. Where is Reed? You should be asking him these questions."

"Addie...Reed is dead. He was found lying next to you with his throat cut. Now tell me what really happened."

FORTY-FOUR

I MUST HAVE DRIFTED off while talking to Chief Abbott, because the next thing I knew, I opened my eyes and Spencer was sitting beside my bed.

"Hey, Addie. How are you feeling?"

"I feel tired and out of it."

"You've been through a lot." He took my hand into his. "The doctor said you were in shock earlier, but other than that, you should be okay. They just want to hold you over for one night, for observation. You'll be free to go in the morning. Are you hungry? The nurse brought a tray of food for you."

"I don't feel like eating."

"That's fine. You can eat later."

"Spence, I need a lawyer. Chief Abbott thinks I killed Reed, but I didn't. He was trying to kill me, I swear."

"Don't worry about Chief Abbott. He's just doing his job. Netty is talking to your family lawyer, Gary. They're working on it. She was here earlier, but you were asleep. Do you want to call her now?"

I shook my head. "I'll talk to them later."

"Your lawyer will help you navigate through this. And just

for the record, I believe you. Reed was twice your size. Do you remember what happened?"

"I remember running from him, and he tackled me from behind. I hit the ground hard. He was so angry, Spence. He really had me scared."

"You're safe now. Everything's fine. But why were you walking in the woods?"

"Because of my car. I thought I'd come into town and go to your shop. We've walked that road probably a million times. Everyone does. I never thought anything would happen."

Spencer shook his head. "You should have called me, Addie. I would have come and gotten you."

"Does everyone think I killed Reed? Tell me the truth, Spence."

"As far as I know, no. And I'm being honest here. Of course, people are curious, but I don't think anyone in their right mind thinks you manhandled Reed and then cut his neck. All the police know is that they found you lying next to Reed. He was dead, and you were unconscious. Plus, they haven't found the weapon."

Spencer gently touched the side of my face, and it stung.

"There's a little bruising. You might end up with a shiner."

"I got hit?"

"Something hit you. Probably Reed."

"I wish I could remember."

"Relax, Addie. Maybe with time, the rest of your memory will come back to you."

"Does Chief Abbott have any other suspects besides me?"

"If he does, he's being quiet about it. But that's expected. The police usually don't divulge much information when they're investigating. Can I ask what you were doing at the school? You didn't go back to the darkroom, did you?"

I nodded. I realized then that Spencer knew nothing about

my encounter with Lane at my house; only Netty did. In fact, I was pretty sure I hadn't mentioned it to Chief Abbott earlier when he was questioning me.

"Lane showed up at my house."

"What?"

I brought Spencer up to speed on Lane's visit and what he had told me.

"You don't believe that psychopath, do you? Sheesh, Addie. Why on earth would you go looking for him after that?"

"Because things don't add up. Lane was on the verge of telling me more—more that would answer all of our questions— but he got spooked when Netty showed up at the house."

"I still can't believe you went looking for him and found him. Addie, you're not even supposed to be on school property."

"I know that, but I needed to find out what Lane knew. I had a hunch he'd been following me and would know about these places. And I was right. He was inside the darkroom waiting for me."

"You're kidding? Sheesh, Addie. Do you know how dangerous that was? Things could have gone bad."

"I know, I know. Thinking back, I realize how stupid it was."

"Did you at least get your answer?"

"Sort of... I'm not sure. He basically said Kam never wanted to bully me."

"Huh? That makes no sense. She was part of the bully group."

"I'm not sure if I ever told you this, but Kam never bullied me when we were alone. It was only when she was with Virgie or one of the others. It made complete sense when Lane explained Kam's past experiences with bullying and her fear of becoming a target again."

"Yeah, so she turns around and bullies you? I don't know, Addie. I still think Lane might be bullshitting you."

"Maybe. At this point, I'm just as confused. Lane thought Reed was the culprit. Did you know Reed had a huge crush on Kam and used to get possessive of her?"

Spencer shook his head. "I didn't, but I believe it. That guy was a major asshole. But now someone killed Reed, so how could he be the one behind it all?"

"I know. Nothing makes sense. Maybe I really am Addie the Maddy."

"Stop with that nonsense. You're the innocent one in all of this."

"I know, but somehow I'm still at the center. I told you, Spence, this town is a curse for me. I'm not meant to be here, period. Three people are dead, and everyone's pointing the finger at me."

"That's not true. As far as I know, Jude's death hasn't been officially ruled a murder. It looks like he lost control of his car while driving in the rain."

"We'll see how long that theory holds up."

"Virgie's the last one left in the bully group."

"You think she's in danger of being next?"

"Actually, I think it's the opposite. Virgie was the leader of the bully group. She was the driving force between Felisa, Jude, Reed, and Kam. They all bullied you because of her."

"Wait, what are you saying, Spence?"

"I'm saying Virgie has always despised you. It begs the question, how far would she go to do you in?"

FORTY-FIVE

THE ATTENDING physician at the hospital had cleared me, and all I needed was for someone to take me home. Chief Abbott walked into my room.

"Good morning, Addie. I heard the doctor gave you the okay to head home."

"That's right, I'm heading home. But somehow I don't think you're here to give me a ride."

"No, I'm not. Netty is waiting outside for you. I just asked for a few minutes, if that's all right with you."

"Ask your questions, Chief."

"First off, I want to let you know I have no intention of arresting you now, and I appreciate your ongoing cooperation."

"I'm happy to hear that."

"But..."

"There's always a but, isn't there?"

"Unfortunately, in this situation, it's unavoidable. You were found lying next to Reed's body. Right now, you're the best hope I have for figuring out what the hell happened. Based on the evidence collected and the brutality of the crime, I find it hard to believe a woman of your size was able to overpower Reed and kill him."

"It's a relief to hear that."

"But on the other hand, I've seen people under duress exhibit unexplainable feats of strength."

"Chief Abbott, what exactly are you getting at?"

"I believe you know who did this—whether you realize it or not."

"You might want to take out a pen and paper. I have a lot to tell you, and you may want to take notes."

Over the next thirty minutes, I walked Chief Abbott through everything that had taken place, from when Lane showed up at my house to when Reed tried to run me down with his car. During that time, the Chief kept quiet—listening, occasionally nodding, but never interrupting. I thought he had taken things reasonably well.

"I gotta tell you, Addie, I've never come across someone so desperate to get out of the limelight but who continuously drags themselves right back under it. What on earth were you think-ing? Are you simply daring me to bring charges against you? Because you are pushing me to my limit."

"I was on my way to tell you all of this. You can ask Netty."

I told a tiny fib. I wasn't on my way to find Chief Abbott, but I was sure I would have told him everything once I found Lane and got my answers.

"And what happened? You just decided to trespass on school property after I repeatedly told you to stop? I've racked up three murder investigations in one week, I can't be dealing with this, too."

"I've had three encounters with Lane. My way may give you headaches, but it can help where the law has your hands tied. You know what I found out is important to your investigation."

"Addie, the last thing I need is to find you dead. Things

could have gone differently in those woods. Do you understand that?"

"I do. I mean, I know it's reckless of me."

"Damn right it is."

"You need to find Lane. I know you're searching for him, but he's the key. I still believe he knows more than what he's told me."

"What makes you think he's telling you the truth? You know it wasn't long ago that you were dead set on the idea that Lane was responsible."

"I know I sound like a yo-yo-ing lunatic who can't make up her mind. I can't explain it. I just have this feeling...someone else is the killer."

"And if Lane isn't the guilty one, who the hell is? You know, you're not helping your case. There is motive for you to go after them."

"I realize that. But it's not me, and I don't for a second believe you think that, either. Felisa, Jude, Reed, Kam—they're all dead. There's only one person left: Virgie."

"You think Virgie's behind it?"

"I don't know, but she's the last one. You need to stick her in protective custody for her own safety, and you can start questioning her."

───

After my conversation with Chief Abbott, Netty helped me check out of the hospital. I was happy to see her.

"It's not a good idea for you to be alone," she said. "You're stuck with me. Even Chief Abbott insisted that, for the time being, someone should always be with you."

"What did Gary say about the defense lawyer?"

"He spoke with one about your situation. From a legal

standpoint, that lawyer doesn't think you have to worry. Chief Abbott has nothing, aside from your trespassing, to charge you with. They lack evidence that you had anything to do with Felisa's or Reed's death. I know the police haven't finished their investigation, or even finished processing the crime scene evidence. Still, I don't think they'll find anything to suggest you killed Reed. To even think that sounds absolutely ridiculous, if you ask me."

"I appreciate you being in my corner," I said.

"Where else would I be? I just hope that they find that Lane boy soon. And Addie, I want you to promise you won't try to sneak off and find him yourself."

"I won't. I think it's time I let Chief Abbott do his job."

"He needs to do a better job. If I were Lane, I'd be on the first flight out of the country. I know Danville is small, and they might not have the resources of a big city police department, but Sherry McDermitt is his mother. Surely she knows more than she's letting on."

When we reached my house, Netty parked as close as possible to the front porch. The rain had started, and she'd forgotten her umbrella.

"How long do you intend on keeping that dumpster?" she asked.

"Until I have the house cleaned out, then I'll call to have it removed." I climbed out of the car.

"You need to get that window fixed," she said as we walked up the stairs.

"I need to be around for them to do that," I said.

"Well, you'll have the time now, because you're staying put."

"I'm in the mood for coffee. You want some?" I asked as I headed toward the kitchen.

"Sounds good."

I returned to the living room with two mugs of coffee and handed one to Netty.

"Addie dear, I don't mean to pry, but have you decided what to do with the house?"

"I'm still in the selling camp. As much as I love this house, I can't see myself living here, especially after everything that's happened."

"I'm sorry that you had to endure these terrible things during your visit. To think, you ran away from here because of these problems, and now when you finally return, they come back twofold."

"And that's being generous."

"I really wish it wasn't this way, but I am glad to finally see you after all these years, even if it's because of your mother's passing."

"Same here, Netty. Have you ever thought of leaving Danville?"

"Leave? Now that's a thought that hasn't crossed my mind. I'd always been content here, but your mother played a huge role in that. With her gone, there's no real reason to stay, aside from familiarity. Why do you ask?"

"Spence wants to come with me when I leave."

"For a visit?"

"No, like he wants to get out of Danville. He's even figured out a way to keep and maintain his store online."

A smile formed on Netty's face. "You two have gotten close, haven't you?"

"We have. Spence was my best friend all through childhood. In fact, he still is. Honestly, I was a little worried about having a romantic relationship with him. Sometimes sex can mess things up, but in our case, it hasn't."

"I think you two traveling together is a wonderful idea. You can watch each other's backs."

"Yeah, we can. When he first suggested coming with me, I was hesitant because I wasn't sure what his expectations were. But he made it clear that our relationship had nothing to do with his decision. If we decided it was best to remain friends, he would be cool. He's pretty hands-off. He's never pressured me about our relationship; he's not in the least bit possessive or anything like that. So I've grown to embrace the idea."

"Sounds like things are working out well between you two."

"It is. I'm happy about it."

"Good. Well, while you two are gallivanting around the world, I'll be here in Danville holding down the fort."

FORTY-SIX

NETTY and I spent much of the day doing nothing but chatting and eating. A worker from the hardware shop stopped by and fixed the window. I felt like things were finally returning to normal, aside from the shiner I had on my face.

We got onto the topic of what to have for dinner. It was a tossup between ordering out or fixing that pasta dish I'd previously cooked for Netty.

"I did like that pasta," she said. "Why don't we just go ahead and make the pasta. That way, I can learn how you cook it and fix it for myself when you're not around."

Netty's cell phone started ringing just then. She picked up and listened. After a few seconds, the look on her face told me it wasn't good news.

"What is it?" I asked when she finally got off the phone.

"It's Virgie. She's gone missing."

"You've got to be kidding me. How the hell did that happen? This morning I told Chief Abbott he needed to watch her."

"I can't answer for him, but she's missing. That was my

neighbor. She said word of Virgie's disappearance has spread pretty quickly over the last hour."

"How did she disappear? I don't understand why Chief Abbott wouldn't just park a squad car outside her place."

"She said Virgie's car was found at her company, that place where you were working."

"The Cubbyhole."

"Yes, that's it. But rumor has it she might have been missing since last night. If that's true, Chief Abbott would have been too late anyway."

"Oh, my God. Maybe she wouldn't have gone missing if I had told him what I knew earlier, about Lane. Maybe it would have made him look harder for him or something."

"Now, Addie, don't you go blaming yourself. You couldn't have known this would happen."

"I know, but I waited. That's the point. I waited when I didn't have to."

"Virgie is not your responsibility. That fact that you're even showing concern is enough. That girl never cared about you."

"No, not until recently... What else did your neighbor say?"

"That was it. I guess the police are out looking for her. We all know who took her. He needs to just throw Sherry McDermitt into jail. That'll get her talking."

"But Netty, don't you see? Mrs. McDermitt thinks *I* killed Kam, not the others. So why would she and Lane want to kill them?"

"I'm not sure, but you did mention that Lane told you Kam was afraid of Virgie and her gang, right?"

"Yeah, and?"

"Okay then, if Lane believes it was them, he could have convinced his mother of that, and now she's in the same camp as him: They think the bullies were responsible, and they changed direction to go after them, instead."

I shook my head. "I don't know. This is all too crazy."

"Or maybe the bully group realized Kam was pulling away, and..."

"And that made them want to kill her back then?"

"Maybe not all of them, but one of them: Reed. You always thought he was the rotten egg, and I'm with you on that."

"So because Lane and his mother didn't know who was responsible for Kam's death, they decided to get rid of them all? I don't know..."

The landline rang just then, and I answered.

"Hello?"

No one spoke, but someone was on the line. I could hear them breathing.

"Lane, is that you?"

A second later, I heard a click, and the line went dead.

"Was that Lane?" Netty asked. "What did he say?"

"They didn't say anything. I just heard breathing."

"It's got to be that psychopath. I'm calling Chief Abbott for you and telling him."

"But we don't know if that was Lane who called."

Suddenly, a loud crashing sound made us both jump and scream. Another rock had been thrown through the window—the same one I had just gotten fixed.

This time, I didn't need Netty to warn me that whoever threw the rock might still be outside and possibly getting ready to throw another. "Stay there," I said to Netty. I crouched and made my way to the front window and looked outside and caught a figure disappear around the hedge.

"You see anyone?" Netty asked.

"I saw someone running away. They're gone now." I walked over to the rock.

"Be careful of the broken glass," Netty said.

This rock also had a piece of paper wrapped around it. Another note. "It says, 'Stop interfering! You can't stop it.'"

"Well, that sounds like something Lane would say," Netty said.

"At least it's not written in blood this time."

"I don't care how it's written. I'm calling the police."

I didn't try to stop Netty. For once, we were on the same page. If I could prevent Virgie from becoming a victim, I had to do it.

While Netty reported the rock to the police, I ran the vacuum cleaner over the floor and rug. I was bummed about the window—not because of the cost but the effort it had taken to get it fixed.

"They said Chief Abbott is in the neighborhood and will personally stop by," Netty said after getting off the call.

Ten minutes later, there was a knock on the door. Chief Abbott had arrived and was already inspecting the broken window from the porch.

"Same one as the last time," he said.

"I know. And I just got it fixed today. I'm beginning to think this is a racket run by the hardware store."

"It would make my life easier if it were. Where are the rock and note?"

"It's on the coffee table."

I stepped off to the side, and the chief came inside.

"Hello, Netty."

"Hello to you, Chief Abbott."

He slipped on a latex glove and examined the rock and note.

"Just so you know, I handled the rock and the paper with my bare hands," I said.

"That's fine," he said as he put both items into an evidence bag. "Did you see anyone after the rock was thrown?"

"I saw a man running away, but he was too far away for me

to tell who it was," I said. "Chief Abbott, do you have anything you can tell us about the investigation?"

"We spoke extensively with the McDermitts. They admitted that Lane had visited and was staying with them, but he's since left, and they have no idea where he is. They'd assumed he went back home to Oakland. We're working with OPD, and they haven't seen him. Lane's residence and the McDermitts' were both searched, but so far nothing has come up to indicate any of them are involved with the murders."

"So what happens now?"

"We keep looking for Lane. We've issued a statewide APB, so all law enforcement, including the highway patrol, are on the lookout for him or his car."

"They've got to be hiding him someplace. I can't believe they have no idea where he is."

"The guilty always run," Netty said.

"Any leads on Virgie?" I asked.

He shook his head. "I have all my deputies and group of volunteers searching. If there's nothing else to report, I need to keep moving. Are you two going to be okay here?"

"We'll be fine. Thanks for stopping by."

I stood on the porch until the chief's car disappeared. I still had some of the wood that had initially covered the window, so I hammered it into place from the outside, hoping it would be harder to remove that way, as they'd have to pull the wood off the windowsill instead of simply pushing against it. I looked across the front of the property, paying extra attention to where I always saw the shadowy figure, before heading back inside and locking the door behind me.

FORTY-SEVEN

THE SUMMER WHEN I WAS 18

THAT SUMMER TURNED out to be the worst summer ever. It should have been amazing, because Spencer and I had finally graduated from high school and we would be free from the bully group. We both planned to take a year off and just do whatever we pleased before we stuck our toes back into school. Neither of us had aspirations of attending a top university. We weren't athletic, so the schools with outstanding sports programs didn't grab our attention. Spencer even considered attending a junior college, but I talked him into applying to San Francisco State University. It would get us out of Danville, but we wouldn't be far from our families.

Five days before commencement, Kam was found dead inside the darkroom. Mr. Clark was replacing the inventory of chemicals when he discovered her body. She'd been strangled to death. Everyone in town immediately thought I must have done it. People thought it was a revenge killing. The only ones who didn't were my mother, Aunty Netty, and Spencer.

"Addie, hurry up," Spencer called from the chair on the front porch.

"I'm coming." I stepped outside as I adjusted my backpack.

Spencer had suggested we spend the day in San Francisco just to get away from Danville and the hate that was being directed my way.

"Sorry. I wanted to make sure my mom was okay with me leaving," I said.

"Is there a problem?"

"I just feel bad. It's not just me that's getting hated on. Some people aren't saying nice things about her, either. But my Aunty Netty is coming over to stay with her."

"That's good. People in this town are assholes. If I could banish them all with the wave of a wand, I'd do it." Spencer made a slashing movement with an imaginary wand.

Just as we got into his car, a police cruiser pulled up behind us, blocking us into the driveway. It was Officer Abbott.

"Can't he see that I was getting ready to back out?" Spencer said as Officer Abbott approached.

He knocked on Spencer's window, motioning for him to roll it down.

"Good morning, Spencer," he said.

"Uh, hi. We were just leaving."

"Well, it's a good thing I got here when I did." Officer Abbott lowered his head a bit more to look across to the passenger seat and into my eyes. "Hello, Addie."

"Hi. If you want to speak to my mom, she's inside the house."

"I'll have to speak to her, too, but I'm actually here to talk to you. Addie. I need you to come to the station and answer a few questions."

Officer Abbott had a short conversation with my mother, and then she drove me to the police station.

"Everything will be fine, Addie. I don't want you to be scared," she said. "They just want to ask you some questions about Kam McDermitt."

"But I didn't have anything to do with what happened to Kam."

"I know that. And now you need to repeat that to the police, so they're clear. That's all this is."

"It's so stupid. I already told them everything I know."

When we reached the police station, it seemed everyone was giving my mother and me a suspicious side eye. Officer Abbott led us into a small room that had a table and three chairs. There was a tape-recording device on the table, a pad of paper, and a pencil.

Officer Abbott pressed a button on the recording device.

"I'm Officer Abbott, and I'm interviewing Addie Baxley. The time is 9:53 a.m., June 3rd. Addie, did you know Kam McDermitt?"

"Yes, you know that already."

"Is it true that Kam bullied you in school?"

"Yes, you know that, too."

"She teased you often, didn't she?"

"Well, yeah, but it wasn't just her. Virgie, Felisa, Jude, and Reed also bullied me. They were the worst. Kam wasn't as bad as they were. Sometimes when we were alone in the darkroom, she didn't say anything to me."

"You mean you and Kam, right?"

"Yeah, she was also into photography."

"Were you often in the darkroom together? Is there a set schedule for students?"

I shook my head. "Any member of the school's photography club can use it whenever they want. I didn't see her a lot. And sometimes there were other students in there with Kam and me."

"The day Kam was discovered, did you use the darkroom?"

"Yeah, I was there for a couple of hours in the morning."

"And was Kam there during that time?"

"No. I was alone."

"Did you see her at all that day?"

I nodded. "When I left, I saw her in the parking lot with Virgie."

"And did they also see you?"

"Yeah, they started calling me 'Addie the Maddy.'"

"They would call you that name a lot, wouldn't they?"

"Yeah."

"I imagine it can get to you after a while—you know, just start grating on you."

"Of course. How would you like it if someone bullied you every day?"

"I wouldn't like it at all."

"That's right."

"You wanted them to stop, right? But they didn't."

"No, they wouldn't. Virgie and her friends bullied me since I was ten. Kam only started when we were in high school. But it was nonstop from Virgie and Felisa since I first met them."

"That's a long time, and I imagine a lot of resentment can build up inside. Is that what happened, Addie? Did it get to a point where you just couldn't take it anymore?"

"Well, yeah, but that's why I tried to avoid them whenever possible."

"But you couldn't avoid Kam in the darkroom, could you?"

"Obviously, she had a right to use it, just like I can't avoid them in the bathroom or in class."

"You mentioned earlier that only students who were members of the photography club had access to the darkroom, right?"

"Yeah, there's a lock on the door. We have to punch in a passcode to gain entry."

"Were you having a bad day, or were you stressed that day you ran into Kam and Virgie in the parking lot?"

"No. I was fine."

"So you were in a good mood?"

"Yeah, because the pictures I took came out great."

"So you were feeling good, and then you saw Kam and Virgie, and they started calling you names. That must have been a downer for you."

"I just ignored them."

"What were they doing in the parking lot? Could you tell?"

"It looked like Virgie had dropped Kam off."

"So she gave Kam a ride to the school. Did you see Virgie drive off after?"

"Yeah."

"And did you see where Kam went?"

"She walked into the school grounds."

"School was out for the year, so it's safe to say you had an idea of where Kam was heading."

I shrugged. "Well, yeah. I guessed she was heading to the darkroom."

"That must have been a relief, right? To finish up what you were doing before Kam got there."

"I already told you. It doesn't bother me when she's in the darkroom with me."

"But she just got done calling you 'Addie the Maddy.' That must have gotten under your skin. You were having a great day, and then you ran into Kam and Virgie. I think it's perfectly normal to confront Kam and want to tell her to stop. Is that what happened, Addie? You decided you had enough and followed Kam to the darkroom?"

"No, that's not what happened."

"Did you wait until she was inside before going back into the darkroom?"

"No, I went home after that."

"You mean after you went inside the darkroom?"

"Officer Abbott, I don't appreciate you accusing my daughter of hurting Kam. She did no such thing. This meeting is over. If you want to have any more conversations, you'll do it only when we have our attorney present."

Officer Abbott smiled at me. I remember it distinctly. It was the sort of smile that people give when they're trying to cover up their true intentions. Officer Abbott was no different from the others, I thought in that moment. He was a bully.

FORTY-EIGHT

NETTY and I didn't have much appetite for dinner after Chief
Abbott left. Instead of pasta, we settled for toast with jam, a pot
of green tea, and some conversation. But it wasn't as satisfying as
our talk before we had learned about Virgie. That and the rock
busting through my window had ruined the entire evening. It
had me shaking my head. I was convinced I wasn't welcome in
Danville, and there would be no chance of that ever changing.

Netty usually went to bed early, so by the time nine o'clock
rolled around, she had started to doze off on the couch. I fixed
up the bed in the guest room and bid her goodnight. After I
showered, I headed to my bedroom. I found myself drawn to
looking out the window. It was like an addiction; I had to know
if someone was outside watching. I flipped off the light switch
and crept over to the window, parting the drapes a tiny bit, just
enough to peer out. I knew where Lane would be standing if he
dared return. But I didn't see the familiar outline that night.

I took a seat on my bed. I wasn't tired. The shower had
cleared any thoughts of sleep right out of my head. Not wanting
to stay in my bedroom, I headed downstairs. I saw Netty had
left her purse on a chair, which reminded me that Netty had

asked about my mother's suitcases. She'd wanted to know if I was keeping them, because she could use one. At the time, the question had gone in one ear and out the other.

I had thought about donating them, as I didn't need suitcases. Netty could have all of them if she wanted. I thought I might have moved them out to the front porch. I decided to check, since I had the time and wasn't the least bit sleepy. I picked through the pile I'd kept off to the side of the porch but didn't see the luggage. I definitely remembered seeing them and hauling them out of the basement.

Could I have tossed them into the dumpster?

I stepped down on the first porch step and put my palm up to the sky to feel for rain. There was barely a drizzle, more like mist. I headed back inside, grabbed a flashlight, and put on a pair of trainers. I thought briefly about swapping my shorts for jeans but figured I would probably just need to shine the light into the dumpster and not have to climb inside and move things around.

I walked over to the dumpster with the flashlight and a chair. I stepped up onto the chair so I could see inside. For a minute or so, I looked around with the flashlight. There was more junk inside the dumpster than I had remembered. I'd probably have to jump inside if I wanted to be thorough.

How badly does Netty really need this luggage? Maybe I'll just buy her a new set.

I was about to climb off the chair when the anal side of me made me climb into the dumpster and search. There was an old rug in the dumpster covering sizable square footage. I picked it up by the corner and flung it back. Just some old plastic lawn chairs. I was about to call it quits—the misting was annoying me —when my eye caught sight of something. I moved a chair off to the side and gasped.

"Virgie!"

She lay there, unconscious, under the chairs. I quickly moved them off of her.

"Virgie!" I called out once again, but there was no response.

I didn't see any blood on her face, but it was beaten like Felisa's. I checked for a pulse.

She's alive.

I stood on the porch next to Netty with a coat draped over my shoulders. Virgie had just been lifted into the ambulance, and the doors closed. I still couldn't believe I'd found Virgie. Netty wrapped an arm around me and gave me a comforting hug.

"I'm still in shock," I said. "If I hadn't gone into the dumpster to look for that luggage..."

"I know. I know."

I turned to Netty. "We would have never found her had I not lifted up that rug. She might have remained in the dumpster until it was hauled away and the contents dumped into a landfill."

Netty pulled me against her shoulder and rubbed my back. "But you did find her."

Chief Abbott stood near the dumpster talking to a crime scene investigator. When he glanced back at me, I knew what he was thinking: Addie the Maddy's in the thick of it again. He made his way over to us.

"How is she?" I asked.

"She's been badly beaten, but she should pull through. If you hadn't found her when you did, we'd be having a different conversation. From the looks of it, she was put there recently. Did either of you see or hear anything strange?"

We both shook our heads. "I wish we had," I said. "I still can't believe the odds of finding her. It was totally by chance."

I'd already given Chief Abbott the rundown of how I had discovered Virgie. I thought he believed me.

"He's gotten to all of them," Netty said. "What do you intend to do about it, Chief Abbott? You have a madman running around dropping bodies wherever he pleases, and yet you and all your men can't seem to find him." Netty folded her arms across her chest and clenched her jaw.

"I understand your frustration. I'm frustrated, as well. We're doing everything we can to track that man down. Trust me when I say that he can't hide forever."

"He's not. He stopped by and put Virgie in the dumpster."

Chief Abbott flinched a little with that last barb Netty had hurled at him. But I agreed, he was screwing up this investigation just like he had Kam's. He'd made a big deal about catching the killer back then but came up empty-handed. And it appeared he was heading down that road for a second time.

"Chief, do you have any other suspects besides Lane?" I asked.

"Spit out what you really want to say, Addie."

"Okay. I told you earlier that Lane denied killing Felisa—and Jude, if he was murdered and not just a terrible driver. So it might be smart to start looking at other people in case it comes out that he isn't responsible."

"You know, I don't get you, Addie. One minute you're telling me that Lane is the one who's responsible, and the next minute you're touting his innocence."

"I'm not saying he's innocent. I'm just saying it might be a good idea to look at other people instead of putting all your eggs in one basket."

"And who would you suggest I look at?"

"I don't know. You're law enforcement. That's your job."

"That's right, so why don't you keep your nose clean and mind your business?"

Chief Abbott headed back down the steps and walked over to his car.

"Well, that was rude," Netty said. "I guess the truth really does hurt, doesn't it?" She turned to me. "You don't really believe Lane is innocent, do you?"

"It's hard to say. If his intention was to frame me for the murders, it's not working. I don't think the chief believes it."

"Still, he needs to do his job and catch that man. He's dangerous. He might try and do something worse if he can't frame you."

"What? Like, kill me?"

"And why not, Addie?"

"He had a couple of chances to do just that, especially when we were alone in the darkroom."

"Well, I'm just saying. The best thing we can hope for now is for Virgie to recover. She might be able to tell Chief Abbott who did this to her."

"I hope so, too. It goes without saying, but I hope he keeps an officer outside her hospital room twenty-four seven."

FORTY-NINE

When I woke the following morning, I peered out my window and saw news vans parked at the bottom of my driveway. I headed downstairs and found Netty cooking breakfast: scrambled eggs, country ham, fried potatoes, and toast.

"Good morning," she said as she stood over the stove.

"Good morning, Netty." I filled a mug with coffee and leaned against the counter. "This is nice."

"You've cooked enough for me. It's time I return the favor."

"I see we have visitors outside. Do you know how long they've been there?"

"They were here pretty early, as soon as sunrise. I don't know how they have so much to talk about. Take a seat at the table. Breakfast is ready."

I did as Netty asked, and a moment later, she placed a plate in front of me.

"This smells wonderful." I picked up my fork and dug in.

Netty took a seat opposite me with her food. "I thought of shooing those reporters away, but the last thing I want is my face on TV. So I just let them be. We'll keep the drapes drawn on the windows until they're gone."

"I hope they don't plan on staying all day." I bit into my toast. "Any news to report?"

Netty was dialed into the town gossip and reliable with most of her information. She'd know the latest news about Virgie.

"I've heard Virgie's condition has stabilized, but she's still unconscious. So, no word yet on who did that to her. But the chief has had men at the hospital guarding her room since she arrived in case Lane tries to finish the job."

"I'm glad to hear she's doing better. I hope she can ID who did this and stop this madness."

Netty and I worked on the house for the rest of the morning. We got a lot done, even considering she continually stopped to reminisce or tell me a story about her and my mother. I began to realize that that house was as much hers as it was mine. She'd forged so many memories there with my mother.

"Netty, I've made a decision."

"And what's that, dear?" she asked without looking up from the box she was sorting through.

"I'd like to give the house to you."

She stopped what she was doing and jerked her head up. "What? Oh, no, no, no. I can't afford to buy this house." I could tell the wheels in her head were spinning from the amount of money that would be needed to buy this house.

"Netty, I don't want to sell it to you. I want to give it to you —that is, if you want it."

"Now, why would you want to do that? You could sell it for a lot of money."

"I know, but I don't need it. My online businesses do just fine. And plus, my mother left me money. I would really like to gift the house to you. You've forged just as many memories here as I have. It should stay with you."

Tears welled in her eyes. "Oh, Addie. I don't know what to say."

"Say 'Yes, I want the house.'"

"Yes! Yes! I want the house."

She shuffled over on her knees and threw her arms around me.

"Thank you so much, Addie. You have no idea how much this means to me."

"I think mom would have wanted it this way. And everything that's still here, you can decide if you want to keep it, donate it, or throw it out. It should be your decision. I'll notify Gary and have the title transferred to you immediately."

"This is beyond generous."

"It's meant to be."

Netty was like a little girl on Christmas morning with the latest and greatest toy. She had already started walking around the house, telling me her plans to redecorate.

"Your mother and I always wanted to repaint the walls and the outside of the house."

"Will you keep the house the same color or mix it up?"

"I don't know, what do you think? Is it better to keep the same color?"

"That's entirely up to you now. It's your house."

"The floors could also use refinishing," she said.

"Now, *that* I agree on. They're pretty tired-looking, but if they're restored, they'll look fabulous. Netty, I'm thinking...this house has gotten pretty run-down ever since I left home. There are a lot of things that need repairing, not just the floors. The roof, for one, and finishing the basement would be great, maybe some new pieces of furniture... What I'm trying to say is I'd like to help with the cost."

"Oh, I can't allow you to do that," she waved off my offer. "I'm sure I can take a loan out from the bank."

"Netty, I've already made up my mind. I'm paying for it."

A smile formed across her face as she tilted her head. "You'll always be welcome here. It's your home, too, you know."

"I know."

Netty stuck around until noon helping me with the house. It was a lot easier deciding what to trash and what to keep with Netty involved. She wanted new furniture for most of the house, but wanted to keep the dining room table and chairs. It was a lovely antique wooden table with eight matching chairs. My mother had gotten it at an auction. Netty planned on restoring the table and chairs to their former glory. She said she'd had so many conversations there with my mother, she just couldn't part with it. The dumpster outside was still an active crime scene, so we couldn't throw anything into it until I got the okay from Chief Abbott. But a quick walk through the house told me I was about ninety percent done.

The news vans had cleared out before Netty left, which we were both thankful for. Neither of us felt like being bombarded with questions. She had checked her gossip sources for the latest on Virgie, but as far as anyone knew, Virgie remained unconscious.

"Are you sure you'll be okay?" Netty asked as I walked her out to her car.

"I'll be fine. Spence is coming over tonight after he closes his shop."

"Good. Until Virgie can tell Chief Abbott who tried to kill her, and until he can track the guy down, you have to be careful."

"I will. I promise."

After Netty left, I called Spencer to confirm he was still coming over. He was busy at the shop and couldn't talk but said he'd come as soon as possible. I spent the rest of the afternoon maintaining my online business. The slow internet made it painful, but I had nothing better to do.

Before I knew it, evening had rolled around. My eyes were tired, and my back hurt from hunching over my laptop, so I decided a soak in the bath was in order. While decompressing in the bubbly water, I sent a text message to Spencer for his ETA. He replied that he was almost finished and would be over shortly. I asked him what he wanted for dinner, to which he replied: *I can eat anything.* I had planned on ordering delivery for dinner, most likely that fried chicken joint Spencer had introduced me to.

I went ahead and ordered the food; my stomach was growling. After I finished my bath and dug into some chicken, I put the rest of the food aside for Spencer. I was up in my room gathering my dirty clothes for a load of laundry when the urge to look out my window bubbled up inside me.

Don't do it, Addie. It's pointless.

I tried to ignore my feelings but decided there was no harm in looking outside. Surely, Lane wouldn't be hanging around my house after what had happened to Virgie. Chief Abbott had already said he would keep up the increased patrols on my street, though I wasn't sure how much they helped.

I shut off my bedroom light before peeking out the window. Even though I had been looking for it, the shock of seeing the outline of a person near the edge of my property caused me to gasp and pull away from the window.

Lane!

FIFTY

I PEERED out the window once more. I wasn't mistaken. Someone was standing near the bushes. A number of responses went through my head: Call the police, call Spencer, or confront the person.

I grabbed my golf club and readied myself. The plan was to rush outside and run straight toward him. Swing, if necessary. I drew a deep breath before marching toward the front door. I opened the door and rushed right into Spencer. He reached up and grabbed hold of the club.

"Sheesh, Addie. I know I'm late, but I don't think I deserve a beating."

"He's here! Lane!" I shouted as I looked beyond Spencer. "He's over there, where he always is."

Spencer looked back over his shoulder to where I'd pointed.

"There's no one there, Addie. I would have seen someone when I pulled into your driveway."

"I swear, Spence. Someone was standing there just a few seconds ago."

"All right, let's take a look, just in case."

Spencer led the way, wielding the golf club he'd taken from me. When we reached the spot, no one was there.

"Your car must have scared him off," I said.

"Maybe..." Spencer's voice trailed off.

"I know you don't believe me, but I saw someone. It was Lane, and he was watching the house."

"Okay, okay, I believe you. I'm here now, so he'll have to deal with me if he wants to start any trouble."

I sniffed and wiped my nose with the back of my hand. Spencer looked out into the night sky before throwing an arm around me. "Come on, let's head back inside before you get sick. Plus, I have good news to tell you."

Back inside, Spencer sat me down on the living room couch. His eyes were wide with enthusiasm, and he had a toothy grin.

"I did it. I got rid of the store. I mean, I sold it to my assistant."

"What? I can't believe it. When did this all happen?"

"Over the last few days. It's why I've been so busy, especially tonight. The other day, I helped her secure a loan from the bank. Tonight, I ran her through a checklist of how to operate the store, which she basically knows how to do, but I want to make sure she can keep the store profitable."

"That's amazing, Spence."

"I know. I decided leaving Danville meant leaving everything. I didn't want to be tied back here by the shop. It was better to just cut ties; that way, I could do exactly what you did when you first left. Disappear into obscurity."

"'Obscurity'? It sounds depressing when you put it that way." I chuckled.

"It'll be great. You and me on the open road, traveling the world like a couple of vagabonds. I can't wait to get started. And I did exactly as you told me. I reduced everything I owned so my belongings could all fit into one small piece of luggage. Also, my apartment is cleared out, and the lease is paid out. I'm free of any and all ties to Danville."

I must have looked confused.

"What? Is something wrong?" he asked.

"Um, don't you think you might have jumped the gun a little? You could have taken it a bit more slowly. When I told you what to do, I didn't mean to do it all at once."

"But I had to. How else could we leave tonight?"

"Leave tonight? Surely you're joking."

"No, we have to leave."

"Spence, I can't leave right now. I still have things to do with the house, and I still have a bit more paperwork that I'm waiting on from Gary."

"What's the big deal? Gary can email you the paperwork, and you can sign it electronically. As for the house, just have Netty take care of things from here on out." Spencer took a quick look around. "And you've got most of the work done anyway. Just pack your bag, and we'll be on our way."

I kept waiting for Spencer to laugh and tell me he was joking. But the look on his face told me he was dead serious.

"Spence, you have to understand why I can't leave tonight. I mean, you mentioned none of this before. I thought we'd plan a date to leave together."

"In an ideal situation, that would have been the plan. But things didn't quite go the way I expected. It's crucial we leave this town—ideally the country—before Virgie regains consciousness."

"What does Virgie have to do with this?" I asked.

Spencer kept his mouth shut while he kept his gaze locked onto me.

"Spence, I asked you a question."

His continued silence told me something wasn't right. I scooted away from him.

"Do not move away from me, Addie." His voice was no longer filled with excitement. "You know we need to leave before Virgie wakes up."

"Spence, what did you do?"

"What did I do? I helped you."

Spencer's eyes seemed to darken right before me as his body stiffened. The muscles in his jawline rippled as he clenched his teeth.

"I made the problem go away." He spoke in a controlled and steady voice. "It took longer than I had anticipated, but I did what I always told you I wanted to do since we were kids."

"What's that, Spence?"

"I stopped them. Your bullies."

I shook my head slowly as realization set in. Spencer was my closest friend. Someone I had trusted since I'd first met him. But he sat a few inches from me with a stony face that I didn't recognize.

"Spence, did you hurt Virgie and the others?"

"I did it for you, Addie. Once I got rid of Kam, I knew I could easily deal with the others. I had it in me to get the job done. But then you left town without any notice. And now, you're back. Listening to your stories and how you reinvented yourself, I knew that's what I wanted for myself. But first, I had to finish the job I had started. Each one of them deserved it. You might have been able to put the past behind you, but I could never forget."

"Spence, that's not what I wanted. I didn't ask you to hurt them...or to kill them."

"No, you didn't, but someone had to stand up for you. You always let people trample over you. So I took care of it for you."

"Those notes...that was you. You weren't trying to frame me?"

"Of course not. I didn't expect it to be perceived that way, but in hindsight, I can see why it would be. That's why I needed you to stop interfering. You were seriously screwing things up. I also couldn't have peace between you and Virgie or any of the others. The last thing I needed was you all becoming friends. My plan wouldn't have worked. Of course, when Lane entered the picture, I couldn't believe how lucky I had gotten. He became the perfect fall guy. And if Virgie remains in her little coma, he'll take the blame. That guy made it easy because he followed you around like a crazy stalker. And he tried to run you off the road. What a psycho, right? And Reed was just an asshole who had no idea how much he was helping me. Between you and me, slicing Reed's neck open was pure joy."

At that moment, everything clicked. I realized why things never quite added up with Reed or Lane being the guilty ones.

"I know what you're thinking. You don't have to thank me, Addie. I did it for you because you're my best friend—and now my girlfriend. There's nothing I wouldn't do for you."

"Spence, don't you see what you did was wrong?"

"Wrong? If solving a problem is wrong, then I don't want to be right. It's over, Addie. We're both free. And they'll never be able to hurt anyone again. Well, Virgie is the odd man out. Maybe she'll stay in that coma I put her in. Or maybe she'll have brain damage and need to be spoon-fed for the rest of her life."

I scooted farther away from Spencer. "I want you to leave right now."

"I will. We'll both go as soon as you get your stuff."

He snatched my wrist and yanked me to my feet as he stood.

"Oww! Spence, you're hurting me."

"Yeah, and you're testing my patience. Now let's get your stuff so we can leave!"

My gut told me I had to fight. I couldn't allow Spencer to force me into his car, because then the chance of me ending up like the others was real. I tightened my hand into a fist and swung with all my might, landing a solid punch to Spencer's face. His head snapped back, and he let go of my hand.

"What the hell, Addie?" A trickle of blood appeared under his left nostril, where I had struck him.

I sprinted toward the front door. I had to get out of the house. Spencer's fist latched onto my hair as I opened the door and pulled me back. I landed flat on my back, and a sharp pain ran up my spine. The next thing I knew, Spencer had straddled me. Forceful breaths of air blew from his nostrils as he bared his teeth at me.

"You ungrateful little bitch. After everything I did for you, this is how you repay me?" A drop of blood fell from his nostril, landing on my cheek.

"Please let me go, Spence."

"Nah, I can't do that now. You've already shown your true colors, haven't you? Why do stupid bitches always screw things up? I had it perfectly planned out. In fact, even with the Virgie mishap, my plan still worked. All we needed to do was skip town tonight and disappear into the wind."

I bucked my hips to throw Spencer off me, but his thighs clamped tightly around my waist. Then he delivered a stinging backhand.

"Be a good girl, Addie. Don't make me do things to you that you will regret later."

You mean things you'll *regret, right?*

"Now, let's try again. I'm going to get off of you, and then we're calmly heading up to your room and packing your stuff. Is that clear?"

I didn't answer him quickly enough, and he slapped me again, harder.

Spencer got up from his knees. He was still straddling me, and instinctively, I kicked as hard as I could right into his crotch. He groaned as he fell over to the side, and I flipped over to my stomach and began crawling away. I spotted the golf club leaning against the sofa and made my way to it. As I reached for it, I felt Spencer's hand clamp down on my ankle. He yanked me back in one quick movement, and I fell against the floor. I kicked as hard as possible, but Spencer had a tight grip on my legs.

With each tug, he brought me closer to him until he latched onto my hair and pulled.

"You made me do this," he said, out of breath.

He punched me in the back of my head again and again. The pain was excruciating. No matter how hard I tried to wriggle out of his grasp, I couldn't get loose. Then, he flipped me over and scooted back on top of me, pinning my arms down with his knees. Just then, a shadowy outline appeared behind him.

Lane!

Lane raised his arm, a table leg grasped in his fist. He struck Spencer across the back of the head. Spencer fell on top of me, unconscious.

"Addie, are you okay?" Lane shouted as he moved to pull Spencer off of me.

"I'm fine, I'm fine. Spencer, he's the killer."

"I know." He helped me up. "I told you I didn't kill them, but I eventually figured out who was doing this. There was only one other person with a vested interest in what was happening. It had to be Spencer, so I started following him."

"Lane, if you knew he killed the others, why didn't you go to Chief Abbott?"

Lane walked me over to the couch and sat me down.

"I had no proof. And everyone already thought I was guilty. Even my own mom started to believe I was responsible."

"I'm so sorry. I didn't know. I thought... Lane! Watch out!"

Spencer struck Lane from behind, pummeling him. Lane

dropped to one knee, and Spencer kicked Lane in his side, causing him to groan and fall to the floor. Spencer looked at me with a smile. His head was a bloody mess, but it didn't stop him from kicking Lane repeatedly.

"You bastard. You think you can get out of this?" Spencer shouted. "Now I need to kill both of you fuckers, and you have no one but yourselves to blame."

Lane did his best to counter Spencer's kicks, but Spencer had the upper hand. Then he pounced on Lane and released a barrage of punches. I had to help. I had to stop Spencer from killing another person. I grabbed the golf club.

This ends now!

I swung the club as hard as I could, like a baseball player at bat. But Spencer caught the club in his hand. He laughed as tiny rivers of blood branched out across his face. He yanked the club out of my hand. Lane was already unconscious, unable to help.

"You are one stupid bitch," Spencer said as he stood.

He blocked the way out the front door, so I turned on my heel and ran in the opposite direction toward the back door as fast as my legs would carry me. I reached out for the doorknob, twisted it, and pulled. But the door didn't open.

The deadbolt! Open the deadbolt!

I fumbled with the latch, trying to turn it. I could hear Spencer's footsteps behind me as he closed the distance.

Come on, open, dammit!

Finally, the latch turned, and the door opened. I bolted out, running away from the house. The backyard was pitch black, and the grass was slippery from the rain. I could barely see where I was running, but I knew Spencer couldn't see me, either. I ran toward the large hedge at the rear of the property, where I knew I could slip inside and hide long enough to gain my bearings and make a run for the front of the house, back into the neighborhood where I could get help.

I stood between two tall bushes and kept quiet. My heart was thumping hard in my chest as sweat poured down the side of my face and neck. It didn't help that the rainwater collected in the hedge had drenched my clothes.

"Addie?" Spencer called out in a singsong way. "Where are you?"

I saw the outline of his body walking cautiously toward the hedge. He still had the golf club.

"I know you're here. You can't escape me. I'm too good for that. Who would have thought all those crime books I read would help me plan the perfect escape? And I will escape, Addie. It's a shame we won't be doing it together. We could have made a great team."

Spencer lashed out at the hedge with the club, making contact not far from where I stood.

"Come on, Addie. Are you really making me hunt you down like an animal? It'll only make it worse." He stabbed the club into the hedge again. "Right now, I bet you're shaking, maybe even peeing yourself as I get closer. The suspense would be worthy of Hitchcock's admiration. We just need some eerie shrieking violins in the background."

Spencer was bound to find me. I had to make a run for it before he got too close. At least I'd have a running start in the dark.

Do I run along the side of the house to the front, or inside to a place where I can safely barricade myself?

The back door was wide open. I could slip right in and latch the deadbolt shut before locking the front door and calling the police. Worst case scenario, I could lock myself in my room. The bedroom doors were sturdy, so even if Spencer found a way to break into the house, I'd be okay. I feared Spencer would kill me if I ran to the front yard and he caught me out in the open.

And then, without warning, my nose tingled, and I sneezed.

"Gesundheit!" Spencer shouted as he looked in my direction.

I darted out from the hedge, pumping my arms and willing my legs to move as fast as humanly possible.

"Addie!" Spencer shouted. "I see you!"

As I closed in on the house, I still hadn't decided—straight through the back door or veer to the house's left side? The right was too narrow, and the ground was uneven.

Make a decision, Addie. Now!

I opted for the house. I ran inside, and just as I shut the door, I saw Spencer's smiling face. As soon as I slid the deadbolt into place, he slammed into the door.

"You can't escape me!" he roared as he punched the door, rattling it.

I was already running to the front door to lock it shut. It was only then that I remembered the broken window with the piece of wood covering it. It was only a matter of time before Spencer broke through. Time for Plan B.

FIFTY-ONE

I SAT STILL, crouched in the dark corner. My legs were pulled up tight against my chest as I struggled to calm my breathing. I kept expecting to hear Spencer's taunts, but the house remained silent.

Maybe he cut his losses and took off.

He was on the clock. I had to believe he didn't want to be caught by the police, and the longer he stuck around, the greater the chances of that happening. A loud crashing noise made my body jump.

He's inside.

A few seconds later, I heard stomping as he slowly walked up the stairs.

"Addie, I counted to one hundred, and now I'm looking for you. Reed tried running from me in the woods, but I found him hiding in a ditch like a little bitch. He begged for his life. All bark and no bite.... What makes you think you can get away, when Reed couldn't?"

Spencer's voice was clearer and louder. He was on the top floor.

"Dragging him back to where you were wasn't easy. But boy, was it satisfying slashing his neck open. I wish you could have seen it. But then my plan wouldn't have worked."

I could hear the hallway floor creak as he walked. The sound of a door being forced open rang out.

That's the guest room.

"Nothing behind door number one!" he shouted.

There was the sound of another door opening forcefully.

"Ah, your mother's bedroom. Well, that leaves one bedroom left. Of course, I knew you'd be in there. That's why I saved it for last."

His footsteps moved down the hall quickly. A beat later, splintering wood rang out as Spencer crashed through the door.

Got you. Nothing behind door number three, either.

I was pretty sure Spencer wasn't aware of the attic. I'd never mentioned it to him. I'd already called the police and knew they'd be arriving any second. I just needed to stay out of sight. I peeked out the window. The road leading up to my home was dark. There were no flashing lights or sirens wailing in the distance. I couldn't understand what was taking so long. Danville wasn't that big.

Suddenly, my cell phone rang. By the time I switched the ringer off, it had already rung twice. I might as well have had a microphone amplifying it.

"Addie? Addie, are you there? It's Chief Abbott."

I had accidentally answered the phone in the process. I brought it up to my ear and whispered. "I'm here. It's Spencer. He's the killer."

"I know, Addie. Virgie is awake, and that's what she told us."

"He's in the house, Chief."

"Addie, there's an army of police, including myself, on the way. Are you in a safe place?"

"I'm hiding in the attic. I don't think he knows about it. But hurry."

I disconnected the call, wondering if Spencer had heard the ringing. I returned to the dark corner and made myself as tiny as possible. I listened and watched the attic door for any signs of movement. Perhaps Spencer hadn't heard anything.

Then the attic door moved.

I drew a sharp breath and held it.

A second later, it opened, and the stairs unfolded, allowing the light from the hallway to glow around the opening.

Stomp!

Stomp!

Stomp!

The ladder shook and creaked with every step he took.

I scooted as far as possible into the corner, thinking Spencer might not see me in the dark. Chief Abbott would be arriving any second, but still, no sirens were wailing in the distance. Tears streamed from my eyes. Was this how it ended?

The top of Spencer's head poked through the opening, the back of his head facing me. He stopped, clinging to the top rung of the ladder. What was he doing? Was he listening? Was he unsure whether I was up here? I clung to a sliver of hope.

I heard him breathing calmly and steadily.

In.

Out.

In.

Out.

What kind of psycho is entirely at ease in a situation like this?

The one who wants to kill you, that's who.

For a brief second, I thought he'd begun to step back down the ladder, but he turned instead.

Slowly, methodically, his head rotated. I could only imagine his eyes focused on every inch of the dark attic they passed over, searching carefully, acclimating to the dark. His face came into view. The light from the hallway lit it with harsh shadowing. Spencer was unrecognizable—a monster, if I had to put a word to it. His gaze settled on the length of the attic, focused on the window at the very end. I was off to the side, crouched tightly in the corner.

Does he see me?

"I see you, Addie."

Spencer's shoulder bounced as a low laugh gurgled up from his throat.

"You almost got away, coming up here."

Spencer placed his hands on either side of the opening and climbed all the way up into the attic. He stood there, staring at me. He moved his arm, and I noticed the meat cleaver he was holding. It glinted in the hallway light.

"Everything had been thought through," he said as he slowly walked toward me. "The plan would have worked. Why did you have to go and screw it all up, Addie? I'm beginning to think you brought the bullying on yourself. Maybe your actions are the reason for your shitty childhood." He shook his head disappointedly. "I can see that now."

Spencer was halfway to me.

"You're a bully just like them," I said. "You're no better."

He coughed out a laugh. "I was bullied right alongside you. Talk about selective memory."

"You were bullied, and now you've become one. Bullies pick on the weak because they don't have a way to defend them-selves, or the will to try. You're taller than me, stronger than me, heavier than me, yet you still chose to bring a weapon. That's what a bully would do: create a situation where the odds favored them."

"This?" Spencer held up the cleaver. He swung it, striking a wooden beam and driving the cleaver into it. He released his hand, and the cleaver remained embedded in the wood.

"Are you happy now?"

When I'd scooted into the corner, I had sat on a wire hanger. I spent the last minute or so twisting the metal head to pull apart the shoulder and fold the wire into a makeshift handle with a pointy tip. I stood up and moved away from the corner.

"Spencer, the police are on their way. Chief Abbott will be here any second."

"Chief Abbott hasn't done a damn thing to keep you safe. Do you think he'll suddenly be able to do that now? He's incompetent."

Spencer started moving toward me. His arms were down by his sides. I had the element of surprise on my side. I just needed to strike at the right moment. I gripped the hanger tightly, waiting.

Now!

Spencer was two steps away when I lunged forward, swinging my arm as I aimed for the fleshy part of his neck. But Spencer caught my hand at the last second, stopping the pointy tip a hair's breadth from his neck. I leaned in, using both hands to try and drive the wire into his neck. My thighs burned as I pressed hard against the floor for leverage.

Spencer slapped his other hand down on mine and began to push the wire away from his neck. His face may have been streaked with blood, but his smile hadn't once dimmed. He pressed a thumb against the pointed shaft and slowly bent the tip so it angled away from his neck.

"Now what?" he growled.

"I don't need it. I have a golf club."

A crinkle formed on Spencer's brow.

A sharp cracking sound rang out as the iron club slammed into the side of Spencer's head, splitting it open and sending him to the floor. He lay there motionless, and standing behind him was Lane.

FIFTY-TWO

THE CAVALRY SHOWED up seconds later. I hadn't had seconds to spare. I was sure Spencer would have ended my life in that attic if it weren't for Lane. Lane took a moment to look me over before helping me down the attic ladder. I could hear the police downstairs in my living room.

"Addie? It's Chief Abbott!"

"We're okay!" I shouted. "We're up on the second floor. Lane is with me. Don't shoot."

The pounding of boots on the stairs grew louder. Chief Abbott appeared first, with his gun drawn. Behind him were four other officers.

"Hands up, Lane!" Chief Abbott shouted.

Lane did as he was told, and I stepped between Lane and Chief Abbott. "Lane saved me. We can explain."

"Where's Spencer?" he asked.

"In the attic," I said. "I think he's dead."

Abbott ordered his men to check it out, and a few moments later, they confirmed what I said was true.

Chief Abbott looked at Lane and then at me with utter confusion.

"What the hell happened here?" he asked.

I explained to Chief Abbott how Spencer wanted to skip town together and eventually admitted to the murders.

"That includes Kam, too. He confirmed that he was responsible for her death."

"Kam?"

Chief Abbott looked dumbfounded. Spencer had never been a suspect or even called in for questioning, apart from giving a statement on how we had found Felisa.

Chief Abbott turned to Lane. "And how do you fit into what happened tonight?"

Lane initially admitted to causing a little trouble, even going so far as to try to run me off the road. Still, he said in his defense that he had allowed his mother's bitter talk to get the better of him.

"So why did you stop?" Chief Abbott asked.

"The more I thought about it, the more I realized Addie couldn't have been the one who killed Kam. Kam had always told me that she felt forced to act a certain way in school so she didn't become bullied. Part of that was pretending to bully Addie. Addie also mentioned that Kam never bothered her when they were alone. I knew she couldn't have done it."

"So, how did you come to suspect Spencer?"

"He was the only other person I could think of who was involved but hadn't experienced any collateral damage yet. I kept an eye on him and watched Addie to see if I could catch the person messing around with her." Lane glanced over at me. "I know now that it came off as stalking, but that wasn't my intention. But then Felisa died, and then Jude ended up in that highly suspicious accident. I knew someone was targeting them. I couldn't keep an eye on everyone, and with the heat on me, I stopped watching Spencer and focused on Addie. When Reed died, I knew

Virgie was next, but I felt hopeless. You guys were hunting me."

"So, how did you know to show up here tonight?"

"After Reed died, I focused even more on Addie, watching her at the hospital and at home. So yeah, that's why I was here when Spencer showed up."

We'd said enough that night to satisfy Chief Abbott for the time being. However, we still ended up back at the police station, answering questions. Chief Abbott had four murders—five, if you included Kam—to process. But with Spencer dead, there was no satisfying closure.

Ultimately, the prosecutor decided not to charge me or Lane for Spencer's death. I learned later that Mr. and Mrs. McDermitt had accepted that Spencer was the one who had killed their daughter, not me, though no apology ever came my way. I was okay with that. I just wanted to be done with them and this town. I wanted it all to finally end.

Lane wasn't completely out of trouble. Chief Abbott investigated him for animal cruelty. There was still the issue of Felisa's dog being killed. Spencer might have murdered the others, but he hadn't killed the dog; he was with me when it happened. Reed might have done it, but since he was dead, that left Lane. Of course, he denied it. Deep down inside, I knew it was him, but there wasn't enough proof for Chief Abbott to move forward and charge him. But even if Lane had done it, I can't for the life of me figure out why, unless his mother's whispering was heightened at that moment and he wasn't in his right mind.

As for Virgie, she recovered from her injuries. I did visit her once while she was in the hospital. We had each thought the other was guilty of dredging up the past when, in fact, we were both wrong. A lot of apologies were made on either side. She was absolutely distraught over losing her best friend and her boyfriend. The once popular girl with all the cool friends was now alone and broken. I honestly didn't think Virgie was able to comprehend how much danger she'd been in and how close she'd come to joining her friends. Grief consumed her. Virgie and I would never be friends, but I was sorry about what had happened to her. I told her to remain positive and not to give up on life. I knew from experience that it does get better.

It took another month for Gary and me to settle my mother's estate. All monies were transferred over to my accounts. The house title was turned over to Netty, and she moved in. During that month, we were able to have the house painted, the roof repaired, and new furniture ordered.

As for Lane and I, we were in an awkward situation. We hadn't known each other before and weren't introduced as friends. Lane stopped by the house one day. He had decided to give up his place in Oakland and move to Alaska. He'd always wanted to live there.

"What's in Alaska?" I asked as we sat on the front porch.

He shrugged. "A simple life. I don't know if I'll stay there forever, but it sounds good. I'll work on the fishing boats like the ones on those television shows."

"Sounds like you got it all figured out."

After a moment of silence, Lane cleared his throat. "So, like, are we supposed to be friends now or something?"

"Why don't we simply say goodbye and wish each other luck?" I said. "How does that sound to you?"

"That sounds good."

We shook hands, said good luck, and parted ways. I didn't expect to run into Lane ever again, and I was pretty sure he had the same thought about me. But we had both gotten something out of the experience: closure.

When it was time for me to leave, Netty cooked our final dinner together. She invited Gary over, and the three of us had a delightful meal as we talked about all the good times we'd had under that roof. Leaving Danville felt different this time. I wasn't trying to escape from anything. I wasn't sure if I would ever return, but I was certainly more open to the idea than when I'd first left.

"You're always welcome here, Addie. This is your home, too," Netty said as we stood on the porch the following morning, waiting for the taxi to take me to the airport.

I gave Netty a big hug. "You're always welcome to visit me on the road, anytime and any place."

That was the way we left things. No false promises, no expectations, just simple invitations. That's how it ended.

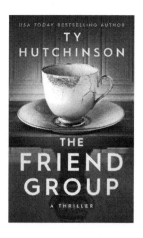

The Friend Group: A psychological thriller.

There are rules one must abide by if they are to be a part of the group. Break one, and you'll be reminded with a courteous smile. Break two, and you'll disappear. Click here to make new friends.

A NOTE FROM TY HUTCHINSON

Thank you for reading IT ENDS NOW. If you're a fan, spread the word to friends, family, book clubs, and reader groups online. You can also help get the word out by leaving a review.

Sign up for my Spam-Free Newsletter to receive "First Look" content, and information about future releases and giveaways.

I love hearing from readers. Let's connect.
www.tyhutchinson.com
tyhutchinson@tyhutchinson.com

ALSO BY TY HUTCHINSON

Sterling Gray FBI Profiler

Hunting the Mirror Man

The King Snake

The Butcher of Belarus

The Green Samurai

Sei Thrillers

Contract Snatch

Contract Sicko

Contract Primo

Contract Wolf Den

Contract Endgame

Dumb Move

Clean House

Done Deal

Mui Thrillers

A Book of Truths

A Book of Vengeance

A Book of Revelations

A Book of Villains

Mui Action Thrillers

The Monastery

The Blood Grove

The Minotaur

Darby Stansfield Thrillers

The Accidental Criminal

(previously titled Chop Suey)

The Russian Problem

(previously titled Stroganov)

Holiday With A P.I.

(previously titled Loco Moco)

Darby Stansfield Box Set

Other Thrilling Reads

The Perfect Plan

The St. Petersburg Confession

Published by Ty Hutchinson

Cover Art: Damonza